WIDER
THAN
THE SKY

WIDER THAN THE SKY

Katherine Rothschild

SOHO
TEEN

Published in the United States by Soho Teen
an imprint of Soho Press, Inc.
227 W 17th Street
New York, NY 10011

Library of Congress Cataloging-in-Publication Data
Names: Mason, Lizzy, author.
Title: Between the bliss and me / Lizzy Mason.
Description: New York, NY : Soho Teen, [2021]
Identifiers: LCCN 2020012353

ISBN 978-1-64129-113-2
eISBN 978-1-64129-114-9

Subjects: CYAC: Dating (Social customs)—Fiction. | Musicians—
Fiction. | Schizophrenia—Fiction. | College choice—Fiction.
Mothers and daughters—Fiction.
Classification: LCC PZ7.1.M37614 Bet 2021 | DDC [Fic]—dc23

Interior design by Janine Agro, Soho Press, Inc.

Printed in the United States of America

10 9 8 7 6 5 4 3 2 1

to my dad
when I said
I'll study law
you said
what about writing?

HOPE AND OTHER
FEATHERED THINGS

You know how you can read a poem, like, ten times and still not get it?

Teachers say: just read it again because something magic happens and suddenly you'll get it. Well, the day my dad died I totally understood this Emily Dickinson poem called "'Hope' is the Thing with Feathers." Not like the understanding helped. Poems can't bring people back to life. But suddenly getting poetry was a weird little gift that got me through what happened next.

On that day, my sister, Blythe, and I stumbled into a windowless, overly air-conditioned room in Huntington Hospital. Inside we found a doctor, my cashmere-sweatered mom, and a cluster of silent machines. And my dad's dead body. No one said he was dead—no one had to. The space his soul had taken up in the room had vanished.

The doctor unhooked one more monitor and put her hand way too casually on my dad's dead leg. "Take as much time as you need."

Like *time* was what we needed.

When the doctor was gone, my mom reached for us and we ran to her like we'd survived a plane crash or something. Which I guess we kind of had. We were surviving this empty room, weathering it the way our bikes did the ocean air, oxidizing and cracking—and crying. There were tears, teary questions, and more tears. When we finally stepped back to wipe our noses, the air filled with the silence only hospitals can achieve: a bustle and racket in the outside, but in here? No more beeping. I felt a stone in my heart, round and cold, sharp against my sternum.

Then someone cleared his throat. A man stood in the doorway. For a blink of mind-time I was sure it was my dad. He couldn't be *dead*. He had barely even been sick. He was fine. He was right there.

"May I . . . ?" He let the question hang in the air, like Southerners do. Like my dad did. *Had.*

Maybe we were all thinking the same thing, because no one said a word. Then he stepped into the room, beneath the glaring fluorescent lights. He was not my dad. Of *course* he wasn't my dad. My dad wasn't anywhere. When we walked through the jerking automatic hospital doors, the stone in my heart knew. My dad was gone. And this man? He was just some random middle-aged guy with sandy hair. Standing beside us. Staring at a dead body. Like a total creeper.

Blythe and I turned to our mom. She was looking from my dad to this guy and back to my dad. When she spoke, her voice cracked. "Charlie?"

He nodded. She swept the salty mascara from her cheeks and pushed her short curls behind her ears. She cleared her throat. "Girls, I have to take a moment—I'll be back. Stay with your father." As if he needed supervising. Then my mom walked into the hallway with a stranger.

I took my sister's hand and squeezed.

My mom's voice rose above the din. "No. Not for at least a month."

"We don't have a month," the man said.

Silence. I held my breath, listening.

"I thought we agreed to see this through." His voice was almost too soft to hear. "Allies."

"We are." My mom's voice hitched. "We *are*."

"I won't stay even though . . ." He coughed, and I lost the words. "I won't attend the memorial. But you must come up by next week." There was a long silence when I wondered if she would ask, *Come up where?* But she didn't. Footsteps fell behind us, and I finally looked away from my dad long enough to see that she'd come back alone.

"Who was that guy?" Blythe asked. She squeezed my hand so hard I felt her bones.

My mom didn't say anything, and Blythe didn't ask again. And I didn't want to know. Because we were all staring at this *dad* who wasn't breathing, who wasn't *alive*. This dad who would only be there until the orderlies had their turn. I should have been falling apart, with tiny pieces of myself flicking into the curtain and rolling under the metal bed. But instead, that stone in my heart stirred. It softened. It shuddered and shaped itself around my heart, not hard like a stone anymore, but soft, like feathers. Then I felt a flap, like wings. Like a second heartbeat.

I rubbed my thumbnail over my lower lip. Back and forth. Back and forth. Blythe saw and shook her head. She knew what I was about to do. But it was too late.

"Hope. Hope. Hope. Hope is the thing. Hope is the thing. Hope is the thing with feathers. Hope is the thing that perches in the soul. Soul. Soul. Winged soul." I heard the words before I knew that I was whispering them. *Chanting* them. I swallowed the words down, and they dove inside me. All the way to my toes.

And right then, I got it.
Hope is what's left when nothing else is.
"Hope" is the thing with feathers -
That perches in the soul -
And sings the tune without the words -
And never stops—neverstopsneverstopsneverstops—*at all.*
The next time we saw Charlie, we were moving in with him.

A DEATH BLOW IS
A LIFE BLOWN UP

It only took a week. Seven days to find a resting place for my dad, to fill our house with friends and casseroles, and then to empty it of everything. Even us. And then it was over. Even our bikes were sold to the kids down the street. A six-hour drive later, we pulled into a completely new life.

A moving truck blocked the driveway, so we parked on the street. I stepped out of the car beneath a street sign. It read: WELCOME TO THORNEWOOD: WHERE EVERYONE KNOWS EVERYONE. Right. Everyone except us. It felt personal.

I turned and got my first look at our new home and stared for a long time at number six Magnolia. I'd expected *none* of the strange and terrible things that had happened to us this past week. Not a single day felt less than surreal. But this? This was a new level.

"Dad died and left us Hill House," I said. Blythe squinted up at the ramshackle mansion, maybe trying to make out if that was a raven on the roof, or just a splatter of jagged shingles. We blinked at the monstrosity.

"It's closer to *Amityville Horror*. Or the house in *The Shining*."

"*The Shining* was in a hotel," I said.

"Semantics."

"Realities." I turned to my mom, who was in the back of

the minivan, half swallowed by bags and boxes. "Are we seriously living in a house possessed by evil?"

She pulled herself out of our life shrapnel and handed me a house key. It was plain silver, shining, and newly cut. It looked like our old house key. I'd half expected it to be made of human bone.

"You love old stuff," Mom said absently. "Just watch out for floorboard holes." Holes? *In the floor?* She gave me a pat on the back and marched toward the offending moving truck.

When Mom was out of earshot, Blythe turned to me, mimicking Mom's tinny voice. "You love old stuff, don't you, Bean?"

"Good old Maryann Interiors." It was something Dad had called her. It was the name of her company, but it was also *her* when she was being . . . like this.

Blythe waved a hand to the house. "Just throw some fabric over it." Mom's catchphrase. Stained duvet? Throw fabric! Cracked window? Fabric drape. Boxes for bedside tables? Guess what will fix that!

"Too bad fabric can't cover holes in the floor," I said.

"And she's going to have to be Maryann Interiors *and* Exteriors if she wants to make something of this place." Blythe tapped the crumbling brick walkway with one foot. I gave her a rueful smile.

We hauled our bags and ourselves to the wrought iron gate. It fought opening, but we yanked, flecks of rust coming off on our palms. It gave. Balancing our bags, we gingerly made our way across a dead, gopher-holed lawn.

Blythe stumbled, and I caught her arm, then kept her upright until we were back on brick. She shot the crispy yellow grass a dirty look from the walkway. "She didn't warn us about the holes in the *lawn.*"

I managed a laugh. "When you're going through hell . . ."

"Keep going," she finished.

It was a Winston Churchill quote. But really, it was a Dad quote. He'd had a lot of them, but I was afraid this one would stick with me. We'd been standing in his hospital room, my mom pacing after the doctors had told us that Dad's infection wasn't responding to antibiotics. As always, he'd tried to lighten the mood. His eyes had been closed as he'd spoken, his voice low and hoarse. "But Churchill was a notorious drunk," he'd added. "So who knows if he even said it. History is a game of telephone." I tried to think of something that would lighten the mood in this moment, like my dad had in that moment. But I had nothing.

I let go of Blythe and made my way up the warped steps to the buckling porch. I pulled out the completely normal key and unlocked the door. As I pushed it open, a long-drawn-out creak emanated from the house. It was like a horror film parody. I lifted a brow to Blythe and in a whispery voice said: "After you."

Blythe shoved her way in, batting dust motes away. "How is this an 'unbelievable decorating opportunity'?"

"The key word is *unbelievable*." But I couldn't fault my mom for trying to look on the bright side. Our lives were pretty dim at the moment.

"How many people do you think died here?" Blythe whispered, mimicking my horror film voice. "Don't go low. One of the ghosts will know for sure."

"Stop it," I said, and stepped inside behind her. The foyer paint was peeling in long strips, as if the walls were shedding skin. A chandelier tilted precariously over an antique entry table, the mahogany coated with a thick layer of dust.

Everything was covered with dust. If there was ever a house in need of Maryann Interiors, this was it. As I squinted into the gloom, a corner of gold fleur-de-lis wallpaper caught the sun and glinted. Gold wallpaper. Classy. This place might have been beautiful. Once.

Blythe scanned the high ceilings and smirked at the admittedly suspicious-looking water stains, edged in a coppery red, like dried blood. "My money's on ten. With at least one window-sash beheading."

"Just don't tell me there's a poltergeist," I said.

My sister held her hands up to test the air, as if taking a psychic reading. She nodded. "Two, actually." She left me standing beneath the skull-crushing chandelier.

I followed her into what could only be called a parlor lined with thick moth-bitten velvet drapes. In the hall I passed, I spied a built-in wooden telephone booth, a tiny private room with a glass door and its own light. An old-fashioned rotary telephone hung on the wall. I tried to pull the door open, but it was stuck. Blythe was ahead of me, so I left it and followed her to the dining room. A door to the side said BUTLER'S PANTRY, but the handle was locked or stuck, too. Beyond was a barren conservatory, the decorative tile gray and yellow in the afternoon light.

I blinked, thinking of my dad's office, with its Lucite desk and Eames chairs. "This doesn't seem like Dad at all. He loved modern. Modern everything."

Blythe popped back around the corner. "I doubt he was planning to keep it this way."

My mood lifted when we found a completely renovated kitchen. A new kitchen island looked recently cleaned, as if . . . well, as if someone lived here. I guess they did. We did, kind of. Still. I couldn't imagine my dad's coffee cup on this new kitchen island. Or his gardening gloves on that antique entry table. My dad smelled like Old Spice and manila folders. This place smelled like mold.

Outside, the moving truck blared, backing up toward the house to make way for the Momobile.

"Do we dare go upstairs?" Blythe asked me.

"It's that or sleep in the car."

Mom had told us what to expect: it would be livable. Now, as we walked through the second floor, I saw what she meant. We walked past four musty bedrooms full of broken furniture before we got to the end of the hall, and our room. I felt queasy as I pushed the door open, but it was the only room that didn't look like it needed to be ripped to the studs and renovated. The windows were thrown open; clean air wafted in. Our Jenny Lind beds were already set up, and a new chaise in pink velvet was waiting beneath the bank of back windows. There was a view of a dry terraced backyard leading up to the only living thing I'd seen so far. A willow tree.

"How did someone manage to put a regular room into the middle of a decaying mansion?" I leaned out the open window. The air smelled like rose water with an undertone of low-VOC paint.

"Mom must have redecorated. It *is* her job." Blythe removed her laptop before she dropped her bag to the ground.

"In a week? From home?"

Blythe looked at me. "Maybe it was . . . that guy. From the hospital."

I was about to speak his name when my mom walked in, leading with jazz hands.

"You love the chaise, don't you? It's custom. You have no idea what it cost to have it done so fast." I raised an eyebrow. She raised hers back, ruffled the velvet, and smoothed it down.

"We had to move because of money," I said, "but you got a custom chaise?"

"I wanted something special for you." She smiled.

I petted it, too. I couldn't help myself. So far, ruffled-velvet feel was the best part of my day.

"Besides," Mom said, "we moved because of *taxes*. That's different from money."

Blythe snorted from the corner, where her desk was almost set up, her screens already glowing. "Wi-Fi code?" Blythe asked, pulling out her phone.

"Oh. I don't know. For particulars you'll have to check with . . ." My mom flipped a hand. As if he'd been waiting for us all along, Charlie walked in. I looked between them. His smile was a sliver of ice down my back.

I'd never lost a parent to unspecified reasons before, but I was pretty sure most moms didn't decide to share their lives with a new guy soon after their husband's funeral.

I rubbed my thumbnail over my lower lip. "A death blow is a life blow, for some. For some. For you, maybe . . ." I pushed my hand down and pressed my lips together.

Too late. The weird had gotten out.

Blythe pretended not to notice. Or maybe she was oblivious by now. Since my dad had died, I'd been poeting more than usual.

I'd always had a little habit of reciting poetry. Poeting. Not on purpose. I wasn't winning poetry slams or anything. This was more inadvertent. It happened before I knew it, and it seemed to strike at random. Like the time I was supposed to be giving an oral report on the great state of Delaware (home of the Punkin Chunkin pumpkin-throwing contest), and ended up reciting half of e. e. cummings's "in Just-." Or the time Blythe and I saw our first horror film in the theater (*The Babadook*), and she said I ruined its scare-ability by whispering, "I took the road not taken, taken, taken." Or when we were saying goodbye to our dad in the hospital, and I couldn't stop saying "*neverstops.*"

But now it was becoming a thing. A *noticeable* thing.

Charlie cleared his throat and looked at my mom. She smiled as if I were a prodigy rather than a teen suffering from a potentially undiagnosed literary medical condition, which would make her a for-real negligent parent, and not just inattentive.

"I don't think we were properly introduced," he said. Blythe looked up from her phone. Our eyes met across the room. That drawl and those Southern manners. So much like Dad's. It was disconcerting.

"I'm Charlie Parker."

My mom gathered my hair behind my shoulders, about to go into the ritual of who was born first, but Charlie held up a hand and pointed to me. "You're Sabine."

I stepped back. No one tried to tell us apart right away. Seriously. NO one.

He gestured to today's tan boots. I'd chosen them because Vivienne Westwood calls them Pirate Boots, and I needed pirate-level courage today. And I'd chosen them because tan was noncommittal, which was exactly how I was feeling about my life. "I knew your father for many years. You've had a boot fetish since you were knee-high to a grasshopper. Your first pair was white with rainbow unicorns. Am I right?"

I blinked. I loved those boots. The rainbow part was iridescent. How did he know about that? I glanced at my mom, but she looked confused. Only Blythe's mouth twitched with a knowing smile. "Remember when you wouldn't take them off for circle time?" she said. "And you screamed so loud Dad had to pick us up from school?"

No. I shot her a glare, and she buried her head in her phone.

"That makes you Blythe." Charlie smiled again, flashing perfectly straight white teeth. He shook his head, glancing between us. "With your father's green eyes and your mother's pretty curls, you've grown up beautifully." Gross. I frowned at my mom's boy-short "curls." Did Blythe feel as creeped out as I did?

"Do you have everything you need?" he asked.

Blythe and I answered at the same time.

"Wi-Fi password?" (Blythe).

"Where's the bathroom?" (Me).

Mom laughed nervously. "Sixteen-year-olds are impossible to please. But deep down, I'm sure they love their room."

"I know it's a mess. I'm sorry," Charlie said apologetically. "Most of the house is as useful as a screen door on a submarine, but this room was completely refurbished." He placed a hand against the wall. "New drywall. Eco-paint. Recycled oak floors. And speaking of bathrooms, it has one you wouldn't believe."

He raised his eyebrows to me, clearly thinking I was the easier twin to please. So wrong. When I glared back, he gave Blythe the Wi-Fi password.

"I'll be driving you girls to school and making some dinners," he said. "You'll have to tell me what you like. But for now, we'll let you settle in." I looked to my mom. What was he? Our manny?

"Just one more thing." His smile faded. "If a woman named Mrs. McMichaels stops by, don't speak to her. Come get me right away. I'll be staying in the garage apartment for the time being."

"Thank you, Charlie." Maryann Interiors gave him a gentle arm pat. "For everything. While they settle, let's talk about scheduling and other . . . issues."

Uh-oh. I knew that tone. Mom sounded like she was about to send back an unacceptable piece of furniture. Either he didn't know that tone or he wore the same poker face that my dad had. Had. Had. Had. Had. Had. They walked out of our room, their footsteps echoing down the wide hallway.

I flopped onto Blythe's bed. "Did that seem creepy to you?"

Death blow/life blow. Life blown away. Life blown apart.

"Not creepy." Her fingers flew over the screen, pulling up all the games and apps she had been separated from on our long, Wi-Fi-free ride. "Odd."

"Off?" I asked.

"Odd," she repeated.

I stared out the window at the sky. It was still bright blue. Just a streak of pink reminded me that the end of the day was coming.

"What's with the cooking dinner?" I asked. "And driving us to school? Are we toddlers? We've never met him before in our lives. We'd never even heard his name. Not until—"

"I guess he's Dad 2.0."

"That's not funny," I said.

"At least he's not moving in here with us."

"Close enough."

Blythe put on her headphones and sank into her social media world. So I got up and claimed the closet. She could have the armoire. Almost nothing in her wardrobe needed to be hung anyhow. I hung up my dresses, pushing the folds out with my hands, then lined up my boots by height beneath the shelf under the closet window.

On the shelf I set out Emily Dickinson's *Final Harvest* because I was reading that one a lot. Then I stacked her letters, her critical essays, and a bunch of other poetry collections. I arranged them around my prized Emily possession: a handbag silk-screened with the text of one of Emily's love letters to Susan Gilbert.

I heard the skitter of gravel and straightened to peer out the open window. My mom and Charlie were walking below, their shadows long.

"You should have consulted me." She was shaking her head. "What's the rush?"

"I've been waiting for years. How much longer would you have me—"

"Forever would be the only long enough."

"I thought we were past that kind of talk." Charlie stopped and stared out at the overgrown garden.

"I'm sorry." She didn't sound as if she meant it.

"Maryann. This plan has been talked to death. Let's just do it."

"There are things to consider. Like the girls." My mom plunged her hands into her hair, making the waves stand on end. I leaned farther out the window.

"They're stronger than you think. And smarter, too," he said. I had to stop myself from nodding.

"That's not it." Her voice caught in her throat. She'd

started to cry the last time I'd heard them talk, too. Charlie took her elbow gently, like he'd done it before. "I will tell them," she said. "I *will*. But not today." Tell us what?

He turned and the setting sun hit his face, making it glow. For a minute, he wore a sweet expression. "If we don't go forward with our plan now, we might never."

"I need time to mourn my husband. And the girls need to mourn their dad." Just as I was sighing in relief that my mom hadn't forgotten my dad completely, Charlie took her by both shoulders and said something low under his breath. I expected them to start making out like in the Spanish soap operas I used to sneak-watch, but she wrenched away from him.

"I know that," she said. "Don't you think I know that?"

She stalked off toward the moving truck. It was emblazoned with a huge logo: BIG FAMILY MOVERS. It felt like a joke at our expense. Maybe we should have called Newly Small Family Movers instead.

Charlie brought a hand to his mouth, like he'd been slapped. Then he crunched over the gravel toward the driveway.

"Why are you hanging halfway out the window?" Blythe was right behind me. I nearly fell out.

"I'm spying on Mom and Charlie." She peeked past me, but they were gone. "Or I was. You don't think they're . . . together?"

She scowled at the idea. "Dad died *a week* ago," she said.

I nodded, swallowing the pain of hearing *died* and *Dad* out loud. She was right. Of course they weren't together. But then, what just happened? I turned back to see Charlie carrying a box from the moving truck to a black rehabbed Mustang. He stopped and carefully placed the box into the trunk. I poked Blythe, who'd begun sifting through my clothes.

"He's taking boxes from the moving truck." Blythe leaned over my shoulder again, watching as Charlie stepped away to reveal a trunk full of white boxes.

"Those are Dad's," Blythe whispered. "I used the fancy boxes to pack his office."

Ah yes, of course she had. Because that was Blythe. Neat, orderly, *the way I like it* Blythe. But this was me: I didn't care how good a friend Charlie was to my dad or who he was to my mom—he wasn't taking my dad's things. Because even I couldn't take anything of his—not yet. Blythe had taken Dad's fountain pen, Dad's leather briefcase (which now housed her electronics), and two of Dad's old V-neck sweaters. But I'd taken nothing but the book of Emily Dickinson's poetry that was once his but now already belonged to me. Because . . . how could I choose? It was like saying: *I want this part of you, but not that part.* As if there were good parts to keep, and others to toss out like last year's fashion after a Milan show. I could never do that to my dad.

Charlie had left the trunk open, like he planned to keep filling it. I turned to Blythe. "We have to stop him," I said.

Blythe groaned. "It's probably just books."

"I don't care what it is. He can't have it."

No one was taking a single piece of my dad from me.

THE HEART IS THE
CAPITAL OF MY MIND

I ran to Charlie's Mustang, but the trunk was closed and locked. I glanced around, but the only people nearby were a couple of guys in navy BIG FAMILY MOVERS T-shirts. What was he planning to do with my dad's stuff, anyhow? Maybe it *was* just books, but he didn't have the right to take them. Beneath the trunk's SHELBY insignia was a keyhole. I pushed it like a button; no luck. I walked around the car to see if it was unlocked. Maybe it had one of those trunk-opening levers. But the doors were locked, too.

I had to get in there.

What if Charlie was planning to take the boxes to the Salvation Army or to the dump? And where was he, anyhow? I glanced around again and tried the trunk one last time. I dug in with both hands, bouncing on my toes. Nothing. I let my hands flop down on the warm metal.

"Need some help?"

I spun to find a young guy with dark wavy hair and light brown skin watching me, his thumbs hooked through his belt loops. He glanced from me to the trunk then back again. I met his eyes—and they were bright blue. You know how beauty's in the eye of the beholder and all? I just don't think so in this case. Mover Guy was hot. No question. He was my age or maybe a year older, his hair a rich brown, with eyes that were . . . ultramarine. He flashed a lopsided smile.

I stroked my thumbnail over my lower lip. "The heart is the capital of the mind."

He kept looking right at me as if I'd said *hi* instead of bursting into poetry like a literary mental patient. "Not biologically," he said, still smiling.

"Poetically."

"Figuratively?" I opened my mouth to argue or explain, but he nodded at the car. "You're not trying to hot-wire this thing, are you? Because first, you're on the wrong side, and second, I don't have my wire strippers handy."

"No. Of course not." I laughed *way* too loud. "I live here. This is my . . . haunted mansion. I just need to get some boxes out."

"Did you try the key?"

"I lost it," I said. "I left it. It's gone."

"It's lost, left, *and* gone?" He laughed. "Okay. I can help."

"Are you a locksmith?"

"No." He pointed to the logo on his shirt. "I'm a mover, among other things. I'm Kai." I wondered if he was one of those guys who knew he was hot and used that knowledge to his advantage for discounts at places like Abercrombie & Fitch. But when he held out his hand to shake mine, it was shy and formal. So I shook it.

"I'm Sabine."

When my sister and I meet people, it's almost always together, and I'm compelled to say things like: My sister was born seventeen minutes before I was. No, we've never pretended to be each other at camp. And yes, we're identical. Blythe ignores people who ask if we're identical because it's painful for her to point out the obvious. But I don't think anything's obvious.

"So, you're a twin," he said.

It turned out I'd said all of that out loud. "Identical."

"There's no such thing as identical." He bent over, his eyes on the lock. He pulled a narrow screwdriver from his back pocket, tapped it in, twisted it, and popped the trunk open. Then he looked at me through a blur of dark lashes.

"Like snowflakes?" I asked.

"Like people." He winked. "Do you both have voodoo smiles?"

My heart skipped. "What?"

"It's from the Cure."

"Oh." The Cure. Lyrics. "I don't know about our smiles, but I guess our hair is a little different." He stopped lifting the trunk to look, and I wished I hadn't just experienced what a six-hour car ride does to curly hair. I pushed it back.

"Hers is more peanut butter," I said. "Mine is more toffee."

"The Candy Store Method. So, licorice?" He pointed to his hair.

"Black licorice is very one-tone. I'd say seventy-three percent dark cacao chocolate."

"Only seventy-three percent?" He flashed another smile. I forgot why I was standing there.

"Nobody's perfect." But I was thinking the opposite.

"Everyone screws up. Hence, forgiveness."

"Speaking from experience?" I asked.

"With forgiveness?"

"With screwing up."

He squinted against the sun setting into the trees, and his

lips turned up in a small smile. "Is this your way of telling me I helped you break into a car?"

I ducked into the trunk. "I'm not breaking in. I'm getting in."

I threw open the top box, thinking to riffle through the contents, grab some stuff I wanted, and drag as much as I could back inside. It wasn't a well-thought-out plan. But the first box was filled with neatly pressed color-coordinated shirts and sweaters I didn't recognize. I flipped through them, hoping something would trigger my memory. But no.

"I can bring these boxes in for you—"

"No, that's okay. I was looking for something specific." I threw open the next lid. It was men's argyle socks and those boy-short *underwear*. I shoved that lid back on and dove deeper. Where did he put my dad's stuff?

Kai reached for the top box. "You can look for it inside. We're getting paid to—"

"It's okay." I stopped him. "I . . . um, I just need a minute." I wedged open another box below. Camera equipment? That's when I realized. He hadn't put my dad's stuff anywhere. Because *this wasn't my dad's stuff*. I shook my head. But . . .

"Blythe is never wrong."

"Who?"

"Blythe. My sister. She's is never, ever wrong."

But she was this time, and I really *was* breaking and entering. I reached up to close the trunk and stopped. Why had Charlie's stuff been in our moving truck? Had he moved from Dana Point, too? I opened the trunk back up and rummaged through the first box again, looking for an answer.

"Hey." Kai elbowed me. "My dad is watching. Give me

an excuse to keep standing here when I should be working."
I scanned the contents of the box, but nothing looked important. So I just reached and grabbed. My hand closed around a smaller box. I yanked it out, and Kai took it from me. "Yep. That's it." I looked at the box and cursed. Great. Exactly what would tell me what was going on with Charlie: a pair of men's size-ten Salvatore Ferragamos. Nice.

"I can carry more," Kai said. "Load me up."

"That's it." I slammed the trunk down and squinted up at the house. The windows might have been broken or dirt-rimmed, but there were a lot of them, and anyone could have seen us. My heart hammered. But even if Charlie saw, what could he do to me? Serve me leafy greens at dinner? I told myself to relax.

"So, you're part of the 'Big Family Movers' family?"

"My two brothers, my mom, my dad, and me. My oldest brother will probably take over when my dad retires."

"Moving's not for you?"

"Big Family is a monarchy, and I'm the third son. So I'm expected to work for them, but not take over." He shrugged. "But I want to go to medical school."

I glanced over at him. Blythe wanted to be a computer programmer and make "awesome badass games for chicks." But I couldn't think of anything I wanted to be, or do, or have. Not anything possible, at least.

"Do they mind that you want to do something different?"

"Yep. But I'm family. They have to take the good with the bad."

Inside, voices carried from the living room. My mom and Charlie.

"Paint color is the least of our worries." He sounded tired

21

of their conversation. "But it *has* to be from an approved list."

"What about greige?" As we passed the doorway, Charlie was saying he was pretty sure "greige" was neither on the list nor an actual color. I slid around the corner and ducked upstairs. Kai followed, the box under his arm.

At the doorway to the pink bedroom, I paused. Blythe looked up from her laptop and gave Kai a once-over. "Is he what you found in Charlie's trunk?"

Kai smiled. But it was different from the smile he'd given me. It was a professional mover smile. "She found me *near* his trunk," he said. Then he handed me the shoebox carefully. It was heavier than I'd expected.

"Thanks for your help."

"Did I just commit a federal crime?"

"Municipal."

Blythe cleared her throat. I was afraid to look. She was probably rolling her eyes.

"If the police stop by, I was never here." Kai turned to me and let his nonprofessional lopsided grin linger before he headed back downstairs. When he was gone, I leaned against the doorjamb. I might have stood there indefinitely reexperiencing the last ten minutes, but the box was too heavy. I lugged it to the bed.

Blythe raised both eyebrows. "You wanted a pair of Dad's shoes?"

I gave her a sidelong glance. Blythe really hated to be wrong. "It wasn't actually Dad's stuff. The shoes are Charlie's . . ." I turned back to the shoebox. It was way too heavy to be shoes. I flipped open the lid. No shoes. No shoes! Inside was a stack of raffia-wrapped letters and a few trinkets—a

Montblanc pen, a large crystal paperweight, and a thick box of new stationery.

"You stole Charlie's shoes?"

"I stole Charlie's *correspondence*." I picked up the letters.

"You shouldn't have taken anything if you knew it wasn't Dad's."

I ran a finger over the address on the envelope. Charlie Parker, Eighteenth Street, San Francisco. I would have recognized that narrow, slanted cursive anywhere. It was my dad's handwriting. I pulled out the first letter and opened it, my eyes flicking over the contents. The letterhead was from my dad's mediation firm. It began *Dear Mr. Parker*—blah, blah, *mediation*. My shoulders sunk. It was practically a form letter.

"Sabine? Mail theft is an actual crime. Give the box back."

"They're letters from Dad," I said.

"What does it say?"

"Nothing. I guess Dad represented Charlie in a mediation."

"Then give them back."

"But why is *his* stuff in *our* moving truck?"

"Maybe they picked it up on the way here."

"Why is he living here?"

"To help." Blythe was always so logical. I rewrapped the letters, closed the lid, and shoved the shoebox under my bed.

"Don't get caught putting it back," she said. I turned to find her watching me. Her eyes flicked under the bed, but instead of calling me out, she gave me a little smile. "If Dad were here, he'd give us all the grit on Charlie."

"He would have roasted him. That slick hair?"

"Laminated. And the reef tuck? He probably has a diagram for folding shirts."

I imitated Dad's Southern lilt. "And his teeth and shoes are shined to a bright *ne*-on."

"Yeah." Blythe smiled a little. All at once her eyes filled with tears. She stared hard, not blinking. Then her tears dissipated and my own eyes filled, as if she had somehow transferred them to me. "I can't believe he's gone."

I shook my head. Me neither. I sat down hard on the new chaise. Just days ago, we'd chosen Dad's final resting place. His drawer. That's what they look like: drawers with cheap Little League trophy plaques. At the mausoleum, we'd gone from one alcove to another, through hallways decorated with soothing fountains, ferns, and plaque after plaque. All had awful sayings, such as, "They're always with you . . . in spirit." My mom talked the whole time, narrating.

"He wouldn't want to be across from those cheap American flags. He'd want to be near a window. Under a window." As if Dad would be there any moment to make the final decision. But as she perused the list of prices, she revised his opinions. "He'd want to be not too far from a window. And not too close to the administration, because it's noisy." It was like she was choosing a table in a restaurant.

Blythe had kept silent, stoic. I just kept thinking, Who wants to spend the hereafter in a drawer? I guess I'd imagined someday spreading my parents' ashes in a field of wildflowers or into crashing ocean waves. Never had I imagined a new-agey building with fake-marble walls.

That building should be banned along with those dumb plaques. The dead weren't with you in spirit. I didn't feel my dad's presence. I could barely feel my own. I felt empty of spirit, any spirit—as if once there had been a whole city inside me, buzzing with life, and someone had come along and blown it up. Boom. Now there were just ashes. And not even a drawer to put them in.

I MUST HAVE DOZED OFF because I woke to a clang. I jumped and looked outside. The willow tree was coated with the yellow light of dusk, and my mom and Charlie were just beneath it. The sound blared again.

"Is that the *doorbell?*" Blythe removed her headphones.

"I'll get it." I hurried downstairs, thinking of movers.

On the other side of the glass door was a long-limbed old woman in a wide gardening hat. I opened the door. I caught the smell of mice and wondered if we had an infestation, or if that smell was her.

"Has your mother finally arrived?"

"She's in back," I said. "Can I help you?"

"I'm Mrs. Bernadette McMichaels, president of the Thornewood Beautification and Historic District Society. Mr. Parker likely mentioned me." I opened my mouth to say that actually, he had, and that I was to call him immediately. But she didn't give me the chance. "Beautifying is a life's work. Once my father passes, I'll be able to dedicate even more time to Thornewood beautification. This place needs full-time help."

I peered outside. What was she talking about? Thornewood *was* beautiful. It was all arching street maples and big white houses and corner pocket parks full of bougainvillea. Our house was the only eyesore.

"You're Mrs. McMichaels?" Maybe she had something to do with the "plan" Charlie was so excited about. I held the door open for her.

She stepped into the foyer and wrinkled her nose. The space was now filled with boxes and plastic-wrapped furniture, but it didn't look much better than it had a few hours ago. Maybe worse. Backstepping, Mrs. McMichaels jerked open her tote bag and pulled out a thick envelope. "I have documents for your mother to sign," she said, her eyes flicking over the room. She shoved the envelope in my hands and pulled out a clipboard. "Can I trust you to give these to her and not leave them between the couch cushions?" With a big, startlingly fake smile, she held out the clipboard and tapped for my signature.

"Uh, sure?" My eyes swam through a sea of fine print. "You work for the city?"

She snorted. Not delicately, either. "I do not *work*. I volunteer to ensure our taxes are going to the schools, where they should. That's been my platform for thirty years, and it will be for another thirty."

I nodded and scribbled my name in what seemed like the right place. "So, what do the schools have to do with the house?"

"Thornewood has high standards." She snatched the clipboard and shoved it back in her tote. "So, as far as I'm concerned, our town is obliged to restore this house to its former glory."

I glanced up at the creaking chandelier, then behind me at the mahogany telephone booth. "That would be awesome."

She stiffened and smiled the tiniest smile. "As you say." She tipped her hat. I waved as she stomped across the porch boards, afraid she'd fall right through. When she was gone, I closed the door and leaned against it, sighing. I glanced at the envelope in my hands. What could this be about? I listened to the quiet house for a count of three. Then I flipped the envelope open and yanked everything out.

On top was a bound document: "The Thornewood Historic District Neighborhood Preservation Rules and Guidelines for Owners/Renters." *Owners* was circled in red ink. I flipped through.

Page 72: Acceptable house paint colors are Benjamin Moore's Eggshell, Egg-white, Ecru, Off-white, Dandelion White, London Fog, Decorator's White—

Page 106: All shrubbery must be boxwood or similar, such as *Myrtus communis 'Compacta'*—

No wonder Thornewood looked so perfect. I dumped the whole packet on the foyer table. A loose page beneath the rule book skimmed off. I picked it up.

To: Mrs. Maryann Braxton & Mr. Charles Parker, as if they were a couple. As if they were married. *Agreement to Adhere to Historic District Codes and Rules of Project Review.*

"In engaging with permitting for projects on a property zoned residential, owners must remain in compliance with all rules and guidelines at all times or risk the fines and liens capable of being placed by the city of Thornewood until such a time as the property is rezoned." It went on. And on. I skimmed to the end.

At the bottom was a "permanent reconciliation date" of November 3 and Charlie's graceful signature, *Charles Parker, Esquire*, and there beside it was a blank space for Maryann Braxton. That sliver of ice I'd felt when he walked in came back. How could all this have been set up in just a week? It was almost as if it was planned . . . as if Charlie had been waiting for our mom to get here.

Or . . . waiting for our dad to die of unexplained causes so he could show up in his hospital room and whisk his family away. A chill ran down my arms. I pulled out my phone and searched for: *Charles Parker*.

Every entry was a variation of: "Charles Parker was a jazz musician who played the saxophone and went by the name 'Bird.' He died in 1955." Great. Even his name was a mystery.

I looked over the documents for something that would tell me what he had planned. And why my mom was so angry about it. But it was just a bunch of historic rules and regulations. Nothing to tell me what I really wanted to know.

Why were we here? And what did Charlie want with us?

WELL ENOUGH FOR HIGH SCHOOLS

Blythe and I stood outside the Rolls Edward admin building, waiting for first bell. I scanned the crowd, not quite believing what I saw. Was there anyone who looked remotely like our friends back home? Anyone who didn't look outfitted to attend an interview at an Ivy League college? Or a hedge fund? But there was nothing but plaid and pastel. What kind of dress code was this?

"See any non-lemmings?" I asked.

Blythe glanced up from her class printout. "Are there ever?"

"Should I have worn jeans?"

"Do you *own* jeans?" She was right. I owned exactly one pair of jeans. Today, I was wearing a sparkling silver sweater dress and unignorable tall black boots because: that's me. And Blythe had on her usual drawn-on hoodie/jeans combo because: that's her. We hadn't dressed the same since I could pull out dresser drawers. Being different was always better than blending. Except, maybe, at a new school.

Blythe leaned into my shoulder. "Bean. You look more like me than you do like them. Does that help?"

I relaxed against her side. "That helps." I might be at an unfamiliar school in an unfamiliar life, but I still had the most familiar thing. I had Blythe. Blythe—who I hadn't *yet* told about sneaking a peek at the suspicious house documents. But I would. Today. She pulled away, holding up her printout. She had Honors Bio first. I had French.

"Why didn't we take the same language?" I grumbled.

"I don't want to be late." Her eyes were sparkling. Of course. She was excited, about to have new adventures in biology.

"Have fun." I waved, and she was off. I gripped my leather backpack straps more tightly. People were filling the breezeway and sending me curious looks. Being new and alone = no good. Head down. Move. My legs obeyed, and I found my classroom without having to raise my head to eye level. I slipped inside to lean against the wall, waiting for everyone to file in. My face tingled from the pressure of everyone's eye scans. The bell rang, and I could see only two empty seats—both in the front row. Great.

"Bonjour!" Monsieur Cade called out and shut the classroom door. He introduced himself and welcomed me to French III, then gestured to the front corner desk. I sat down, a wall on one side and an empty desk on the other. Monsieur Cade pronounced my name the French way, "Sabina," then started talking about how a whole group of people were once named *Sabine*. He called them a colony. I was pretty sure I wasn't the only one thinking I sounded like a disease that had been quarantined in this corner. I could feel eyes on the back of my head, probably imagining it rolling off. From colony disease. I was seriously considering making a run for it when the door flew open. Kai, Mover Guy, jogged in and sat down. Next to me.

He was breathing heavily, like he'd run to school. "Pardon, Monsieur Cade."

"Pas de parler, Monsieur Thompson." Monsieur Cade leveled his dark gaze on Kai. The silvery wings in Monsieur Cade's hair flared. Note to self: he doesn't like to be interrupted. Kai muttered something under his breath and glanced over at me. He did a double take, then lifted his hand in greeting.

I bit my lip to keep my smile from becoming scary.

Monsieur Cade was talking, but all I could think was: Mover Guy was here. Mover Guy—Kai—went to my school. And sat at the desk *beside mine*. I mean, I'd have to get Blythe to calculate the odds, but I was pretty sure they were slim. Finding him sitting beside me in my first class was like something out of a novel, or a poem—stop! No thinking about poetry. *No poeting*. I imagined sealing my lips closed to keep myself from word-vomiting all over the classroom.

Midway through class, Kai slipped a folded piece of paper under my spiral-bound. I waited until Monsieur Cade was writing on the board to open it.

His handwriting was neat and tidy.

S— Want a Rolly tour guide? —K

He knew which twin I was. What did it matter that I'd already had a tour? I crossed out *want* and wrote in *desperately need*. Then I slipped the note back. He glanced at it but didn't smile. Maybe the word *desperate* wasn't funny. It was just *desperate*. I slumped as far as my spine allowed.

At the end of class I lingered, but Kai was talking to a guy wearing a Rolly Soccer sweatshirt. So I hefted my bag and headed out. Then at the door, I looked back.

He was watching. My heart hammered. He mouthed: *Find me at lunch*.

I waved and ducked out, afraid my smile would outgrow my face and fall off.

I WASN'T ABLE TO TALK to Blythe until we were in line for what Rolly generously called "haute cuisine." The cafeteria did smell a little better than our old school's. As we moved up in line, I thought of telling her about the house documents, but instead blurted everything about seeing Kai. "He said to find him at lunch."

Blythe looked approvingly at her chicken in a bun with a side of fries. "I'm thinking this place is a seven. If our old school was, like, a three."

"Did you hear what I said?" I frowned.

She rolled her eyes. "Yes. We've been at this school for four hours and you already have a crush."

"I met him yesterday," I said, knowing this was as much encouragement as Blythe was capable of. "Fine. Your talking time." She hesitated for a single second before it all fell out: she hated her honors lab partner, which alone accounted for Rolly being a seven and not an eight. She loved her bio teacher, the Guru, who wore aloha shirts. Then she paraphrased his lecture until I made her stop.

"Four hours, and you already have a teacher crush?" I teased.

"More like four minutes," she said. "It was my first class." We laughed, but it was short-lived. The quad was crowded, and there was no sign of Kai. I searched the picnic tables (made of fancy hewn wood Maryann Interiors would appreciate), but they were packed with guys in navy team jackets and girls in pale sweaters. It was very Bay Area, with a mix of people of lots of different races and hair colors—but none of them blue. Or lavender stripes, like the underside of Blythe's. And their clothes. It was like the unofficial dress code was pastel color wheel. And everyone held textbooks; it didn't matter if they had a big 'fro or a sleek ponytail, or were wearing navy or a petal pink, they had a book. We'd been warned about the rigorous motto in the office: "Achieve the honorable." Or maybe it was: "Achieve the impossible." Whatever.

But we couldn't achieve even the slightest noticeability. And we were *twins*. At our old school, we got a lot of attention. Like people asking if we had superpowers. Or if one of us was evil. Or if we could we read each other's minds. But here? Nothing. Nothing but the occasional fish-eye.

Was it my dress? My boots? I knew it wasn't my gigantic hair. Other people had bigger hair than I did. I glanced at Blythe, wondering if she noticed our invisibility. She did not look concerned. I took in her hoodie and the half a quadratic equation on her sleeve. Oh. It wasn't her fading purple streaks. No, the problem was Blythe's bold admission that she was a walking GPA threat. My heart sank. There was no way we were finding a friendly table.

I was about to slink back to the cafeteria when I saw him: Kai. He was with a lanky Asian guy with spiked black hair and a blond white girl with rhinestone cat-eye glasses and a black beret. Finally! Someone who knew khaki was only acceptable for the Boy Scouts.

I started toward their table, but Blythe caught my elbow. "No way. That guy's in my Honors Bio. He's an idiot."

I shook her off. "Blythe. That's Kai. He helped us move in, remember?"

"Not him. The guy next to him." But I didn't wait for her to come around. I made my way through the picnic tables, my eyes on Kai. I was hoping he would look up and wave us over. I was hoping that we'd plan the most amazing tour, not just of Rolly, but of all of Thornewood, and it would include a romantic viewing of a vista with—

"Watch it!"

Icy liquid hit my chest with a punch, and icy pellets smacked my face then trickled down over my silver vintage found-in-a-thrift-store Alexander McQueen. One-of-a-kind *Alexander freaking McQueen*. I froze, blinking. Three girls stood before us, two holding trays of lunch detritus, one no longer holding anything, because her tray, alongside mine, and all of their contents, had landed on me. And then the ground. Everyone in this school just saw me get double tray-splattered. Words started bubbling up inside me, and Blythe pinched my arm, hard, to get my attention.

"Bean? Are you okay?" I couldn't look. I couldn't move. My silver dress. They'd all seen. Kai. Beret girl. *Everyone.*

"*Bean?* Like *jelly* bean?"

"Like lima bean?"

"Garbanzo bean?"

"Pinto bean?"

"Coffee bean!"

"Navy bean!"

I blinked through the sting of carbon filtration; I couldn't hold the words back anymore. I dropped my empty lunch tray and swept my thumbnail across my lower lip.

"It's well enough. It's well enough. For high schools, for my life, for schools, for my high schools—" Blythe hooked my arm and pulled me back.

"Don't open your eyes. Just keep walking." Her voice was strong. Calm. "We'll get paper towels."

I kept my eyes closed tightly as she led me through the

jeering and laughter of the quad. When it was quiet around us, I opened my eyes and saw Blythe and I weren't alone. The blonde who'd been sitting with Kai was walking with us.

"I have something for you, new girl." She smiled. "A dress. An Emma McMichaels original."

She had me at *dress*. I glanced at Blythe, who shrugged, and we followed Emma into the school's costume room. She went straight for a clothes rack holding everything from T-shirts with detailed seam stitching and pinwheel necklines to full-length dresses with ruffled layers. She glanced at me and pulled down a black dress with a knee-length golden vertical ruffle skirt and a black T-shirt top with a single line of gold stitching down each arm—one long sleeve, one short— like all her designs.

"Gold will bring out your eyes," she said. I felt like I could breathe again.

"Did you . . . make this?" I reached for the dress, forgetting my damp, sticky fingers. I quickly pulled back. "I don't know how, but even your ruffles are sexy."

She laughed. "Unfinished seams. I'm hoping to get a scholarship to FIDM"

I smiled at her. "I bet you will."

Emma's blond hair was straw-straight from too much peroxide, and a long nose made her face serious. But even without the beret, she'd have une certain je ne sais quoi. She brushed a hand over the nearest dress. "This is my admission collection." Then she held out the dress. For me to wear. On my body.

"What if . . ."

"You run into jerks again?"

I blushed. Emma twisted her lips. "Don't worry. They'll

leave you alone now. So let's get you into this." She tilted her head, and the rhinestones in her glasses sparkled. "Now take off that McQueen and let me stain-treat it."

"Why are you being so nice? Are you my fairy godmother?"

"Ha!" She winked, taking my wet dress. "Maybe I am." Her smile dropped a little when Blythe came in bearing a stack of grayish wet paper towels, but Emma recovered quickly, and Blythe slapped the mass against my bare shoulder. Even my bra was damp, so she just de-stickified me and patted me down. Emma laughed as she awkwardly safety-pinned me into the dress. But it fit.

After a long moment of admiration, Emma took a picture of me with her phone.

"I'm sending this to Kai." She grinned. "You're my first model." Blythe raised an eyebrow, but I shrugged. I was not about to argue with an up-and-coming designer.

At the picnic table, I tried to sit without drawing attention to myself, but Kai looked up right away, his phone in his hand, my picture staring out at me.

"Emma made the outfit she's wearing now, too," Kai said as we sat. I began to admire her dress, but a cough drew my attention down the table.

"I've met one half of this dynamic duo already . . ." Kai's friend was so tall and slim it looked like a challenge to fold and unfold his limbs. "I'm Nate. Blythe's best chance for an A in bio." I gave her the side-eye. He must be the "idiot" because he was competition.

"She might not need help," I told him, and looked back to Emma. It was quieter now; several lunch tables had emptied out. "Do you make all your clothes?"

Kai was looking at Emma with something I couldn't quite

place. But it made me nervous. "Pretty soon her art will be in Paris or Milan."

"It's not art," she said, but she flushed. "And that's impossible."

"Like a polar bear," Kai said, and they exploded into laughter.

No, no, no. People only laughed like that if they had history, if they had trust, if they had years of inside jokes. If they had a serious relationship. The girl I liked and the guy I liked could not like *each other* . . . it was too unfair.

When she stopped laughing, Emma gave me a significant look. "I don't make clothes out of necessity. I love working with textiles. I'll make anything. Even a pillowcase into—"

"Art," Kai interrupted. They laughed again.

I glanced at Blythe, whose glare told me I was crazy for being into Kai. I wished I could tell her it wasn't just his looks. It was how, when I'd poeted in front of him, he'd just gone with it. He hadn't judged me or said I was weird.

"You know . . ." Nate reached across the table to tug Blythe's sleeve. "Anything can be art."

"That's not art." She yanked her sleeve away. "It's homework."

"I want a pillowcase covered with words," I heard myself say. "Then maybe the ones in my head will fall out while I'm sleeping and I could read the story of my life." I didn't mean to be funny, but Emma laughed.

Kai leaned across the table. "You could read your dreams."

"Or nightmares," Nate said.

"I could make a pillowcase for you," Emma said.

"Show-off," Kai said and met my eyes. He smiled. I held my breath. "Hate to break this up, but I promised Sabine a

37

school tour." He stood, grabbing his backpack and gesturing for me to follow him, but Emma put a hand on his wrist.

"You have class. You can't be late." Kai looked at his watch and the flutter in my chest died as he frowned. "Maybe tomorrow?" I didn't get a chance to respond because a second later, the bell blared. We all grabbed our bags. I tried to wave goodbye, but Blythe was rushing us toward our next class—thankfully together.

When we were across the quad, I couldn't stop myself from looking back once more. Blythe saw, and said: "She's not prettier than you."

"You know you're giving yourself a compliment when you say things like that."

"I know." She shrugged.

She also knew this: I'd never had a boyfriend. I'd never even had a *real* kiss. The closest I'd come was a pseudo-boyfriend. And I'd stolen him from her. In sixth grade, she'd started hanging out with a white guy named Gerard who wore glasses that were so wide and thick, he was unrecognizable without them. His hair was lank, mousy, and hung behind his glasses in little clumps. He liked first-person shooter games, Skrillex, and old episodes of *Star Trek: Deep Space Nine*. I tried to talk her out of dating him, for all the above reasons. But she ignored me, and he started hanging out more. I saw them kiss a few times. And when they were together, she smiled a lot. It seemed nice to have someone. Even someone like Gerard.

One day we all went biking together. They were riding side by side, and I had to ride behind. I guess I was jealous. So I flirted. And it took exactly eight minutes for him to decide he was done with Blythe and into me. Twin swap.

When Blythe stopped speaking to me, I realized I didn't even like him. I'd just wanted to feel special. I tried to apologize, but she wouldn't listen. Her silent treatment went on so long, my dad got involved. Who was this Gerard? he wanted to know. What was so special about him? We hadn't spent fifteen words describing Gerard—including *glasses, skinny*, and *sweaty hands*—before our dad had us both laughing over the annoying way Gerard said *identical sis-thhhhhers*.

Thinking of Dad made me remember the house documents, and I turned to tell Blythe, but she gave me a big smile, and I hesitated. Then, without warning, she unzipped her backpack and pulled out her Sharpie. She grabbed my arm, drew an arrow on my wrist pointing at my sleeve, and wrote: *Is this ART?*

I burst out laughing.

Then I swiped the pen, grabbed her sleeve, and wrote: *Is this LIFE?*

IT'S EASY TO
INVENT A FAKE LIFE

We'd never had a babysitter. And definitely not one who brought in a construction crew the second Mom disappeared. But we did now—in our entry hall. We had a full-on construction crew with four sawhorses, a ton of two-by-fours, and a deafening circular saw. And Charlie.

Blythe glared at them all. "How am I supposed to work?!"

I shook my head and covered my ears. "How am I supposed to think?!"

"I have snacks!" We both jumped as Charlie shoved a tray between us: cheese-and-cracker stacks. A solid choice. He shouted over the circular saw that Mom was gone to Los Angeles for Topanga Vintage Swap and a client consult. I thought of the sparkly dresses, vintage boots, and long necklaces I'd miss out on because I had school. "She's gone through the weekend!"

The saw cut off abruptly, and *weekend!* echoed through the house.

"Does my mom know about this?" I gestured to where the crew had ripped up half the entryway floor. The saw started up again.

"Of course!"

Blythe rolled her eyes, grabbed half the contents of the tray, waved, and headed upstairs. I glanced after her, then back to Charlie. I still hadn't told Blythe about the house documents. And I hadn't returned Charlie's letters. All week I'd thought about doing both, but there was never a good time to irritate people. Besides, maybe there was something in the letters about Mom? Or, with Mom gone, maybe I could go right to the source? It was the first time I'd been alone with Charlie in the week since we'd moved in.

I raised my voice over the construction. "How long have you known my mom?"

Charlie gestured for me to follow him into the kitchen. I did, and he let the swinging door close behind us, muting the noise. "We're getting to know each other."

"Is that code for *dating*?"

"Absolutely not." Charlie set the tray on the kitchen island. "I was good friends with your father, Bean—"

I prickled. "Don't call me that." My dad started calling me Little Bean when I was a baby, because I was the second, smaller twin. It was a nickname I'd hated all my life, until I realized he'd never say it again.

"*Sabine.*" Charlie smiled the way Southerners do—like his smile had nothing to do with the rest of his face. "I was about to make my famous Mississippi hot cocoa. I'm from a small town not far from where your dad grew up. Why don't you sit."

"I thought you met my dad through work," I said, thinking of the letters.

"His firm assisted me with a personal matter." Charlie opened one of the old-fashioned fridge cubbies and took out milk, then a container of Cool Whip.

Cool Whip?

"So, you were his client?" I asked.

41

"At first I was," he said, fussing with the burner to get it to light beneath the pan of milk.

"Then one day . . ." I said, "you woke up and decided to help his widow raise her kids." If there was one thing my dad had taught me, it was that people always had a vested interest in the outcome. What was his?

Charlie measured the hot cocoa and leveled it, then tipped it into the mugs. "There's more to it than that." On the stove, the milk popped.

I waited until he was pouring the milk to speak. "The city's letter listed your names together. Like a couple. Is that what's more?"

His eyes flicked up to mine, and he winced as boiling milk trickled over his thumb. "I told you not to talk to Bernie McMichaels." He set the Cool Whip on the burn like an ice pack.

"How was I supposed to know who she was?" But I knew. And he knew I knew.

He leveled his eyes at me. "What do you want to know, Sabine?"

"Who you are? Why you're here? If you're with Mom." Keeping his eyes on mine, he spooned a huge flap of fake whip into one mug, and then the other. As if he weren't doing anything wrong. As if he weren't ruining the integrity of hot chocolate.

"I already told you. The answer hasn't changed in five minutes." He held the mug out to me. When I ignored it, he set it down.

"If you were friends with my dad," I asked, "why don't we know you?"

"It's not possible that we've met?"

"I knew everything about my dad." Except one thing, I thought. Except how he died. The official line was: infection. But when we asked Mom for more, she said she couldn't talk about it. We didn't press her. But I didn't think Charlie was going to cry if I asked him. "If you knew him so well, how did he die?"

Charlie covered his mouth, then he walked to the bank of windows looking out on tangled rosebushes. He splayed his hands on the countertops. "Here's what I know. Your father liked salmon in his eggs. And he would take it like that at dinner just as easily as brunch. He never had more than one drink at a time—ever—but it was always a double. If he drank vodka, it was Grey Goose. If he drank bourbon, it was Maker's Mark."

Maker's Mark was the bottle topped with red wax, like a candle. After he died, I found an empty bottle in his desk drawer. Charlie looked over his shoulder at me. I stared back. "Still don't believe me?" He lifted his slim blond brows. "His favorite shirt was a short-sleeved polo, and he had them in every color known to Ralph Lauren. He read you and your sister poetry at bedtime. His favorite was Emily Dickinson. I think yours is, too."

I'd asked to hear this. I'd asked, but now my hope bird was caving in on itself from all the knowing. Words bubbled up inside me, Emily's words in my dad's drawl. I skimmed my thumbnail over my lower lip. "It's easy to invent a life. Easy to invent—any life, just any life. A fake life, a real life. It's just that easy." I gripped the edge of the kitchen island to stop the words.

Charlie waited. When I spoke, it was to my hands. "How do you know all this?"

He ignored my question and walked back to the island, close enough to touch me. But he didn't. "I know something else about your dad, Sabine." When I looked up, Charlie's eyes shone with tears. As if he really did know my dad. As if he'd lost him, too. "He'd want you to try my famous Mississippi hot cocoa."

I closed my eyes. Charlie even knew my favorite drink: hot chocolate. I took one.

Charlie swept the back of his hand across his eyes. "Take one to Blythe." I picked the mugs up, and, without thanking him, I walked out through the construction zone. In our room, I handed Blythe her hot cocoa.

She smacked her lips. "What did you use? Whole milk?"

"Charlie made it." I put mine aside. "With Cool Whip."

She looked into the hot cocoa as if she could read the recipe there, then drank deeply. She savored it while I watched before she set the mug down. "Prepare yourself," she said. "You may never hear this again." She flopped onto her stomach on the bed and tapped the heels of her graffitied Converse together. "I think you were right."

My stomach clenched. "Charlie and Mom?"

She nodded, holding up her fingers. "First, Mom has a type. Southern charm. Second, if Charlie were a friend of the family, he would have made lasagna or sent flowers like everybody else." She went on with a five-point rationale. But nothing could explain Charlie's name beside Mom's on the house documents. Except maybe . . . cheating. I opened my mouth to tell Blythe about the house documents, but she was holding her empty mug, her face close to her textbook, murmuring to herself, a faint smile on her face from figuring out the sticky problem of our lives.

I walked to the window and stared out at the willow tree on the hill, alone and swaying. I could almost imagine my dad there, looking up at the tree. I felt a tickle in my heart, like the brush of feathers, then a deep pinch of pain. That's when it hit me. That heart squeeze that lets you know you've lost something. A little squeeze for your phone, a bigger one for a fight with a friend, and one that almost makes you pass out for a lost person.

But my dad wasn't lost. He wasn't misplaced. He was gone. Forever.

I curled up on the pink chaise with a first-edition Emily and lifted my thumbnail to my lips. I let the words fall out. When silence filled the room again, I stared out at the willow tree, the vast sky leading, in the distance, to the Bay Bridge. Charlie had answered my questions, but nothing he said convinced me that he belonged here, or that we did. I had to figure out what he wanted with us before his presence became a permanent situation.

THE HEAVEN WE CHASE
INVITES DEPRESSION

On Monday at lunch, I found Emma in the costume room to return her dress. She was smoothing a bolt of fabric over the huge counter-height table, so I hung the dress up. Then I presented her with a thank-you card I'd made from card stock, scraps of fabric, a glue stick, and a real paper clip I'd bent to look like a hanger holding a ruffly dress.

"So crafty!" She hugged the card to her chest. "Maybe I'll make this one next."

With Blythe studying through every lunch, I'd spent most passing periods and lunches with Emma, talking life, boots, and design. Being with her was a vacation from thinking about Charlie and my mom and how much I missed Dana Point.

"Let me know if you need a model," I said as I sifted through the costumes on one rack. It was a mix of *A Midsummer Night's Dream* romantic and 1950s poodle skirts and sweater sets.

"Speaking of, I have a new one." She pulled out a short black dress with a skirt of silver and black alternating ruffles. Like all her dresses, it had one long sleeve and one cap sleeve, and I wanted to ask about the sleeve lengths, but artists can be sensitive about stylistic choices.

"It's amazing," I said, gently lifting the hem.

"Your McQueen was the inspiration." She flipped the skirt into the air. "Where did you get that, anyway?" I told her about the beachy vintage stores I used to frequent as I skimmed my hands over the detailed stitching on the skirt.

"Well, there may not be a McQueen waiting for you in San Francisco, but there are some awesome vintage shops. We should check them some weekend."

I agreed, trying to hold on to the warm feeling that vintage shops gave me, but there was a tickle of worry in my chest. I shouldn't get attached to this place. "Emma? Do you know how to find out about someone's history? Like, beyond what's on the Web?"

The warning bell rang, and we grabbed our bags and headed out of fine arts and toward the quad. At first, Emma didn't answer, and I told myself I should be having this conversation with Blythe anyhow.

"Well . . ." She paused. "Kai could help you." I sucked in a breath. She flipped her glasses down over her eyes, not noticing my nerves. "He works in the library. Let's head over there." I nodded, my heart already pounding at the thought of speaking to him in something other than French. Even at lunch, we'd only just nodded and said, "Hey." And as yet there had been no tour. We gathered our things and headed toward the library.

Emma bumped my shoulder. "What top secret intel do you need?"

"I haven't even told Blythe yet," I glanced around, like Blythe might overhear, but she was probably already in class.

"You don't have to tell me," Emma said quickly, and I felt a stab of guilt.

"It might be nothing." I bit my lip and dug my thumbs

into my skirt. "But there's this guy we live with? Charlie? His name was on these documents right next to my Mom's, as if they were married. But when I asked, he said they were platonic. But it seems . . ." I wasn't sure what, exactly, it seemed. "Suspect." I pushed my hair behind my ears, containing it.

"You live at number six Magnolia, right?"

I stopped walking. "Yeah."

"I'm not a stalker." She laughed. "My grandmother is the president of this beautification organization. Yours is the oldest house in Thornewood."

"Your grandmother isn't . . ." I cringed. "Mrs. McMichaels?" I couldn't imagine Emma being related to a topiary lover like *her*.

"Yeah." Her eyes widened at my expression. "So you've met her. She's intense. But she does good work. Oops, I mean good volunteering."

I laughed. "So, what does this beautification society do?" And what did they want with my mom? And our crumbly mansion?

"Everything." Emma swung her hair out of her eyes. "Grandmamma oversees the rose garden, the street trees, the permits. She keeps this place perfect."

"So that's what I need to look up. I mean, I just want to know why we're here, and how Charlie knows my mom, but no one will give me a straight answer."

"I could poke around. See if they have any permits filed?" Her eyes twinkled behind her cat-eye glasses, and I feel the twist of fate that we met on that first disastrous day at Rolly.

"Thank you." I'd barely met her, and I'd thanked her more in a few days than I had my friends back home in a year.

"So, do you still need to go to the library?" I tensed, not knowing what to say. After a week of close observation, I was pretty sure Kai and Emma were just friends. But I was still working up the nerve to ask about their status.

"Yeah," I said, wondering if I could find a way to ask him. "I just can't stop thinking about why we're here. I may not find anything, but . . ."

"Kai's your guy for library machinations." She took my arm. "I'll go with you."

"That's okay," I said, gently pulling my arm away. "It will be boring. I'll meet you after." She shrugged, and even as another pinch of guilt twisted my stomach, I waved and walked quickly through the breezeway toward the library.

The entrance to the library was on the second floor. It had a wide landing hovering above a two-story space lined with windows overlooking the quad. I had a bird's-eye view. The labyrinth of mahogany stacks of muted hardbacks wound into rows of deep tables where students studied, laptops and papers scattered around them. Beyond the desks were deep leather couches, and beyond them, rows of silver computer desks. I scanned the space, first for Blythe, then for Kai.

Blythe was nowhere in sight, but I saw Kai. He was inside the stacks, a book cart at his side. Each time he shelved a book, he adjusted the nearby bindings so they lined up evenly. I watched, biting my lower lip at how careful he was.

Before I could think about it, I swept down the stairs, through the book-theft detector, and to the end of his row. He looked up, raising his eyebrows.

"Looking for a book?" He turned back to the stacks, sliding a finger along the row to check for evenness.

"No." I tried not to chew my lower lip, since his looked so shiny and pink and *unchewed*. "I'm actually looking for . . . someone's history?"

"Hmmm." He placed another book on the shelf and threw me that crooked smile it seemed as if he saved for me. "Did you try . . . Google?"

My cheeks flared. "Yes." I opened my mouth to explain, to tell him that Charlie's name belonged to a famous musician, to a man named Bird. But my thoughts suddenly seemed like nonsense, and I wondered if I'd really looked him up, or if I'd dreamed it. And while I was thinking my nonsense, Kai was staring at me with that intense blue gaze, and . . . I lifted my hand to my mouth and brushed my thumbnail over my lower lip. "The heaven we chase invites the race, the race to tears, the race to insanity—" I yanked my thumb away from my face. "Google didn't help."

"Oh." He pushed the cart out of the way and walked over to me. He opened his mouth, an inquisitive look on his face, like he was going to ask about my poeting—about my little word disorder. But he didn't. "I'll show you the databases. They can search paid content. Even government stuff, like births and deaths."

He led the way to the bank of computers and sat down. "What do you want to find out?"

I lifted my eyes and swallowed. Was there any way this might sound normal? "Well . . . remember the Mustang?"

"How could I forget our first break-in?" Kai logged into a portal for Rolly staff and students.

I tried to look like my insides were not turning into a pile of spaghetti straps. "I want to find out a little bit about the guy who owns it. Charlie Parker. But there's another Charlie

Parker, and . . ." I trailed off, and Kai turned to look at me, his hands still on the keyboard.

He searched my face for a moment, carefully, the way he'd reshelved the books. "Charlie lives with you, right? But he's not your dad?"

"No." My thumb twitched, but I held my hands together tightly. "My dad died a few weeks ago." I hadn't meant to say that. I really hadn't.

"Oh." Kai sat back, his face slack. "I'm so sorry."

Tears stung my eyes. I wished I hadn't told him. As if my poeting weren't weird enough for one lunch hour. Now everyone at this school would know I was weird *and* dad-less. "Thanks," I said, because that's what you say. You have to thank people for feeling sorry for you. I waited for him to ask how it happened. Or if my dad had been sick long. Or if it was unexpected. Why does everyone ask those questions? It's not my job to reassure them about the relative safety of their lifestyle.

But Kai didn't ask any of those questions. "I meant I'm sorry I was so nosy." He shifted closer to me. "Are you okay?"

I didn't trust words, so I nodded.

He pressed his lips together and leaned toward the screen. "Okay. You know search basics." He typed in *Kai Thompson*, putting quotes around his name. A dozen articles popped up. Future Physician of America, volunteer for Doctors Without Borders, center-half for Rolly's winning soccer team. I took the cursor from him to pause on one: "as the only Rolls Edward High School junior to make the all-star team, Kai Thompson is a front-runner for a scholarship to UCLA, known for—" He put his hand over mine and shifted the mouse away.

I kept my hand perfectly still beneath his. For a moment, I couldn't concentrate on why we were even sitting there because: he was touching me.

"Now let's try Charles Parker." He moved his hand away to type, and I took a deep breath. I didn't know if I was more nervous finding out more about Charlie, or being so close to Kai. But even using quotes, even using location, the databases knew what Google did: the other Charles Parker. Kai sat back in his seat, his cheeks a little pink. "We need a narrowing term. Like his profession. Or a family member's name?"

I hesitated then typed in *Maryann Braxton + Charles Parker.* The first hit was a real estate listing for our house— *number 6 Magnolia. Sold: 2009. Owners: Mick Braxton and Charles Parker.*

"What?" I stared at the names. Charlie owned the house with my dad? In 2009? Why would they buy a house together? My dad was a mediator, not the contractor star of *House Flippers.* I clicked further. Beneath was a mess of encrypted gibberish from Thornewood city records.

"Is that him?" Kai scanned the screen.

"Yeah." I hesitated, thinking about what I knew. They'd been friends. Maybe my dad helped him with money or something? A loan? "Keep scrolling."

Kai scrolled, finding repetitive listings. Then he stopped. *Intent to Modify Zoning.* The city document read: *Business Permit Application*, and a stamp on it said DENIED. It was dated just last year. I pressed my fingers into the desktop until it hurt. "Mover-librarians don't know anything about city permits, do they?"

"This one does." Kai glanced at me, a hint of his lopsided smile playing over his lips. He pointed to a zoning square on the document. "Zone C is for commercial properties. Like my dad's warehouse. They want to change the house from residential to commercial." All I knew was that Charlie had a "plan" for the house—one that we were unwilling accomplices to. Maybe it included turning the house into a commercial property? Or maybe it included marrying my mom.

I printed the documents—the title with Charlie's name and the Zone C application. With this, I could finally talk to Blythe about Charlie. I realized as I held the paper, warm from the printer, that I'd been hesitating to tell her about the house documents because I was afraid that with nothing to show her, she wouldn't believe me. Or she'd think I'd read them wrong. Blythe was an evidence-based-beliefs type of human.

Kai looked over my shoulder at the pages. "Are you going to ask him about this?"

I pressed my lips together. "I'm going to consult with Blythe. Then, yes."

"Must be nice to be part of a permanent team," he said as the first warning bell rang. I'd spent the entire time here, and had eaten nothing. I glanced over at him. He was wearing that real smile again. Worth the hunger pains. "Walk you to class?" he asked.

I smiled and followed him to the circulation desk, where he grabbed his backpack. We started up the steps together, the air between us a little empty without a project.

"Thank you," I said. "I wouldn't have found all that without you." I wondered what I could say that would keep his attention. But all I had was the truth. "And I'm sorry if that was too much reality."

Kai hummed a few bars of a song I thought I recognized. I

watched him, waiting for an explanation. He gave me a new smile, a small, shy smile like a piece of string cut too short. "That's 'The Reasons Why,' by the Cure." He shrugged. "According to them, reality is likely a highly interpretative state."

I tried to keep a straight face. "The Cure has all the answers."

"They're my favorite band." Kai pulled his Hacky Sack out and dropped it to balance on his foot. "They wrote some amazing poetry."

"I'm sorry," I said, and gave him the side-eye, "but song lyrics aren't poetry."

He froze, the ball balanced on his shoe. "I beg to differ. Evidence piece number one: poems were often sung in ancient times."

"Is that true?" I tilted my head, wanting to grab my phone to look it up.

"Yes." He tossed the ball in the air and caught it. "Evidence piece number two: poetry's been used through the ages to court women. And I just used a song lyric to flirt with you."

"But poetry and song lyrics are completely different. They're related, but poetry conforms to a . . ." Wait. Flirt? My eyes caught on his smile.

"Standard?"

"A meter . . ." Everything around me was buzzing. "Did you just say *flirt?*"

"I didn't say I was good at it."

He was flirting with me. Oh. Oh, oh. He was so not dating Emma. Energy coursed around us, and my hope bird shook out its feathers.

"Well, you're not *bad* at it," I said, and Kai laughed and

flicked his Hacky Sack into a high arc. I caught it and tossed the ball back to him, unable to contain a smile. "But maybe you should try *real* poetry next time."

"Maybe you should start listening to the Cure." He tossed the ball to me.

"I could try." I tossed it back. "But can they beat Dickinson for lines that make your heart shudder?"

"They can beat anybody. Even old-fashioned poetry." He tossed the ball to me.

"Nobody beats Emily."

"So, Emily Dickinson is that one you're always quoting?" Our eyes met and the ball fell to the floor.

"Sorry." I picked it up, hiding my frown. I told myself to look up, to meet his eyes, but I couldn't quite manage the confidence I'd had just a moment before when I was catching and throwing a ball. I bit my lip, chewing to keep from poeting. I took a deep breath, ready to see scorn or disgust, and handed the ball back to Kai. He was smiling, that sweet lopsided smile that was like a half-written sentence that ended in the word *forever*. He pushed open the quad door and held it for me.

The rush of students and noise blew in, scattering the shy sparkly energy between us. I took a step toward my next class. But I couldn't help looking back at him.

"Thanks again, I—" Someone bumped me from behind, and I stumbled.

"Sorry," Nate said, his hair flopping in front of his face. He ducked around me and grabbed a fistful of Kai's backpack. "We can't be late for calc. My perfect record will not be marred."

Kai leaned toward me and touched my elbow. "Let me

know what happens, okay? With Charlie?" Charlie. I'd almost forgotten about Charlie. And my *mom*.

Nate's long fingers yanked Kai into the sea of students. As I watched him go, my eyes skipped over someone watching *me*. I blinked back, ready to tell Blythe about Charlie. I had to talk to her—finally talk to her. She'd know what to do. But it wasn't Blythe. It was Emma. I lifted my hand to wave, but she turned her head as if she hadn't seen me at all, and kept on walking.

IMPERCEPTIBLY, AS SUMMER GRIEF

"But why would Dad want to start a business in Thorne-wood?" Blythe had finally put her phone down on the new white bedspread when I'd handed her the printouts from the library. We were sequestered in our pink room, me on the chaise I'd fallen in love with despite grievous attempts not to, and her on the bed. The afternoon light slanted through the bank of windows, turning the room to rose gold. Blythe tapped the printouts with two fingers, as if she could reveal their secrets. I was worried she'd be angry I hadn't told her sooner, but the news of the city documents and the denied permit were a puzzle to her, like math. Or global warming.

I shook my head in answer. "The permit was commercial. Maybe they wanted to start a mediation firm?" Or a mold-and-spore cultivation center.

A wrinkle formed between her brows. "That doesn't make sense. Dad had a perfectly good firm where we lived, in perfectly good Dana Point." Her brow furrowed further. I wondered if she felt the way I did—like she was floating above her life, looking down through a bank of fog. Our dad had had property he'd never mentioned. He had had business plans we'd never known. He had had friends we'd never met. What else would shift and change if we looked hard enough?

"Well. It's a nonissue. The permit was denied." Blythe threw the printouts on her desk, where a snack tray held bologna and cheese squares. Charlie knew his audience. I picked up his note: *Girls. Your mother will be late today. I'm at the store for dinner fixings. C.* "He's 'C' now?" I crumpled the paper.

"Snackmaster C." Blythe nibbled a bologna square.

I paced the floor so as not to give in and eat the tempting snacks. "What if he's a con artist out to marry Mom and steal her . . . dilapidated mansion?" When I looked over, Blythe gave me a slow blink. "I'm serious. That letter from the city was addressed to Mom and Charlie like they were a couple."

Blythe wrapped her bologna around a cracker. "Did it say Mr. and Mrs.?"

"No. But aren't you suspicious? Dad dies suddenly, with no explanation, and then here's Charlie to take over his whole—"

Blythe held up her hands. "All we know is Charlie is part owner. It makes sense. Mom got half the house from Dad, and Charlie kept his half." She was quiet for a moment. "We just don't know why Dad and Charlie owned the house together in the first place."

"And Mom and Charlie aren't telling us."

Blythe licked her fingers of crumbs and picked up her homework, then stopped. "Do you still have those letters?" The letters. How had I forgotten the letters? But I knew how, and he worked for Big Family Movers. I shot up and pulled the box from under the bed. The next letter we read together.

July 23, 2009
Dear Mr. Parker,

I'm so glad the firm has settled adequately over the incident of the mismanagement of your termination. I have contacted the Mission Project on your behalf to let them know that an excellent attorney is in need of a position. They're awaiting your call. This letter concludes our official engagement.

Good luck,
Mick Braxton, J.D.

We glanced at the third letter—advice on how to handle a case at this Mission Project place. Guess Charlie got the job. The next letter was an update on the same case. Blythe flipped through a few more. "I don't know what I expected—a red letter titled. 'Read me'?"

"That would be good." I skipped to some of the last letters in the pile—the most recent ones. When I went to open it, Blythe stopped me.

"The address."

I turned the envelope back over. *Charlie Parker, Number 6 Magnolia, Thornewood, California.* Blythe tilted her head. "How long has he lived here?" The room shifted from rose gold to pale gray as outside, rain began to fall. Above the patter, the Momobile roared up the driveway. We went to the window in time to see Charlie's Mustang roar up behind. They both got out, neither wearing jackets or carrying umbrellas. Mom held up a piece of paper, and they looked at each other for a long moment. Then they both smiled, and he lifted her in his arms.

"Seriously?" Blythe said, her face smashed against the window. I pressed my shoulder to hers, her body warm against me, the window cold against my nose. They were crushing each other. I almost looked away, expecting their next move to be a full-on lip-lock. But it wasn't. They just hugged—for an unnecessarily long time. As if they were being graded. I squinted into the rain. Was it just the blur of the water on the glass, or was Mom crying?

"I can't believe she's letting her hair get wet," I said.

Blythe rubbed her fist against the window, as if she could erase *now*. "What is she holding? It's not a . . . marriage license, is it?" I rarely heard Blythe's voice waver. I wrapped my arms around myself, trying to keep my pieces together. But just standing felt impossible, like holding water. I pulled away from the window and curled up on the chaise and let it happen: I thought of my dad.

I thought of the way he would whistle the 1812 Overture and say the "booms" when he cooked dinner. How every Saturday morning he wore his FEET DON'T FAIL ME NOW T-shirt to garden, even after the cotton started coming apart at the seams. How somber and clear his eyes were the day he went to the hospital. And how he'd been so still as it happened, as the air emptied around us as his life left his body. I felt salt water splashing over me, drowning me, filling the cavity of my chest. I felt tears rush through my veins like a river. I waited for my heart to burst with it. But my heart kept beating.

Blythe sat down beside me, holding a box of tissues. When I looked over at her, I saw the salt water had gotten her, too. I wiped her cheeks with my tissue, then held it so she could blow her nose. We leaned into each other as the waves of grief passed, the tissue box smashed between us. The room lit slowly as the rain stopped and the last rays of sun fell in across the jagged tree line to the hardwood floor. When my eyes cleared and Blythe's breath was even, I sat up.

"We need to talk to Mom."

"HOW WAS SCHOOL, GIRLS?" MOM scrunched her hair as she turned off the hair dryer. Her damp clothes were on the floor, and she'd changed into a silk robe. When Dad was alive, he'd been the one who picked us up from school, made our lunches, cooked dinner. This was how we saw Mom most often—in the mirror above her dressing table. We saw her readying for evening client meetings and weekend furniture events, or returning from them and preparing for bed. I felt a pull to her side, to let her make room for me on the bench, to lean into her and breathe in the scent of Chanel. So I reminded myself why her hair was wet.

I crossed my arms and leaned against the doorway. "At school today, we found out that Charlie owned this house with Dad." Blythe glanced at me and imitated my stance.

My mom's fingers shook as she pinched at her hair to get the water out. She stared at us in the mirror, tight lines around her eyes. But when she turned to look at us, I could swear her hair had grown more highlights.

"That's correct." She gave a bland smile. "We were planning to tell you, but—"

Blythe lifted away from the door frame. "Were you also planning to tell us what business Dad planned to start here?"

Her mouth dropped open. Behind us, her bedroom was dark, and I found myself wanting to turn all the lights on. "How do you know about the . . ." Her mouth clamped closed, and she turned back to her own reflection. "We were planning to tell you. We wanted to let you settle in." Was this what they'd been talking about the day we moved in? Whatever they were allies on? But after what we just saw . . .

"Were you also planning to tell us about your . . . relationship?" I met Blythe's eyes in the mirror. She nodded and spoke: "And how long it's been going on?"

Maryann Interiors slid her eyes from me to Blythe. "I don't know what you mean." My stomach churned, and I dug my fingers into my palms to keep myself from poeting.

"We saw you. In the driveway." Mom gave a short laugh and looked at her wedding ring. It glinted under the task lighting. She twisted back to us.

"It's not what you think." She closed her eyes for a long moment, and as her face relaxed, I saw the mom I knew before Dad went into the hospital. I waited for her to say something that would put ground back beneath my feet. Outside, the rain tapped the earth again. It felt like something was missing, like we were listening to Nature Sounds, not to our life. I thought of Emily's poem about the way long summers end so mysteriously.

Maryann Interiors smiled with all her teeth. "This house was an opportunity to leave our memories behind. An opportunity to make something with what's left of our—"

"Maybe we liked our memories," I said. Blythe reached across the doorway and took my hand. "You told us we *had* to leave," she said. I met Blythe's eyes. When I'd complained about missing riding our cruisers to school, about how there were no vintage shops in Thornewood, and about how I wished we could have taken our beach-glass garden with us, Blythe just nodded. But I could hear it in her voice now—she missed home, too. Maybe she never chimed in because she couldn't bear to talk about it. This was being a twin: sometimes we shared the same heart.

"We *did* have to leave," Maryann Interiors said. "Your father and I thought there would be years to pay back the loans on this house. But he didn't have years."

"Why didn't he have years, Mom?" I asked. We had brought up the reason for his sudden death only once before, and she had turned away and cried. We hadn't asked again.

Mom pushed her hands over her face, wiping away tears. "There wasn't anything anyone could have done. I can't talk about it—"

Something hot unfurled in my chest, like my hope bird was turning into a phoenix. "You can't talk about Dad. You can't talk about the house. It's amazing you can get any words out at all." Blythe squeezed my hand, but I couldn't stop myself. "Who's Charlie, Mom? Was he really Dad's friend?"

"*Yes*," she growled. "He was your dad's *best* friend. And I can't sell the house without his approval." Blythe and I looked at each other.

"What does that mean?" I asked.

"It means make the most of it." Her eyes met mine in the mirror. "We're not going back home." Home. Home with a green sea-glass garden, home with my rusty cruiser, home feeling the ocean breeze in my hair as I rode my bike to school, home where Blythe and I had friends who thought we were quirky, not weird. Home, where it was summer all the time. I brushed my thumbnail over my lower lip.

"As imperceptibly as summer grief, the summer gone. Summer grief, summer gone, summer grief, some are grief."

"That's not as cute as it used to be, Sabine," Mom said. I

ground my teeth. "Blythe is making the most of things. I've had a wonderful report from her biology teacher." I narrowed my eyes. She wasn't turning us against each other. Not tonight. I heard my father's voice chastising my mother for playing favorites, telling her that what I lacked in intellectual merit I made up for in creative spirit. And behind his voice, poetry stumbled through my mind. I swept my hand back to my lower lip, but Blythe saw and grabbed my arm, keeping me from poeting.

Mom took off her pearl earrings and dropped them into her jewelry bowl with two distinct clunks, then held her head high. "I certainly hope I'll be hearing good things from *your* teachers soon, Sabine. It shouldn't be too hard to impress now that you're not on an honors track." I set my mouth, waiting for the right words, but they didn't come.

Blythe rolled her eyes. "Whatever's going on, you'd better figure it out." She clutched my hand. "This move was the last insane thing we'll be putting up with."

All I could say was: "Yeah!" before Blythe marched us out of there.

Back in our bedroom, she slumped against the door. "Well, that went well." Blythe pushed her hair back into her usual ponytail and wiped her nose on her sleeve. "Maybe they're not dating. Maybe they're just . . . hugging friends?"

"Hugging friends? That sounds like Netflix and chill," I said, and Blythe shrugged. I was so confused. I headed toward the bed, ready to curl up with the tissue box again. But when I sat down, I realized something was missing. "Where are the letters?" I asked, patting the bedspread.

Blythe glanced over. "We were only gone a few minutes. Look harder."

I threw my covers back. Nothing. I crouched beside the bed, but there was nothing under my Jenny Lind besides newly formed dust bunnies. "Did we put them on your desk?"

Behind me, Blythe picked up her laptop and shuffled papers, scattering Post-it notes. We looked on her bed, on the chaise, beneath the chaise, and in the closet.

We even looked in the bathroom.

But the shoebox of letters was gone.

AND THIS OF ALL
MY HOPES WILL FLY

As we walked out of the house the next morning, I tripped over a drop cloth then slammed my elbow into a scaffold as the circular saw roared to life. I was still coughing up sawdust and humiliation as I sat down for first period, nursing a bruise. I couldn't believe Charlie had not only stolen those letters right out of our room, he'd also called my morning scowl "the French housewife look." When Kai walked in, I tried to lose the scowl, but it refused to budge.

Kai lifted his eyebrows as he sat beside me, on time for once. "I'm thinking your grump face isn't only over our French project?"

I curled my lip and looked at the board. *Assignment: in pairs, create a project using at least seven verbs of le subjonctif. Get creative; 100 points.* Well, great. "The scowl may be a permanent fixture," I said. "We confronted my mom, but she won't tell us anything. We may have to resort to breaking and entering to get to the truth." I thought of Charlie's garage apartment. That's where he must have taken the letters—letters that must hold secrets, otherwise why steal them back secretly? Why not get us in trouble? I scrunched my face up. "Feel like accessorizing another crime?"

He imitated my scowly face. "I *do* like to carry a purse

during criminal activity." I laughed, ruining my criminal mastermind look.

Monsieur Cade whacked the blackboard with chalk to drown out our chatting. "Fais attention! Le subjonctif! This may seem childish," Monsieur Cade said in French, "but your subjunctive boards will help you understand a most important and difficult tense."

I scanned the class. Partner work. I knew no one besides Kai because this was a third-year class, not a second-year class. I turned back to the front, crossing my fingers beneath my desk. Monsieur Cade passed a hat for students to pick group numbers. I reached in and wished hard to be in Kai's group. I drew a seven. Kai leaned over my desk to see my number. He placed his slip of paper beside mine.

Seven. Our eyes met, and he smiled. I looked back down at the sevens. I felt a flash, like my soul shining, and I wondered if wishing made this happen. "Library after school?" he asked.

I nodded. The library was my new favorite place.

I SKIPPED THROUGH THE QUAD after school, thinking of Kai's eyes, and whether they were more ocean-on-a-sunny-day blue, or more cerulean blue. And I wondered whether I could do a school project with him, given the extreme nervousness that gripped me every time he was around. I tried not to imagine the poetry that could burble up.

"There you are!" Emma clomped out of the fine arts hall and swung her arm through mine. We stopped outside the library in a patch of sunshine. She was sans-glasses today and wearing a slinky glittery one-armed sheath dress with a belt of broaches and a hem of tattered ruffles. She was like something out of a fashion blog. "So, I found something. About your house." She pulled out her phone and turned it to me. "A new permit was filed this week."

My cheeks burned, all thoughts of dresses gone. "What kind of permit?"

"This is all I have." She enlarged the photo. *Permit Application for 6 Magnolia Street filed by owner Charlie Parker on behalf of the Mission Project partnership.* Below that was the name of our construction company, a big ZONE C stamp, and a description of work. In Charlie's slanted cursive, it said: *Transitional housing and meeting center in conjunction with the Mission Project.* "Transitional housing? What's that?"

Emma balked. "How should I know?" I looked again. Why wasn't my mom's name under *owners*? What if she didn't know about it?

"Will you send that to me?"

She tapped her phone. "Sent. But don't worry. Not many permits get the go-ahead in Thornewood. Plus, you already have one for restoration."

"They're replacing the floors right now." I cringed at the thought of the circular saw.

"You know, Thornewood doesn't give warnings for inspections. It's how we raise revenue. But I'll message you before, okay?"

"Okay," I said, but I wasn't thinking about not getting fines. I was thinking about why Charlie had filed a permit for something called *transitional housing.* Not that I was planning on staying long at number six, but it's not like I wanted to be kicked out, either.

"Headed to the library?" Emma twirled the hem of her

skirt, looking down her nose at the ruffles, like they might not be exactly what she'd been going for.

"Yeah, I—" I started, but stopped. Something in the way she was looking at me made me swallow involuntarily.

"To see Kai?" My cheeks flushed, and I reminded myself it was a study session, not a date. "Am I imagining things, or do I see you together a lot?"

"We have a project." I tried to look studious. "For French." I flicked my eyes to Emma's. Had she noticed how I waited for him to sit down at lunch to start eating? Or how I walked the long way to English so I could say hi to him in the hallway? We'd even stopped to talk a few times. Maybe she'd noticed that, too.

"So, are you into him?" She laughed, and I laughed, too. And it came out *way* too loud.

"Uh . . ." My smile slipped into the neckline of my dress. The truth: I'm into him like he's the best book in the world and I want to read his pages until they turn to dust in my hands. The partial truth: "He's nice."

"I adore him." Emma flipped her hair and the light turned it to gold and her dress to diamonds. "It's such a bummer we can't hook up. But he has to concentrate on his future. School, soccer, his jobs." She sighed. "What a waste of a great body."

I squeezed my French text against my chest. So she did want to hook up with him. Fine. That was fine. It'd be much easier to do French homework with a friend. No, a peer. No, a colleague. A colleague with a great body. Oh no. "So . . . what are you saying, Emma? Are you two together?"

Emma flipped her hair and sighed. "You don't get it because you didn't grow up here." She leaned against the wall, her dress sending sparks of light across the quad. "Thornewood looks beautiful on the outside, but it's like quicksand. The longer you stay, the more likely you'll never leave. Kai and I've wanted to get out of here together since we were little kids. And for that to happen, we both need scholarships. So I need to make the best wardrobe FIDM has ever seen. And he needs a sports scholarship even if his dream *is* to join—"

"Doctors Without Borders."

She stood up. "He doesn't need to go to *Africa* or whatever to be a doctor."

She sounded like his mom or something, but I could tell what she was getting at. She liked him, and even if they weren't a pair, she was marking her territory. "I guess not," I said. The last thing I wanted was to mess up my friendship with Emma. Seeing what she wore to school each day was a highlight of my life. I was afraid to say more. If I did, all the feelings I had for him might spill out of me like words onto a dream pillow. And then she'd never speak to me again.

"Say you're not going after him." I'd known it was coming, but it still felt like a slap. Maybe the slap showed on my face, because Emma looked flustered for a moment before she shook out her shoulders. "Because if it weren't for our workload, we'd be together."

I met her eyes and my hope bird shriveled into a pile of feathers and hollow little bird bones. "I'd never go for a friend's guy, if that's what you're suggesting."

She heaved a sigh. "Thank you. Blow off your project. Let's go to the Berry Market for candy."

"I can't." I wasn't about to blow off schoolwork, especially if Kai needed a scholarship. Emma stepped around me and opened the library door. I guessed she was coming, too. As I turned to the library, I told myself that a crush was meant to hurt. That was the whole point. I thought of our sevens: the heart that almost was. It hurt more than I'd thought, thinking of those sevens, and the shy way Kai had smiled at me when he'd put them together. I swept my thumbnail over my lower lip. "This of all my Hopes, of all my Hopes, all my Hopes; this will fly away."

I ducked my head and stepped through the library door.

Inside, I heard Kai before I saw him. There was a smile in his voice. And my stupid hope bird reassembled and took off flying inside my chest. When Kai caught sight of us, he waved his French book. He was on one of the leather couches beside Nate, whose hair was spiked into a faux hawk. Nate's hair: another mystery of life. We stopped at the circulation desk, where Emma dropped her things and grabbed a return cart. I helped her shove it in the direction of the couches.

I hopped up on my side of the cart, looking for a way to ease the tension between us. My dad was so good at that. "Let's take this thing joyriding."

She laughed, but before she could weigh in on the merits of book cart joyrides, Blythe walked up beside us, cradling her Honors Bio book in her arms. "Emma. I think we should switch lab partners. I'm presenting tomorrow, and my lab partner is a complete and total—oh, hi." Blythe pressed her lips between her teeth as Nate rose from the couch, his limbs unfurling like fabric running off a ream.

"Well," he said. "These sea monkeys won't kill themselves." He held up their book and shook it.

"Killing sea monkeys is your department," Blythe said. "If you would accept that my critical mass theory is best, we would already be in first—"

Nate slapped a hand over Blythe's mouth. "A partial

degree increase is the way to—eww!" He yanked his hand away and wiped it on his shirt.

"Did I forget to mention that she's a biter?" I asked, scooting around their tussle and toward where Kai was watching from the couch, one eyebrow raised.

"Take it to a table. I called the couch." Kai motioned for me to sit, and I almost glanced back at Emma for permission. But what had she really said about them? That they're *not* together. Besides, we were studying.

As I sat, Emma pushed the book cart nearer. "Why can't someone fix this wonky wheel?" Nate pushed past the book cart, grumbling as he followed Blythe to a table a few feet away. Kai smiled but didn't look up from our assignment.

"Book carts by nature should be flawed." Kai lifted his eyes. "Thanks for the help."

When Emma rumbled off, I sat back and sank into the couch so deeply my feet swung into the air and my shoulder thumped Kai's. He laughed and pushed me upright.

"Sorry," I mumbled. "This couch should be replaced." I yanked out my assignment. I hoped he couldn't see the color of my cheeks. Maryann Interiors might call it *persimmon*.

"We could form a committee." A little smile played over his lips. "Have a booth in the quad." Rolly had more quad booths than the parking lot on farmers' market day. Everyone from the Mathletes to the Yoga Club wanted you to sign something or buy something. The first day, I'd thought the booths were up because of an event, but they were always there.

I looked skyward, like I was considering it. "We'll need a banner and some flags. Cookies in the shape of couches."

"*Brownies* in the shape of couches," he said, tapping his stomach.

"You're a teen boy. You're not supposed to be choosy about snacks."

"I'm choosy about a lot of things, Sabine," he said. I swallowed, and we both reached for our books. Our shoulders brushed and the sleeve of his T-shirt touched the fabric of my dress and there was no way I could focus on French. I glanced over at Blythe. Blythe pointed to an assignment sheet then to a note on her sleeve. Nate took her arm in his hands and pulled her halfway across the table to read it.

I opened my French book. And pretty soon I forgot how close Kai was sitting because our assignment was crazy hard. In French, the subjunctive is like a future tense, but a future tense that might, or might not, be. In English, we usually say *might* or *maybe*. The subjonctif made me think of my mother's design boards: she called them *worlds of maybe*.

I pressed my lips together. "What if we made a design inspiration board? We could pitch it to the class like they were our clients and we were going to redecorate the classroom." It was a totally girly thing to do, and I expected Kai to say that we should predict next season's soccer matches, but he didn't.

"Can we have a houndstooth sofa?"

"Do you even know what that is?"

"It's pictures of dogs, right?" I didn't correct him. We looked up words like *stripes* and *suede*. Then we found poster board in the library's recycle bin and cut and pasted photos from home décor magazines. I wrote French all over the board, and he used neon highlighters to show the tense changes. We even printed out a "fabric" swatch with an Andy Warhol–like terrier repeat (for the couch).

A few fabric scraps from my mom's discards and we'd be

done. When Emma walked by again, Kai held up the board. "Old-school awesome, right?"

"Old-school rocks." She swished her hair. "I can't believe you're almost done."

Kai looked at me and smiled. "Miss Genius French Speaker is making this easy." Emma nodded and walked on, but when I glanced up, she was still watching us. I schooled my thoughts.

"Will people do PowerPoint?" I asked.

"Yeah. But Monsieur Cade likes personality."

I ran a finger over a picture of long green curtains. It was still damp from the glue. "I don't want to mess up your perfect GPA."

"It's only *almost* perfect." He gave me the lopsided smile I'd started to think of as mine, and I felt it everywhere. I searched for something that would extend our study session, but my head was filled with unthinkable thoughts. We sat silently for a moment, organizing our pens and papers. He put away his highlighters and slowly zipped his backpack. Then he looked over at me, tightness around his eyes. Maybe he was looking for something to say, too?

"So, what are you going to do about Charlie? Pack him in a shipping container and send him back to Mississippi?" I laughed, imagining Charlie shoved into packing peanuts.

"As Blythe has pointed out to me, the most threatening thing Charlie's done is make hot chocolate with Cool Whip." It was on the tip of my tongue to tell him about my mom and Charlie in the rain. But then I would be talking about . . . *hugging*.

"Oh, no. Real whip all the way." His face relaxed into an easy smile. Not *the* smile. But still. A nice one.

"Agreed." I laughed a little, wanting to keep talking, but not wanting to say anything with too much reality. "But I do have a partner in the battle of number six Magnolia. Emma's keeping an eye on the permit stuff."

"Emma's a reliable girl." He nodded, keeping his eyes on mine.

I pressed my lips together. "No. A reliable girl is a Labrador. Emma is a design queen. Emma's a *fashionista*."

He laughed, shaking his head. "An artiste?"

A scuffle came from Blythe's table, drawing our attention. Blythe was frowning, and Nate's cheeks were like two blooming poppies. Blythe was pointing to one page while Nate tried to flip to another page. As they struggled, her elbow caught him in the solar plexus, his hands flew into the air, and they knocked the book to the table with a glorious thump.

Kai leaned close to me. "My money's on your sister."

I grinned. "No bet."

With a frustrated growl, Blythe grabbed the book and packed up. "Well, this was a huge waste of time." Blythe's voice was way too loud for the library.

"Maybe if you'd allow my intimate knowledge of biology—"

"Being human doesn't give you knowledge of human biology." Blythe gave me a *we need to go already* look, and while she was turned away, Nate made a strangling motion. She swiveled back as if she could feel the insult, and he quickly clasped his hands together in prayer. She glared at him then turned to me. "Get up. We're leaving." Blythe tapped her arm as if she wore a watch.

"Don't you all want a ride?" Nate's eyes were on his textbook.

"No." Blythe glanced outside. The fog was in, and a cool mist hung in the air outside the great library windows. "Maybe."

Kai gave me a conspiratorial look. "Take the ride." I smiled and told Nate thank you. As we headed out, Nate offered Emma a ride, too.

"I'll stay and finish the return cart." When Kai gave her a thank-you hug, she closed her eyes and melted into him. I watched, digging my thumbs into my backpack straps to stop from poeting. At the top of the stairs, I could see Emma pushing the book cart below. I wondered if the hug was worth it.

Outside, Nate pointed to a blue Volvo sedan from the age of swooping bell-bottoms. Blythe took the front, so I hopped in back with Kai. As Nate drove, he and Blythe took up all the space in the car arguing over how hot they could allow their sea monkeys to get before they would die. Nate wanted to increase by one-tenth of a degree. Blythe was arguing for a large degree increase to weed out the "loser sea monkeys." By the time Nate pulled up in front of our shame shack, idling the heatless, shaking Volvo, they'd compromised on a half degree daily.

"Compromising is throwing caution to the wind," Blythe said as she got out of the car. "Thanks for the ride."

As Blythe slammed the door, I started to grab the poster board to get out, too, but Kai stopped me, his hand on mine. "Thanks for making this project fun." A little shiver went through me at his touch, and to cover it, I pulled my hand away and rubbed my palms together.

"Cold?" Kai asked, and in a moment that would top the most beautiful moments of all time, he wrapped my hands in his, dropped his head to our hands, and exhaled warm breath between them.

A single shock of pleasure shot up my spine as his lips brushed the tips of my fingers. I pulled away, my heart hammering. Kai's mouth looked soft and just a little surprised. "I'll finish this tonight," I said, then grabbed our project and leapt out of the car before I could poet. I was like a fountain that had been tamped down with dirt and moss for too long—if I wasn't careful, Kai would clear me of debris, and words would splash all over us both.

As the Volvo roared off, I turned to find Blythe waiting on the wall, kicking mortar from between the bricks. "I heard a rumor," she said. "About Emma and Kai? How they're going to get married someday or something?"

I tightened my grip on our project, still thinking of Kai's lips. "Don't worry. Emma gave me the message loud and clear." A tremble of discomfort went through me. If it was obvious to Blythe how I felt about Kai, it was probably obvious to Emma, too. Even if there was no such thing as calling guy dibs, I had more important things to do than nurse an unattainable crush—like expose Charlie for being a liar and a fraud. "I need to show you something," I said, and sent Blythe the photo of the permit application. She read it as we walked to the house.

"Wait, what's the Mission Project again?" Blythe gave me a look like she thought it might be the name of a cult.

"That's where Charlie works, remember? It was in a letter."

"I wish we still had those," she said.

I nodded. "There's definitely something in there he doesn't want us to see." We stopped on the porch.

Blythe bit her lip. "They've obviously been relocated to the garage apartment."

"And maybe hidden," I said, though it was hard to imagine what could be in the letters that was so damning they'd had to be burned or something. Except one thing. "Did you ever wonder why Charlie was there the day Dad died?"

Blythe's face paled as she met my eyes. Her right eye had a tiny black dot in the iris, one of our only physical differences. I focused on that dot as she spoke. "Do you think he had something to do with Dad's death?"

"I don't know. But maybe the letters do?" My throat tightened.

Blythe squinted up at the garage apartment. "I guess we're breaking and entering."

THE DAILY OWN OF ANY LOVE

"It's not like we're robbing a bank," I said as we left number six Magnolia through the side porch. Blythe handed me the key she'd taken off our mom's key chain. It was Saturday, and sunny, and everyone was finally gone, even the construction workers. I took a deep breath. Today was the day. "If we're caught, we tell him what we know and let him hang, okay?"

Blythe nodded. "Got it."

That was something my dad used to say. *Just let them hang.* It's a mediation tactic that means never give more information than you have to. When people ask questions, you ask them why they ask, then stare them down. Hang them. The thought gave me confidence in our plan. Which was: Get inside. Get the letters. Look for any info about the Mission Project. Take photos. Get out. If we found something incriminating, maybe it would be enough to get Charlie to sell number six, the money pit.

At the top of the driveway, the garage apartment rose like a mini-Magnolia. But a nice one, with new paint, new windows, and big brushed-glass windows where the garage doors once were. It was as big as our old house. On the wood-shingled second story, a sensor light flickered on. I glanced around for a camera but didn't see one.

Hurrying now, I fit the key in the lock. It slid in, but the knob wouldn't turn. I tugged at the doorknob, turning it right then left. I shook out my hands and tried again: shimmy, jimmy, shake. It didn't budge. Blythe pushed me out of the way. She tried everything I had, but either Mom had the wrong key, or it was a bad copy. Blood rushed in my ears as I took the key from her again. Blythe was making plans to come another day, but this was the day. I could feel it. I pinched the key between my fingers and pushed down the poetry that threatened to burst out of me.

Think, Sabine. The garage was on a hill, so the apartment backed up to ground that was higher in the back than in the front. "Come on," I said, and we walked around the side of the apartment. Sure enough, I could almost reach the base of the second-story windows. I jumped, and a slice of modern kitchen came into view.

"We'll climb." Blythe placed her foot on a lower window sash. She definitely could not climb up. And unfortunately, neither could I.

"Stop. You'll break something." But the workers had stored a bunch of construction supplies here in the overgrown grass. I threw back a tarp and found planks of wood leftover from the new floors, bags of cement mix, and yards of iron rebar. I grabbed a couple of two-by-fours and dragged them below the kitchen window. Blythe grabbed another, and a few minutes later, we had a short set of wobbly stairs.

I climbed our makeshift staircase and pushed the base of the sash, testing it. It slid open so easily I almost fell over. This window was definitely new. I heaved myself through. For a moment I hung half in and half out before I pitched to the floor. I rolled and slammed my shoulder, glad it was me and not Blythe who'd gone first. I pulled myself up and leaned out. "I'll let you in the front." I closed the window.

But when I turned to the kitchen, I froze. It was the kind of swank my dad loved: all stainless steel appliances, oversized butcher-block kitchen island, and Plexiglas bar stools. It was soothing compared to piles of construction shrapnel. At the door, I told Blythe: "We'd better take off our shoes." She grumbled, but we left our shoes at the foot of the stairs.

In the living room, the views went all the way to the Bay. Number six was huge, but it was at street level and sur-rounded by street trees—the view of the bridges was there, but it was obscured. But up here, at the top of the property, you could see past the Bay Bridge to the mound of Alcatraz and beyond, to the Golden Gate. This apartment had been completely remodeled—and not inexpensively. "Maybe this remodel is what their loans were for," I said.

Blythe sunk her toes in the fluffy white rug, wide-eyed. "I expected it to be like something out of *Southern Living*," she said.

"Gingham check?"

"Matching plaid? Maybe some antlers."

"You know who this reminds me of?"

We looked at each other and both said: "Dad." We stared for a second too long, as if looking deeply into each other's eyes could answer the questions we both had. Blythe looked away first.

"I'll try to find something about the project. Maybe steam open his mail." She slipped down the short hall to the kitchen.

The living room was all birch floors and crisp white leather–and–steel furniture and flokati rugs. Each wall was adorned with a huge, red-framed black-and-white pho-tograph—all of people in cityscapes. And the place was immaculate. It was a stark contrast to the dust, toolboxes, and plastic sheeting shrouding our house. I stood there enjoying how *finished* this place was.

I walked over to his bookshelf and scanned the titles. I didn't recognize very many, but a bright orange book caught my eye: *The History of HIV/AIDS.* I blinked and looked at it more closely. The spine was lined with creases. I skimmed the rest of the shelf—noticing that he didn't organize his books by color (like my mom did) or by author's last name (like my dad had) but by theme. He had a huge row on photography. Another row was law books. And the bottom row was . . . *Safe Space: Gay Neighborhood Histories, The Castro: Then and Now, The UCSF LGBTQ Hospital Survival Guide. The Gay Man's Kama Sutra.* There was a rainbow spine I recognized from a class I took last summer on the art of protest—*The Stonewall Riots.* I blinked, wondering if these books were for Charlie's job? None of it gave me a clue to what he had planned for number six, my mom, or us.

I took a deep breath and looked over the rest of the room. It was white walls and clean air. No letters. Nothing to see. Except—the bedroom door was ajar. I pushed the door open with my foot and peered into darkness. Then I flipped on the overhead light.

It was sparse. The gray comforter was neatly folded to reveal crisp white sheets. A single yellow throw pillow was the only bright spot in the room. I sighed. There was nothing here.

I was about to leave when I saw it: a single photo on the nightstand. I swallowed the impulse to turn off the light and leave. Instead, I took a step forward. And another. And then another, because even though I could see the picture clearly, I didn't quite believe it. The photo was of my dad. With Charlie.

Charlie was looking at my dad, smiling. My dad was looking

at the camera with his arm around Charlie and his mouth open, like he'd been laughing. He held a Bloody Mary. It was dusk and warm, because they were both wearing short sleeves, and behind them were umbrellas and the tall masts of boats. They were at a marina or harbor café. A sign in the background said SAM'S. I picked the frame up. Good friends had pictures of their friends. Sure. I could believe that. But on their nightstands?

I thought of the day Charlie listed everything he knew about my dad. The day he cried. Then I thought of how Charlie had appeared at the hospital the night my dad died, and how my mom wasn't surprised to see him. How, when we asked if she and Charlie were together, she'd *laughed*. I thought of the books I'd just seen—all those books about queer culture. Maybe it wasn't my *mom* Charlie was in love with. Maybe it had been my *dad*. My dad? Charlie? My dad. Charlie. My dad. Charlie. Dadlie? Charad? *Charade.*

My knees buckled, and I sat down on the bed. I had the urge to throw the photo across the room, but instead I held it so tightly I thought I'd crack the glass. A giggle burbled up in me. A panic laugh. My dad and Charlie couldn't have been a couple. You don't live with a parent for sixteen years and not know him. Not know who he is. Not know he's gay? Because—who was in the closet anymore? But people *were*. Celebrities. Politicians. People *were* in the closet. Was my dad? I swept my thumbnail over my lower lip again and again, rubbing furiously. "The daily own of love, the daily own—owe, owned, owe, owned—" I caught my hand against my mouth to keep the words in. But the poem was crushing my tongue to get out. I swept my thumbnail again, the words like my own breath. "Owe, own, owed, owned. Owned. Owe." The words tumbled into the absorbent flokati.

I squeezed the photo. My dad looked so happy. Charlie looked so happy—like my dad was his whole world. Like love. They were *together*. My thumbnail brushed my lower lip again. "The daily own, own, owed, owe—"

Blythe's voice cut through mine. "You'll never believe how he labels his . . ." Blythe froze when she saw me. I don't know how my face said *Guess what? Dad was gay*, but she paled, then took the frame from me.

"You are freaking kidding me." She slumped down beside me on the bed, cradling the photo. Then her mouth flattened, and her eyes snapped to mine. "What are you doing sitting there? Go through his stuff."

I jumped up, my heart hammering as if now, and just now, I'd realized we were breaking into someone else's—well, if not someone else's house, someone else's space. And that even though he was supposed to be working today, Charlie could come home at any minute. I yanked the bedside drawer open and started rifling through it.

And here was the mess. I pushed things aside without keeping it tidy: lip balm, hand lotion, checkbook, pens, receipts. I shoved my hands to the back of the drawer, closing my eyes against the possibility of sharp objects. I felt a familiar stack of papers, wrapped in raffia. I tugged the letters out. But I hesitated. At least some must contain information about their relationship; otherwise, why would Charlie have stolen them back? And I didn't want to know more. I didn't want to know that my dad had never loved my mom. Or that he'd never loved us. Or wanted us. That he'd wanted this other life in an apartment with a view of the Golden Gate Bridge and a man who wore a reef tuck.

A very uncomfortable thought occurred to me then. We

were his, weren't we? I looked at Blythe to see his eyes/my eyes/ her eyes/our eyes. We were his. We *were*. So what more could we learn from these letters? Nothing. I opened the drawer to put the letters back but stopped to brush my finger over my dad's handwriting one more time. Then I yanked a single letter from near the bottom of the stack—the newer letters. I folded it into my palm. Then I tightened the raffia and returned the letters to the back of the drawer. I wasn't going to read the letter. Not ever. I just didn't want Charlie to have it.

"How often did Dad travel for work? Monthly?" Blythe asked, her eyes darting over the bedroom, to the living room and back to me.

"A lot," I said. At least once a month.

"Some of the time, he came here." She looked around in wonder. "He must have."

I clenched the envelope in my hand. For one horrible minute, I was glad my dad had never gotten the chance to tell us this truth himself. I was glad whatever plans he'd had for his new and improved life were ruined. Almost glad that he'd *died*. I tried to push the thought out of my head, to take it back. But it was too late.

"He must have been planning to move here permanently," Blythe said. "The permits. You know."

Heat coursed into my cheeks. What would this have been like? To have a dad who left us for another life? In Thornewood? "Do you think Mom knew?" Did she know that her husband of almost twenty years was in love with someone else? And if so, how long did she know? I felt a pang for how awful that must have been. And was it awful now, to share a life with that someone?

Blythe stood slowly. "She'd have to, right?" I nodded, and

suddenly I wanted to get out of there. I wanted to have never come at all. But before I could voice that, Blythe gestured for me to follow her out of the bedroom.

"I found out what Charlie's big plan is." Blythe showed me an architectural rendering of number six on eleven-by-fourteen paper, titled: *Mission Project–sponsored Transitional Housing*.

It was hard to tell from the drawings, but it looked like most of the house would be broken up into small studios. Number six was too much space for just one family, especially our small family, and I hated the long dark creaking hallways and the smell of basement that permeated most rooms in the house. But if number six became studios, where would we live? And if it was gutted, what would happen to the beautiful chandeliers? "They're going to just tear out all the fixtures and the little signs and the telephone booth?" I pressed my lips together, thinking of the gold fleur-de-lis-patterned wallpaper. "Does Mom know about this?"

"We'd better tell her. Just in case she doesn't feel like living in a studio apartment forever." Blythe gave me a grim look and set the drawings back the way they'd been.

As we walked down to number six, I pushed my father's letter deeper in my pocket. Back at the side-porch entrance, we rested our backs against the door. I tilted my head to Blythe's, and she leaned against me. Her breath rose and fell with mine.

I wished we'd never gone up to Charlie's; then I could forget that my whole life was a lie. Then I could pretend I still knew who my dad was. I could pretend I still knew who *I* was.

I guess that's why people keep secrets. I guess that's why no one told us who Charlie was. Maybe it was safer to keep doors closed and locked than to see what was on the other side.

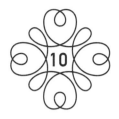

ALL BUT DEATH
CAN BE DISCUSSED

On Sunday morning, we walked into the kitchen planning to grab bowls of cereal and leave only to find my mom holding a whisk and frothing something at the stove. Behind her, Charlie was at the kitchen island, chopping purple cauliflower. I narrowed my eyes—we hadn't eaten vegetables except on vegetarian pizza since before my dad died. Blythe leaned against the kitchen island. "Are we being *Punk'd?*"

"Stop it," Mom said. "I can cook. Your dad was just a better chef." As if in evidence, the milk boiled over and hissed onto the stovetop. She laughed like that was planned and turned down the heat. Charlie pulled fancy hot cocoa mix, fresh flour-dusted biscuits, baby tomatoes, and a bag of loose spinach from a Berry Market paper bag.

"What's going on?" I asked. Since what we'd seen in Charlie's apartment, I hadn't been in a great mood. Blythe and I spent the rest of Saturday in our room, only emerging to order pizza. But we still hadn't come up with a good plan for asking about what we now knew: that our whole family was a farce.

"We thought it would be nice to have a family breakfast," Charlie said. "Maybe some small talk."

"Mom, we . . ." I opened my mouth, but my tongue felt swollen. I should have planned what to say. Planned it and then written it down. And maybe had Blythe say it. "We know that Charlie was Dad's boyfriend."

Maryann Interiors flipped her jazz hands. "What are you talking about?"

Charlie coughed like he'd swallowed wrong. "So you *did* break into my apartment." Blythe and I looked at each other. "I told you, Maryann. And I told you we should have told them the whole truth from the start."

Mom dropped her whisk and whirled on us. "How could you violate Charlie's privacy like that?" *That* was what she was choosing to focus on?

I huffed out a breath, meeting her furious gaze. "How could you lie to us about our dad like that?" Beside me, Blythe cleared her throat as Charlie opened the fridge door to pull out his precious Cool Whip, as if this were a normal brunch conversation.

Charlie slammed the fridge cubby shut with a heavy thud. "They're almost adults, Maryann. I said, 'Let's treat them like adults. Let's tell them everything.' I'm tired of living with secrets, and now look. They're breaking and entering."

"Not technically," Blythe said. "We *got* into the apartment. We didn't *break* in." I leaned into her shoulder as Charlie paced back and forth and Maryann Interiors resumed heating the milk.

"Technicalities do not make such a violation any better," Mom said. Then she took a deep breath and turned back to the stove, as if that ended the conversation.

"Maryann," Charlie said. "Tell them the rest."

"What more do we need to know?" I asked. "Our dad wanted to leave us. So we're unlovable, and you have a really cool apartment. Mom, did you do the décor?" I wasn't thinking—the words were just coming out. Maryann Interiors sagged against the stove.

"I sent Charlie an initial design," she said. Blythe and I looked at Charlie. Our mom decorated an apartment for her husband and his lover?

When Mom turned from the stove, her face was ashen. "Girls, understand. Mick wasn't planning to move until you were both in college." She started to say more, encouraged by Charlie's obvious throat-clearing. She made a sound, a hollow humming, but then nothing. My mom's hair and makeup and nails all looked perfect, but it was as if it was just a pretty coating. As if one day, I would look over and she'd be nothing but a pile of face powder and glitter.

She shook her head. "I can't." Blythe and I looked at each other, then at Mom, whose blond hair flopped over her eyes. Her blouse wilted as she hunched into herself, wrapping her arms around her waist.

"I can't do this for you, Maryann." Charlie's voice was low, breathy, as if he was talking to a wild animal and not a mom. The room fell silent, as if the walls held their breath. Finally, Mom uncrossed her arms and cleared her throat. She spoke so quickly that at first, I couldn't tell what she'd said.

"Your father died of an HIV-related infection. And that's why it was so fast, and that's why they couldn't do anything. I'm sorry I didn't tell you sooner."

My heart suspended for a beat. My dad died of *AIDS*? I looked at my mom. And even though I didn't want to, I looked at Charlie. I thought of his well-worn *The History of HIV/AIDS* book. Did Charlie have HIV, too? Had my dad come up here for treatment?

"Don't worry." Mom wiped the sudden, sparse tears on

her cheeks. "I was tested again just a week ago, and I'm negative. I even have a printout, if seeing it would make you feel
safer. Your dad took a prescription drug that helped stop the
transfer of the infection during intimate . . ." She covered her
face with her hands. "I can't believe I'm talking about this
with my daughters."

I couldn't believe it, either. I felt Blythe press into my side,
but I kept my eyes on the kitchen island. "You knew Dad was
sick," I said. "And you didn't tell us."

Blythe shifted away from me. "People live a long time with
HIV. Why didn't Dad?" I expected my mom to answer, but
Charlie spoke.

"He broke his finger trimming a tree. Trimming that willow tree." I remembered seeing tape around the index finger
of my dad's left hand. I hadn't even asked about it. "He
didn't realize it was broken, and he got a staph infection. It didn't
respond to antibiotics."

Is there anything worse than being told it's just one of
those things? We want reasons. We want answers. We want
someone to blame. I wanted someone to blame. "How long
did you know, Mom? How long did you know he was sick?"

She shrugged, sinking into her blouse again. "Years. Over
ten years. But there wasn't reason for concern."

"Wasn't reason for concern? He *died.*" I wanted to yell,
but my voice was whispery. I gripped the edge of the kitchen
island to stop myself from poeting, and felt Blythe's arm
around my waist.

"It's okay." But she was wrong. Nothing was okay. When
I looked up, the room seemed brighter, louder. The sunlight
angled in through the windows as if it were slicing through
bread. Charlie scuffed his shoes over the linoleum. On the

stove, a drop of milk popped. Maybe if they'd told us when he was alive, it would have made sense. But now the whole thing seemed insane. My dad was with Charlie *while* he was with my mom? And Dad was sick? And everyone knew but us?

And he was gone. He was gone, and nothing made it better. I swept my thumbnail over my lower lip. "All but death can be adjusted, discussed—disgusted. Discussed, adjust, discuss—all but death. All but death." Blythe's arm tightened on my waist, and I stopped. Then I looked up. "I wish you'd never met my dad."

Charlie looked smacked. But I didn't care. He'd stolen something from me, and I wanted to steal it back. I closed my eyes and took a breath. "Sometimes I do, too," Charlie said, and took a long sip of coffee.

"So, is that it?" Blythe asked. "Just the fake marriage to announce?"

My mom and Charlie exchanged a look. "It wasn't a fake marriage, Blythe. Your dad was bisexual, but he was also what's called polyamorous. Our marriage wasn't fake; it was nontraditional."

"What are you saying?" I backed away from the kitchen island.

"Sabine, don't walk away." Mom's face was close to the shade of the dish towel over her shoulder—a pallid gray. "Your dad had relationships with men and women. But being in love with two people is uncommon no matter your sexuality—that's being polyamorous. He chose to love more than one person at a time. I know myself—rather, I knew myself—and I couldn't share him forever. So we decided when you both went to college, he would move here. To be with Charlie."

"But then he died," Blythe said.

I lifted my thumb to my lower lip, but Blythe grabbed my hand in hers. "And you lied about it all. The whole time? Our whole lives?" I narrowed my eyes at Charlie. "We never had to know. If you'd sold the house, we could have *never known.* We could have stayed in Dana Point with our friends, in our house, with the memory of Dad—"

"You mean keep us in the closet?" Charlie said, barely sounding angry. "Keep our relationship a secret so you can feel better about how regular your life is? Would you prefer that, Sabine? Just because you don't say a truth out loud doesn't make it disappear." Charlie's eyes swam—a drowning pool of palest blue.

It wouldn't have been true. Not for us. "Why didn't you just sell the house?" Did they think keeping the house meant keeping my dad? My mom turned to Charlie.

"I told them," Mom said, lifting her chin from her chest. "About the will. That we had to decide together."

Charlie spoke through gritted teeth. "We're not selling."

Mom blanched. "We said we'd discuss all options. The new permit request was denied. Charlie, where does this leave us? We're building without a permit."

"We're *not* selling this house," he said. When I looked up, his blue eyes reflected the morning light. "Your dad's dream was to build a safe, healing place for the LGBTQIA+ community. It was his *dream*—"

"But—where will we live?" Blythe said. Where *would* we live?

When Blythe and I were seven, my dad started building a dollhouse. He traveled so much, it took him two years, and by the time it was done, Blythe was too old for it. But I loved all its perfect shingles, its big front porch. I loved the little rooms where I imagined our life playing out. Now I wondered, as he glued those tiny pieces together, if he was thinking not of us, but of this other life he was building. Did he know that the dollhouse would lose its shingles and splinter front porch rails? And did he know that by that time, he would be living in a new, perfect house, while the one he left behind fell to pieces?

Charlie shrugged. "You'll be in college by the time it's done." It was as if he really didn't get why this completely sucked.

Mom wrung her hands. "The girls will need a place to come home to." She looked between me and Blythe, trying to gauge how angry we were. "On breaks. It's something we need to think about."

"We'll think about that if we get through this without Bernie McMichaels fining us so badly, we'll be too poor to paint," Charlie said. I imagined him thinking about paint swatches. And it made me really, really mad.

"So you're illegally building. And you have no intention of even continuing to let us live here? Dad owned half this house. So half of it should be *ours*." I imagined my mom taking one of her wide hot pink grosgrain ribbons and tacking it down one wall, across the floor, and up another until the house was in two pieces.

"Well, Charlie's right. We'll be going to college in two-point-seven years." I heard the voice from beside me, but I couldn't believe it was coming from Blythe.

"And until then?" I stared at her. "We live in a construction zone and then have no home at all?"

"Once I'm at MIT, I'm not planning to come home. Dad

never did." I didn't know whether it was her mentioning Dad, or the fact that she didn't plan to come home again after she went to college, but suddenly, the brightness and silence were too much.

I covered my face with my hands, blocking out the sunlight, the squeak of shoes on linoleum, the pop of milk on the stove. I shook my head, trying to clear it, trying to find something to say, but without Blythe on my side, all I wanted to do was *scream*. I was afraid I *would*. I had to get out of there.

I pushed through the swinging door and rushed out of the house and up the driveway. I passed through the decimated rosebushes lining the empty pond, and ran up the brick stairs past the willow to Charlie's apartment. *My dad's* apartment.

Did my dad stand where I was standing and look out at his million-dollar view, and imagine how one day he wouldn't have to come back to us? Did he imagine how he'd exchange his family for a house full of strangers who needed him more than we did? Were we nothing but an obligation to him? Time served as "Dad"?

I stumbled to the pile of two-by-fours and lifted the top piece. It was damp with morning dew. I leveraged it over my shoulder and almost lost my balance, but leaned forward just in time. Then I swung it in an arc right into the back window.

I flinched as the glass smashed and I dropped the two-by-four. A splinter broke off into my palm, and I yanked it out before I lost my nerve. A bubble of blood welled. I squeezed and a shooting pain went up my arm. But I kept at it. I squeezed drop after drop of blood onto the stack of wood, feeling like I'd been blind and stupid my whole life.

ONE AND ONE—ARE DONE

Blythe found me kicking around the willow tree a few hours later, still pumping pinpricks of blood out of my fingertip. I was surprised she hadn't found me sooner. Maybe that's what kept me outside.

"Are you mad because he was bisexual or because he had a secret?" Blythe was holding a scone in a floral napkin that Maryann Interiors had clearly chosen as the scone's appropriate wrapper.

"Just the *one* secret?" I sat down below the tree and held out my hand for the scone. She gave it to me and sat down beside me.

"Charlie told me that it was Dad's childhood in the South that gave him the idea to have transitional housing." A frown creased Blythe's forehead. It was the look she got when she was having trouble with an algebra proof: half irritation and half determination. "Did you know after he left home, he was homeless, sleeping in Greyhound stations and parks for a few weeks?"

I swallowed down guilt, lifting my thumb to my lower lip. I looked at my thumbnail, wanting the soothing feeling of the words filling me and spilling out. But I put my hand down. "Yeah. I knew he'd had some adventures."

"Don't you want to hear about Dad's dream?" Blythe

reached across me and stole a piece of scone. A blueberry popped out of the flaky dough and landed in the grass.

I tilted my head back against the tree, wondering why I didn't want to hear about Dad's dream. But—I didn't. I didn't even want to hear about it, let alone live in it. "Why didn't he tell us himself? If this was his dream, and he didn't want to be our dad, why didn't he just tell us?"

"I don't think it's one or the other," Blythe said, her tone even, practical.

"But it was." I sat up. "He was planning to leave Mom, leave you and me, and live here full-time."

"But only after we went to college." Blythe's brow creased further.

"Is that when you're planning to stop being my sister? You'll go off to MIT and leave me at Cal State. Is that when we won't be a family anymore?" I felt the scone crumbling in the napkin. I squeezed it the way I'd squeezed my finger.

"Stop being ridiculous." Blythe stood up and tapped her Converse on the tree. "Just come inside and apologize to Mom for walking out. And apologize to me for leaving me to eat an omelet in the most awkward silence ever."

I sighed. "I'm sorry about the awkward omelet. But I'm not apologizing to Mom. If anything, she should be apologizing to us. And Charlie? He should be getting the house ready to sell."

"Charlie's not that bad, you know." She kicked the tree again, her eyes skittering to mine, then away, as if she knew she'd said the wrong thing. "He's the one who taught Dad snap-crackle-pop." She clapped her hands together and pulled them apart, making a loud pop. When we were little, she and I slapped palms until our fingers hurt, trying to make a pop sound as loud as our dad could. Blythe wore a little smile, as if it were so easy to replace one hand with another. As if you could replace one dad with another.

I stood and threw the scone to the grass, the napkin swirling through the air behind it. "What is wrong with you? Charlie's not our dad. And this shouldn't have to be our life. They need to sell the house. And we need to move away from *him*." I turned and started off before she could stop me, sweeping my thumbnail over my bottom lip. The words came as fast as the sting of tears. "One and one is—one. One and one is—one. Two is done. *Done*."

This was the final proof—twins were nothing more than two people. Two people with nothing in common.

12 I DWELL IN THE IMPOSSIBLE—

At number six Magnolia, no one spoke to anyone for the rest of the day, which meant I had a lot of time to make the fabric on the subjonctif board look just right. But when I walked into class on Tuesday, I saw we were the only ones with recycled poster board. Everyone else had laptops, laser pointers, and those wireless slide clickers. Had we done this big project completely wrong?

As I watched a clearly professionally edited video, I wondered if Kai had been wrong about "old-school." I glanced down at our fabric swatch–covered board. Maybe the poster board we'd made wasn't charming, but boring. "We can't compete with this," I whispered.

Kai turned his head, but shrugged. "We have personality."

I sunk my thumbnail into the edge of the board. "Could we ask for an extension? Just until tomorrow?"

Monsieur Cade's voice rang out: "Pas de parler!" *No talking!* Rolly rules were so strict.

"Seriously," Kai whispered, and the back of his hand touched mine. He brushed his knuckles past mine. Once. Twice. "We're good." Then his fingers twined with mine. My heart tumbled in my chest. He was right. I was worried for no reason. They'd love our décoration intérieure poster board.

Clapping filled the classroom, and the light flicked on. We dropped hands.

"Mademoiselle Braxton. Monsieur Thompson." Monsieur Cade was bearing down on us, his cheek pulsing in anger. "You are dismissed. Return when you can stay silent."

"But . . ." Kai's mouth dropped open. "We were next."

"Ne pas maintenant." *Not anymore.* Monsieur Cade strode to the door.

"Mais c'est notre tourner." *But it's our turn*, Kai said, putting on his best good-student smile.

Monsieur Cade gestured for us to leave. Were we seriously getting kicked out of class for whispering? This was so much worse than a low grade on an assignment. Monsieur Cade nodded to the door. "On y va." *Go on.*

The classroom twittered. I couldn't let this be over. Pinpricks tickled my arms. Kai tossed his French book into his bag with a thud and stood. His face was bright red, and he didn't look at me. I grabbed the subjonctif board and held it up like a shield. I was going to get us out of this. That or get us suspended.

"Arrête!" My hands were shaking where I held the poster board. Kai stopped and turned to me. He gave me the universal look for: *Seriously, do* not *make this worse for us.* A shiver ran down my spine. Breathe. I rubbed my thumbnail over my lower lip—just once—just to calm myself down, but once was too much.

"Je demeure dans la possibilité. Je demeure dans la possibilité—" *I dwell in possibility. I dwell in possibility.* My fingernails sunk into the poster board, stopping my French poeting. I turned to Monsieur Cade, and the worst French of my life tumbled out. "This was all my fault. I was nervous so much. Because of I'm new to—at—in this school. Because all we have is this terrible paper and these other excellent students have cinematographers. Please, please, let us have a turn? Please? Please? Did I mention I was born just the other day?"

Kai's mouth hung open. The classroom twitters became snickers. Monsieur Cade looked at me strangely then let the classroom door close. "Je demeure dans la possibilité? Emily Dickinson, non? Mon poète favori." Emily Dickinson was his favorite poet? He crossed and uncrossed his arms. Then he nodded. "Cinq minute. Et après, Mademoiselle Le Principal."

I stood slack-jawed for three heartbeats. Then I turned to Kai, who was staring blankly at me. I mouthed *Come on* and gestured for him to get up as I fumbled our poster board and dropped my notecards to the ground. When he figured out what was going on, Kai hurried to the front of the class, wide-eyed and nervy, and welcomed our clients. He explained our fabric choices and gestured to where the "houndstooth" sofa would go. But he kept saying the wrong form of the verb as he described what we "had done," instead of what we "would do." So I kept correcting him. And then it began to seem as if he was doing it on purpose, and I began rolling my eyes and pretending to be upset with him, and the class began to laugh. Monsieur Cade even smiled once, right before he sent us to the principal.

Our backpacks thumping along, we walked in silence toward the main office. After the *no talking* fiasco, which was, admittedly, 90 percent my fault, I was afraid Kai would never speak to me again. He kept his eyes straight ahead the whole way through the breezeway, so I did, too. But as we ducked into the office and handed the receptionist our shameful yellow infraction notices, Kai shot me a conspiratorial look. Maybe getting kicked out of class was only 75 percent my fault?

The receptionist lifted his brows and pointed down the hallway. I wasn't sure what was happening, but clearly Kai was, because he trudged to the end of the hall and stopped outside Principal Chambliss's door. He dropped his backpack and sat down in one of two wooden chairs. I did the same, afraid to ask what we were waiting for.

I pulled my knees to my chest, my cheeks burning. "I'm sorry I got us in trouble with my unchecked school-related anxiety." I could hear a litany against my actions in my mind: having side conversations during a peer's presentation, talking back to a teacher, poeting in another language. "Is this going to mess up your GPA?" I asked.

I held my breath as he looked over at me. His lashes were so long they drooped at the edges, casting shadows on his cheeks. I let one of my legs flop down, and he tapped my foot with his. "I guess we'll see." A door opened and closed at the front of the office, and we both glanced down the hall. When it had been quiet for a while, we looked back to each other. He didn't look mad, but maybe I didn't know him well enough to know his mad face. Then he wrinkled his nose. "So, are you the president of the Emily Dickinson Fan Club, or what?"

I was tempted to pull my leg up, curl into a ball, and play wombat until he went away, but then he tapped my foot with his again. I looked at his striped Adidas beside my brown boots with the multicolored stacked heel. "No . . . I just have a weird little habit of poeting when I get nervous."

He let out a short laugh. "Poeting, huh?" He pulled his Hacky Sack from a pocket. "No weirder than most people's habits."

We sat in silence, glancing toward the closed door of the principal's office. "So, come here often?" I asked, not sure what I wanted the answer to be. Too many of the kids at Rolly were so . . . sweater set. I wanted more glitter. More sparkle. More Kate Spade.

He threw the Hacky in the air then caught it, turning it in his hand. "Let's just say it's not my first time waiting in this hallway." He glanced back toward the assistant's desk.

"Should I be worried?" I really didn't need to get into more trouble with my mom, especially now—it was only a matter of time before she found out I broke Charlie's kitchen window. "Delinquency's never gone with my look before, but I could adjust my wardrobe."

"I'm not sure you could stand out more if you tried," he said, leaning into my shoulder a bit, like he was telling me a secret. My face flushed, and I dug my thumbnail into my hip to keep my hands by my sides. The truth was, I'd never wanted to wear anything other than what I liked; my dad said it showed confidence. I wasn't sure I believed him then— when I wore one of my mom's altered prom dresses to the first day of high school—or now, sitting here, trying not to chew my lip. And not, under any circumstance, to poet.

I shook my head. "It's Emma who's truly original. I find cool clothes, and I'm not afraid to wear them, but she—"

"You're not afraid of a lot of things. What did you say to Cade back there anyhow? You saved my ass. I had two games this weekend, and work, and I didn't have time to study. And I should have. French is my toughest language."

"You speak more than one language?" I asked.

He nodded, then shrugged. "For Doctors Without Borders. I know French, Tagalog, and a little English. Oh, and pidgin."

I purred in a pigeon impersonation. "What did I just say?"

Kai busted up. I hadn't heard him *really* laugh. It was loud and throaty and bigger than his wiry frame would suggest. And it kind of gave me the chills. "*Hawaiian* pidgin." He said. "My mom's taught me some. It's like English and Japanese and I don't know what else."

"So you're Hawaiian, and you speak like, twelve languages, and you're one of only seven people at this school who know what style looks like . . . What other amazing things don't I know about you?"

"Well . . ." He cleared his throat. "There are some not-so-amazing things—" Outside, the rising commotion of passing period brought shouts and shuffles, slammed lockers and slapped palms. On the other side of the floor-to-ceiling windows, Emma walked by, a single-sleeved dress swirling around her. She looked over and stopped midstride. She made the motion for: *What in the world did you do to be sent to the principal's office?*

I pointed at Kai. Then he pointed at me. He pushed my hand away, and I pushed back. Then he grabbed my hand, pointing with his other hand, and I grabbed back, and we were laughing, our hands linked with each of us trying to pull away to point blame at the other. When I turned back to Emma, she was walking away. Kai blinked, his eyes still on the place she'd disappeared. I pulled my hands from his quickly.

I didn't know what I'd been thinking. Or, I'd been *feeling*, but not thinking.

"We should be studying," I said, just as he said:

"What you don't know is—" His eyes were wide. My hope bird peeked out from a fluff of feathers. I knew I should shove that bird away, but I just couldn't. I nodded for Kai to go ahead. "I don't have a car." His voice was low. "I don't have a family estate, not even one that's falling apart. I'm lucky to get new shoes when mine get holes. I can't take you anywhere that costs more than five dollars. But I know all the hidden paths in the Thornewood Rose Garden. If you wanted to go. Maybe today?" He tapped the heels of his Adidas in a way that said maybe he hadn't just grabbed my hand in class to stop me from freaking out. Maybe he wanted to hold my hand. "I don't have practice."

He was watching me carefully. I tried to think of Emma, to frown or shake my head. I tried. But I couldn't do anything but smile and nod. He let out a long breath and flashed a gleaming, gorgeous, show-all-his-teeth grin in return. He turned from sharp and striking to warm and sweet, and with a sudden rush I realized he was holding my hand. "So, is that a yes?"

"Don't let me interrupt." An African American woman with long braids wearing a dark suit and amazing purple lipstick stood over us, her arms crossed. "I'm *only* the principal of the high school with the single most excellence awards in all the Greater Pacific West. But I'm sure your side conversations are more important than keeping us in first place. Of course they are." She took off her glasses and twisted her mouth. "But what if I let everyone break the rules? No more awards for my trophy shelf. Then what would I put on my shelf?"

She looked from me to Kai as if *our heads* might be the

answer. "Elevate your flirtation in the hallways. And never on my time." Then she turned and shut the door behind her. We sat in silence for several heartbeats.

"That's it? No detention?" I asked. Kai shrugged. "They keep us in line through fear alone?"

"Do they need more?" he asked, and gave me a wicked grin. He pulled me to my feet, and we hurried toward our next classes, a minute until the bell. In the breezeway, he squeezed my hand, then let go. When I sat down breathless beside Blythe in Civics, I could still feel his palm against mine . . . and his fingerprints on my heart.

13

THE HEART ASKS PLEASURE
FIRST, FIRST, FIRST

The clang of last bell was still in the air when I walked to the quad to meet Kai. I didn't know what I would say to him, but I had to either tell him I couldn't go on a maybe-date to the rose garden, or let him know what Emma had told me: that he was already taken.

As if she could feel me thinking about her, Emma messaged me: *Got a peek at Grandmamma's calendar. Beware surprise inspection Thursday!* My thumb hovered over the forward icon, ready to send it to my mom. But I couldn't deal with it right now.

In the quad, I found Blythe and Emma talking poetic mash-ups, their project for Honors English. Blythe looked like she was about to hyperventilate as she tried to remember the first line of some John Donne poem. I was looking it up for her when Kai came around the corner, tossing his Hacky Sack in the air. When he saw us, he stopped and threw it high, then caught it on the back of his neck. He popped it off and caught it again. Nate ran up behind him and snatched the Hacky out of the air. His hair flocked out from the sides of his head like wings. What was with that hair?

"Juvenile," Blythe said, and I looked from her to Nate.

Nate kept his eyes on her as he hopped up on a quad bench and placed a hand over his heart like a Shakespearean actor.

"Friends. October is nigh. We are in the last days of sunshine. What shall be done about this?" I glanced around. Kai hadn't told Nate about our plans, and Emma clearly didn't know. And I hadn't had a chance to tell Blythe. I glanced at Kai. Why wasn't he saying anything? Why wasn't I?

I realized I could solve the problem of the maybe-date right now. "Let's all go to the rose garden," I said.

Blythe shook her head. "We have homework."

"Come on," Nate said, saving me from an argument. "We can review the great American poets while enjoying the great outdoors." Agreement passed through our circle, but as we walked to Nate's car, I glanced at Kai to find him watching me, his brow furrowed. Then I glanced at Emma.

It was the right decision. No regretting it now.

THE MAYOR OF THORNEWOOD WAS bald, stocky, and stately. Everything a statue should be. Nate ran up to the statue and leapt in the air to high-five him. "Hello, old friend!"

The rose garden grew in the valley of Thornewood's hillside. From the lower entrance, winding trails curved up to a pillared central building, and a stone stairway led to a misting fountain. But the rest of the paths were shrouded with overgrown vines and rosebushes, hidden by crumbly half-stone walls and flashes of wilting, once-colorful flowers. At the statue, Blythe read aloud: "'Johnston McMichaels. First mayor of Thornewood. Founder, Beautification and Historic District Society.' Too many titles? Or just enough?"

"Is the first mayor of Thornewood your great-grandpa?" I asked.

"And he's still alive. Why do you think Grandmamma gets

away with being such a historic nuisance? I should say hello. On Tuesdays she does garden tours." Emma winked at Kai. "I'll ask if she'll give the tour in Latin." She walked up the hill toward the building.

When she was gone, I took a tiny step closer to Kai and tapped his elbow. "You didn't list Latin among your talents."

Kai blushed, not meeting my eyes. "I can read it."

Nate bounded past Blythe and swiped the fine-point Sharpie from her back pocket. "You know who needs a longer title?" He held it over her shoulder. "Blythe Braxton. Know-it-all. Ruler of all things scientifically oriented, master of the lab report . . ." She swiped the pen back and grabbed his sleeve.

What was happening here? I thought she hated him.

"Nate Fong. Insufferable smart-ass. Holder of asinine attendance awards . . ." He ducked away from her and loped into the garden. She gave chase, continuing with the academic insults. Was she . . . flirting with him? Blythe ran past, and Nate caught up to her and yanked her hood. She yelped and took off running again. They dodged up to the fountain, and Nate leapt onto the side, his feathered hair flapping in the breeze.

"When did *this* happen?" I asked.

Kai laughed. "In a very romantic setting. Beside a bowl of dead sea monkeys."

I laughed, watching Kai's profile. Why did he have to look so stormy and Heathcliffy today? It shot a little dart of bittersweet right into my heart.

There were reasons Rolly girls gave Kai long looks. He had great style, even if his clothes were old or faded or, like his fleece, pilled with use, and he was good-looking with his tawny skin and those contrasting crazy-blue eyes. But I knew that the reason they kept looking was because he made life look so easy, so fun. Like life was a ride everyone was on, and he was glad just to be cruising, wearing a half smile and waiting patiently for the drop. It was so different from how I felt. I probably looked like every day was a winding road that made me carsick. I was probably tinged green right now. But when he looked at me, he didn't look like he was having fun. His eyes were dark, as if the sky had taken up temporary residence there. Did he think I'd invited everyone to blow him off?

"I'm sorry I invited—" I said as he said:

"I should have known we'd run into—"

We both stopped talking, and the patter of the fountain filled the air. Storm clouds were gathering, fading the blooms around us to cool tones. I opened my mouth to tell him about Emma, to let him know that it wasn't because I didn't want a maybe-date, because I really did. But what came out of my mouth was what I actually wanted to ask: "Want to find a secret pathway?"

One side of his mouth lifted, and he took the end of my sparkly black scarf and tugged. We ducked beneath a wrought iron archway into an overgrown area of the garden. Along the gravel walkway were beds of roses in all varietals—brilliant red bushes, pale pink garden climbers, and miniature white roses. The colors were brilliant, and the fountain—ornate and huge and beautiful and spraying water into the air—made the garden feel festive.

"This must be where the fairies live. All these alcoves and winding pathways," I said as we walked under a wrought iron arch trailing blooming vines. Kai hummed a few bars from a song I didn't recognize and gave me one of his perfect, lopsided smiles.

"The Cure. It's called 'A Chain of Flowers,' and there's a line about finding a girlfriend in a chain of flowers, and I think it's about being afraid to lose someone? Or maybe being afraid to let yourself feel too much, because you're afraid of losing someone."

I tried to hide the pinch of emotion that caught me at his explanation. I swallowed the feeling down, not knowing why it made me feel so raw. "Still not poetry," I said, and bumped his arm with mine. His fingers wrapped around mine, and I settled at his touch—as if he'd wrapped a blanket around my heart. My hope bird nestled down as we walked on, hand in hand.

We passed "Jude the Obscure," a white rose that looked like any other white rose, and "Double Delight," which was white with beautiful bright pink edges, and "Barbra Streisand," which was a big, fluffy pale lavender rose. Its fresh scent reminded me of honeysuckle and of the first bees of summer. And of my dad. Then we stopped beneath a mammoth Sally Holmes climbing rose. "We had one of these at our old house," I said. "My dad called it Kong, like King Kong. It was twenty feet high and almost feet thirty wide." I pressed my lips together tightly. I didn't want to think about my dad, let alone talk about him.

Kai swept his thumb over my palm, and sparks lit my veins. "Will you tell me more about him?"

"No?" Another pinch caught my throat, and I thought about a girl in a circle of flowers, with crumbling stone around her—was she in a graveyard? I pinched my eyes closed. "Sorry." We passed under the next archway, and he stopped walking.

"Don't be sorry." He glanced through the rosebushes toward the distant sound of Blythe and Nate bickering. "I'm just glad you want to be here with me."

The wind swirled through the trees, lifting his hair from his forehead. He stepped closer, still tracing slow circles on my palm, sending little shocks up my arm. Before I could stop myself, my thumbnail brushed my lower lip. "The heart asks pleasure first," I whispered. "Pleasure, pleasure, pleasure."

Kai met my eyes, watching me carefully. And then he dipped his head, and his lips brushed my forehead. A soft stroke of warmth coursed through me, lighting my heart, stopping the words. I tilted my head back, and his cheek was against mine, his nose cold against my skin. I closed my eyes, thinking of grass, and spring, and flowers blooming. He smelled like cinnamon. I lifted my chin and forgot every word I ever knew as his breath met mine.

The thud of a walking stick hitting packed earth brought me back to myself, and I pulled away, Emma's warning on the tip of my mind.

There was the rustle of leaves beneath feet and then from behind Kai: "Beware—the tour is about to begin." It was Mrs. McMichaels brandishing a mean-looking pair of pruning shears.

"How are you today, Mrs. McMichaels?" Kai nodded in greeting,

"Emma will be along." Mrs. McMichaels grunted and pushed past us toward the statue at the base of the garden. We followed her, our heads down. For a woman who must be approaching a hundred, she walked with long, lean strides. "I hope your mother's considering the society's offer to purchase your property for the city of Thornewood," she called over her shoulder.

She stopped so suddenly I almost crashed into her. When she turned, her wide-brimmed hat cast a shadow over my face. "It doesn't matter how many Zone C applications are put forth. No one can retro-activate a neighborhood vote. But if your mother and Mr. Parker sell, we'll forgive the current fines." She turned back to the garden entrance and strode on. "Imagine. Number six could finally be restored the way it *should* be. Maybe become a museum."

It seemed so simple. Why hadn't they sold? I ground my teeth. Charlie. He must have known about the offer. But did my mom? I was about to ask when Mrs. McMichaels lifted a hand for silence. "Mr. Fong! Do I need a bigger sign to keep people from using my father's statue as a lounge chair?" Nate, who was leaning against the first mayor of Thornewood, stood slowly, his praying mantis legs unfolding like they had two joints. He glanced between me and Kai and smiled. I couldn't stop a blush.

"I'm here!" Emma came down the center path, scattering gravel. She slid and bumped into Kai, laughing. Kai smiled, and buried his hands deep in his fleece pockets. I had the overwhelming urge to put my hands in his pockets, too. I thought of his lips on my forehead, his fingers wrapped around mine. The places we'd touched were white hot, like I'd been burned. But then Emma leaned against my shoulder, and I cooled, pushing away thoughts of Kai's cinnamon breath. Emma hooked her arm through mine, and we followed Mrs. McMichaels into the garden.

At the fountain, Mrs. McMichaels raised her voice over the crash of the water. "Our first mayor, my father, brought well-to-do San Franciscans to this beautiful place. Thorne-wood. A safe, separate community." Something about the way she said *separate* raised my hackles. "And his beauti-fication society thrives today thanks to the original grant he bestowed. Though your parents should consider annual giving."

"How long is this tour?" Nate asked. Mrs. McMichaels ignored him and circled us through the wide, twisting lanes of the rose garden. It was, thankfully, not a long tour. Back at the fountain, Mrs. McMichaels hit us with a stream of Latin botanical names as our eyes glazed over. When we gave a round of applause, Mrs. McMichaels beamed.

"Remember to tell your parents about the fund!" Mrs. McMichaels lifted her pruning shears and walked off into the garden.

"Well, at least the tour was free." Nate kicked a rock, and Blythe kicked it back at him. Emma gave us a grateful look.

"Thank you," Emma said. "She loves giving that tour. And she doesn't get a lot of takers." As we walked toward where Nate was parked, Emma fell into step with Kai. I pulled out my phone to pretend I didn't care, to pretend that I hadn't been on a maybe-date, or had a maybe-kiss. To pre-tend that my heart did not shudder when Kai was around. On my home screen, Emma's message about the house inspection was still there.

And I realized what I needed to do. I just had to give my mom and Charlie *a good reason* to sell the house. Like Char-lie said, if they kept getting more fines, they'd have no choice but to sell. And if they sold number six, I'd never have to see or think about Charlie or the dad I never knew. And our lives could go back to the way they were before. Maybe we could even get the cottage back. My thumb hovered over the message for one more moment. I looked at Blythe, wondering if I should ask her what she thought. But what if she disagreed? I couldn't take the chance.

I pressed delete.

MY FRIEND MUST BE
A FEATHERED BIRD

I tried to ignore thoughts of Kai by spending every waking moment planning the downfall of number six Magnolia with Emma. The day after our rose garden adventure, I invited Emma over to the crumbling mansion, and we sat on the creaking front porch floorboards as I explained about my dad's unique approach to relationships, Charlie's plan for transitional housing, and Blythe and me becoming homeless. She was in.

"Everyone needs a home," she said. "Even if it's just a tiny place in the world that's yours." She looked away, her eyes welling with tears. "Thanks for telling me all of this." She leaned against my side, and I leaned back, and even though Blythe didn't care if we had a home or not, Emma did. And that felt like enough. We began recon right away. While I chatted up the job supervisor and found out they were about to frame a wall to turn the library into a studio suite, Emma took pictures of the Historic District permit check-off sheet. When she left, we were one step closer to selling and leaving the crumbly mansion and the moldy truth behind.

Thursday after school, we walked the block and a half to Thornewood City Hall. As we crossed the entrance, Emma waved to the valet. He was sitting at the edge of a spitting-cupid fountain, looking less like he was there to park cars and more like the handsome owner of a Tuscan villa. I tried not to be surprised by the excess. If Mrs. McMichaels could force everyone in the Historic District to paint their houses some form of white, she could raise enough revenue for a fountain and handsome valet service.

"Glad they're using taxpayer money cautiously at Thornewood Headquarters," I said.

Emma waved, and the valet waved back. "That's Kai's brother."

Inside, I said: "I guess the hotness thing is genetic."

We busted up laughing as we passed quiet offices lit with those money-green banker's table lamps. We were still giggling when we arrived beneath gold letters that read: RECO DS. As if we were there to see Dr. Reco, oral implant specialist. It didn't seem very Thornewood for a sign to be missing a letter.

The door jangled as we walked in, and Mrs. McMichaels stepped from behind her massive nameplate. BERNADETTE MCMICHAELS, THORNEWOOD BEAUTIFICATION AND HISTORIC DISTRICT SOCIETY PRESIDENT, THORNEWOOD CITY COUNCIL MEMBER-AT-LARGE. "My darling girl. Look at you." She seemed about to say more, but she noticed me. "And a transplant."

"You remember Sabine." Emma bounded over to Mrs. McMichaels.

"I didn't realize there were two of you until I saw you both at the rose garden." Mrs. McMichaels adjusted her glasses. "I've always thought twins were redundant." It wasn't the worst or the weirdest thing I'd heard about twins.

"She's checking on the new permit application," Emma said.

Mrs. McMichaels waved a hand in the air. "First let me look at you." Emma gave me an apologetic look, hugged her grandmother, and then twirled, showing off another ruffly one-armed dress. Mrs. McMichaels lifted her glasses. "Why don't you wear some of the clothes I bought? You look so nice in navy." I pinched my eyes closed. How could she not see the amazing talent in front of her? Why buy clothes for someone who made them so well? For someone who stitched her ruffles by *hand*?

I pressed my lips between my teeth and walked into aisles of files like I knew what I was doing. Mrs. McMichaels's hushed voice carried. "Is he keeping your clothes clean? Is he making you healthful meals—"

"Grandmamma, stop worrying. Dad's fine." Mrs. McMichaels pulled Emma close and spoke directly against her cheek. Emma pulled away, and her grandmother raised her voice: "When there's a problem, we deal with it. By whatever means necessary. I want you to consider living in the house instead of—"

"I'll come to brunch, okay?" Emma sounded not angry, but resigned. Brunch. I thought of purple cauliflower and shuddered. I trailed my fingers over the open shelving, through a sea of manila. I had no idea where to start.

"Your great-grandfather will be pleased. You can even bring that boy."

I stopped walking and looked back. Don't let it be—

"His name is *Kai*." My mouth went dry. He had brunch with her? And her grandparents? I turned back to the files, telling myself that Kai and I were just friends. Kai + Me was a harmless nonflirtation. We were an accidental hand-holding moment. That was it. There was nothing between us. There was no reason he should not go to brunch with her family.

So why did my heart feel like it was being pressed through

a mangler? I rubbed my thumbnail over my lower lip. "My friend must be a bird, for it flies—on ruffles in the sky, it flies." I pushed my thumbnail against my teeth to stop the poeting, reminding myself that Emma brought me here because she cares what happens to me. I took a deep breath, let it out, and lowered my hand.

"Kai has to work this weekend." I glanced up to see Mrs. McMichaels flinch. She was seriously allergic to the word *work*. She leaned into Emma with a whisper/kiss then let her go. Emma practically ran down the aisle to me.

"Sorry about that," she whispered. "Let's see what we can find . . ." She ran her hands down the files and pulled one out and set it down on an big table at the back of the room. She opened it, and it was as if someone had taken the contents of the file, dumped them in a drawer, stirred them up, threw them in an oversized folder, and labeled it MAGNOLIA BLOS-SOM. Seriously?

I looked at the mess helplessly. "What are we even looking for?"

Emma blew her bangs out of her eyes and grabbed a stack of mismatched papers. "Zone C apps are light pink. So just find pink," Emma said. "Whatever came in should have been attached to that. But I swear I didn't leave it like this. I don't know what happened." Emma and I dug through and sorted papers into colors. We sorted. And sorted.

When we'd gotten through a good quarter of the documents, Emma lifted her head. "How's Blythe doing with her mash-up?" I stopped sorting.

"Um, I don't know." I'd forgotten Emma and Blythe were in the same English class. I looked back down at the forms. One was for "a residence above the stable for guests and household help." The date was 1934. "It's a poetry slam?" I felt a tinge of jealousy that Blythe got to recite poetry while I struggled through *The Canterbury Tales*.

"A poetic mash-up," Emma said. "Rolly tradition." At least poetry was better than their other tradition: poodle topiaries. "HA!" Emma held up a piece of pink paper. *Application for Zone C Alteration and Reuse of Historic District Homes.* I snatched it.

We read aloud: "'The house at number six Magnolia can be confirmed to have financial backing to be rezoned as a temporary housing facility for the needs of the Mission Project and its subsidiaries." Emma wrinkled her nose. "What's the Mission Project?"

"It's where Charlie works." I pulled off the attached documents and read aloud: "The Mission Project supports the progress of legal and social issues in the LGBTQIA community." Stapled to the back of the pack was a new set of architect's drawings. They were more detailed than the ones in Charlie's apartment. The dining room, library, conservatory, and butler's pantry of the house would all become studio units. The kitchen would be industrialized to serve two meals a day. And upstairs, which I'd just started getting used to, would turn into dormitories.

"This looks like a hostel or something." Emma picked up the drawings of the upstairs rooms. "Isn't this your room?" Instead of two twin beds, the drawing had two bunks—making room for four people. I shook my head, feeling nauseous. The world needed places like this. It did. But this housing was called *transitional* for a reason. I'd always thought there would be a *home* to come to. And I always thought it would be the cottage. I could get used to another home, but

I wasn't sure I could get used to *this*. Behind all the drawings was another Zone C permit dated almost three years ago. It was stamped DENIED. Just below the red stamp was a personal note in flourished cursive.

Mr. Parker: According to the town charter of the beautiful city of Thornewood, no Historic District home may be owned or operated as a business. The only way to bypass this is the neighborhood vote. It failed. There is no recourse beyond the neighborhood vote.—Bernadette McMichaels

"What's a neighborhood vote?" I asked.

"Thornewood is very democratic," Emma said. "Any time someone wants a big change in the Historic District, the residents vote." I was about to ask what major changes they'd accomplished, considering it still looked like 1940 around here, but Mrs. McMichaels was suddenly standing above us.

"It's time to close up, Emmaline," Mrs. McMichaels said, and I glanced at *Emmaline*. Emma rolled her eyes. "I have an inspection soon."

"One sec, Grandmamma." Emma shoved the permit we'd found and the plans at me and motioned for me to take pictures while she complimented her grandmother's newly curled hair. I quickly took the photos, getting as much as I could, then I scooped up the materials up and shoved them back into the folder.

I didn't know what more I'd learned, really, except that the house was for sure in violation of a bunch of Thornewood rules and regulations and was about to be in violation of a bunch more. And that the pink room I'd just started to not hate was slated to become a hostel. I shoved the folder back on its shelf and cleared my throat. Emma took my arm, and after grabbing our backpacks, we headed toward the front doors of city hall.

"So," Emma said just as we were about to leave. "Are you ready for the inspection today? You've got the list of potential violations. What's your plan?"

I shook my head. "I was thinking to make sure she saw the new framing of the library? Maybe bring some paint cans down from the attic so she could see that they're planning to go with greige, and pretend it's a white?"

"Hit as many of the violations we lined up as you can. Paint color, painting woodwork. The framing. It should be easy to rack up a bunch of fines."

"Will you come with me?" I asked, wishing that Blythe was still my partner in crime.

She shook her head. "I can't. I have a meeting for the Mash-Up." She hip-checked the door and popped it open. Sunlight burst into my eyes, and I lifted a hand, squinting. I blinked, not sure I was seeing what I thought I was seeing.

Kai sat on the side of the fountain beside his brother, arms crossed, laughing. My heart thundered, and I gripped my backpack straps tighter. Kai lifted his eyes and found mine. I swallowed, filled with that same feeling he gave me that day in the library: as if he'd turn the whole world away to listen to me. I was just that important.

I didn't know what this was. But it wasn't a crush.

"Hey!" Kai's brother pointed at me like I was famous. "You're French Sabine!"

I laughed, all the nervousness of seeing Kai going into

it. I shook my head and waved. "I'm not French, but I am Sabine."

Kai said: "The one and only." We looked at each other, and my heart hammered all over the place. Emma took the pavers two at a time, leaping to the side of the fountain. She gave Kai's brother a high five and introduced him as Keanu. Then to my horror, she said: "Sabine is about to go destroy her crumbling family mansion by rigging it so they get about a dozen fines."

"I'm starting to think you might be a bad influence, Sabine." Kai smiled to let me know he was joking, but I was starting to feel a little like a criminal. Maybe I shouldn't be sabotaging these inspections. Maybe I should try again to talk to my mom. Or Blythe. Or Charlie. But my stomach turned at the thought. If I did that, they'd say what they'd said before, and I'd miss my opportunity to get us a real home.

"It's for the greater good," I said. "Or the greater good of Blythe and me having a home to come to." I explained to Kai and Keanu what was going on, trying to sound upbeat, as if everyone's parents had open marriages and everyone's houses turned into transitional housing at one point or another. As if it were okay to have a room one day and the next day, a bunk. Or maybe have nothing at all.

"So you're going to go carry paint cans and whatever else from your attic right now, by yourself, before four P.M.?" Kai lifted his brows and exchanged a look with Emma. "I have an hour before practice; I'll help. I'm already implicated in your previous crimes." I shook my head, not wanting to be alone with him. No, I wanted to. I really wanted to be alone with him. But I could *not* be trusted to be alone with him.

"If you're saying no because of the GPA thing, I'm caught

up on my homework. I'm happy to help. I am a professional mover, you know." I tried to say no. My mind formed the words, then something else bubbled up instead: poetry—hope and feathers and stones and hearts—and instead of saying anything, I nodded. He watched me for a moment, then he smiled.

"Let's go do some crimes," he said. With a little wave to Keanu and Emma, we walked back in the direction of the school—and number six Magnolia.

BETWEEN ETERNITY
AND TIME YOU'RE MINE

When we walked up, number six was quiet and the door was ajar. As it swung open, I had a sense of déjà vu. Not of the first day we saw this place, when it was shedding wallpaper like skin, but of another house—a house that wasn't in disrepair or under construction. A beautiful white wedding cake of a house. It was what it must have looked like once, and might again. I blinked, and the image was gone, leaving me and Kai in the entrance hall, batting away sawdust like dust motes.

"You're sure if we do this," Kai asked, "your mom won't get stuck with debt?" He looked around the entrance, his eyes catching on the new windows. They looked much better than the broken ones he'd seen before.

"Mrs. McMichaels promised to buy the house," I said. "If she does, the fines will be dropped." Kai nodded, and we walked deeper into the house, listening for anyone there.

"This place isn't exactly in great shape," he said. "What if the selling price doesn't cover the loans?" I stopped in the kitchen doorway. I hadn't thought about loans. Loans were the problem, weren't they? Or was the money problem taxes?

"Well, it's not all like this," I said. "The garage apartment is gorgeous. Design-mag amazing."

Kai's eyes popped. "Apartment? Is it rented?"

"Charlie lives there right now."

"Only a certain number of apartments are allowed in Thornewood," Kai said. "Our building is one of only two apartment buildings in the whole city. Mrs. McMichaels will want to know if there's another rental."

"Noted," I said, and pulled up the punch list and showed it to Kai. He read aloud. "Watered-glass windows. Real wood trim (use dovetail check). Approved interior paint colors. Aged brick for hardscape. Approved stain colors. Century-appropriate carved details." When he gave me an incredulous look, I smiled.

"Thornewood is a place of rules." I tapped the list on my phone. "The paint colors my mom chose are off list, and I know she was planning to paint, not stain, the woodwork. She hates real wood color. She says it's provincial."

Kai laughed. "I hate to think what she'd say of our place. There's real wood color *and* fake wood color."

"But I bet it's full of a real family with real love." I slipped my phone in my pocket and dropped my backpack on a kitchen stool. Kai followed suit, watching me.

"You know you can't get away from what you know about your dad." Kai dug his hands into his pockets, searching for his Hacky Sack. I swallowed. I'd thought something similar. I couldn't unknow that my dad had a secret life. But . . . maybe I could forget. Kai came up with the Hacky and tossed it once, then shoved it back in his pocket. He scanned my face as if the right thing to say was written below my eye. Or along my jaw. "No house is perfect. Ours is too noisy and too small and it smells like a bunch of guys live there. Which they do." I knew Kai meant well, but I couldn't think about families and secrets right now. I needed to *do* something.

"The paint cans are in the attic. We should bring them down." I attempted a smile, but images of a happy house stuck in my mind, poking and prodding. "You don't scare easily, do you?" He gave me the side-eye. I gave it right back. He gestured for me to lead the way, and we walked up through the house and to a door I'd only glimpsed the other side of once—the day we moved in.

The attic.

I'd seen the workers bringing their extra tools, the fixtures my mom already bought, and the paint cans up there. But I'd never gone up. We stood there for a beat, and the door creaked open on its own. I took it as a sign that number six wanted to be saved from Charlie's nefarious plans.

"In my professional opinion, you have ghosts," Kai said, then he took my hand. I tried to tell myself we were just friends. But my hand knew that was a lie, and held on tight. We climbed, stepping in the deep grooves of the worn stairs. Our shoulders brushed the high walls of the stairway, and my sweater sleeves caught on the splintery wood. At the top of the stairs, we peered into the eaves of the house. The dark, unfinished wood dripped cobwebs, silt, and spiders.

Kai squeezed my hand and let go. "If I lived here, this is where I'd want to be." Kai walked to the windows. Even with the crawly inhabitants, the attic was amazing. It was all uneven floorboards, beadboard walls, and huge windows with a view as spectacular as Charlie's. I walked around the tarp-covered lumps and unpacked boxes littering the floor, keeping my eyes open for paint cans. "All this place needs is a cleaning and a coat of paint. It'll be like the *Swiss Family Robinson* house." He sat down on a deep window seat and leaned his elbows onto his knees.

"*Swiss Family Robinson?*" I swept dust from the seat and sat down beside him. "I never saw it."

"The littlest brother saves the day with his pirate alert system."

I laughed. "Is that how it goes?"

"Yes, and I'd thank you not to make fun of Francis." We both laughed.

"Would it have a hammock?" I said. "We had a hammock once, but a week into hammock ownership, I flipped onto the hardscape. No more hammock." I showed him the scar just below my lower lip.

"Ouch." He touched my chin. I shivered in the thick, close air. "I hate it. It's ugly."

Our eyes met. "Scars are just places where everyone can see your memories," he said. Words bubbled up inside me, itching to get out. I pinched my fingers into the fabric of my dress, but I couldn't stop them. I swept my thumbnail over my lower lip.

"Between eternity and time, time, yours and mine. Yours, mine. You're mine." It was the single most blush-inducing poeting I'd ever done, and I bit my lip to stop. But Kai was just waiting patiently, his fingertips against my cheek. I leaned into his touch. Where he touched me, I could feel his heartbeat thrumming, then syncing with mine, and the world disintegrated. The space between our faces was six inches, but it seemed endless. Him on one side, me on the other, and a sea of energy between us. How do people cross that gap? How do people just lean over and they're *there*? Together?

"Does my poeting freak you out?" I asked. Was it six inches between us? Or only five?

"No." He brushed a curl off my cheek. "Does it bother you that I have a job instead of a trust fund?"

"No." I shook my head, and my hair fell back so he could push it away again. Now it was four inches. "I prefer apartments to mansions."

"And movers to stockbrokers?" Three inches.

"Much better stories with movers," I murmured as we closed the space between us. And I guess that was how it happened.

His lips were warm against mine. The tip of his nose was cool against my cheek, and his palm was rough on the back of my neck. And when his mouth opened against mine, I saw colors: bright red and hot pink. I sucked in a breath.

He pulled back, searching my eyes. "Is this okay?"

I froze; there was something I needed to tell him. But I couldn't think. I nodded, then I closed the space between us. When his lips met mine again, the colors changed to green and then to a blue so bright it had a yellow center. The colors turned to patterns, as if my mind were creating textiles in response to *joy*. I lifted a hand to his chest, feeling dizzy.

How was this kiss so different from anything I'd ever felt before? It was so different from the softness of my dad's hand in mine, so different from the smoothness of my pillow beneath my cheek, so different from my sister's head on my shoulder. I never wanted to stop feeling the way I did right then—like there was no past and no future and nothing in the world but him and me and now. And in my mind not words, but color, and pattern, and light.

Then, from outside, an engine roared. The Momobile. Then the Mustang.

They were home.

16

I'M NOBODY!
WHO THE HECK ARE YOU?

I pulled away from Kai, my heart climbing my throat. Our hands were still linked, and I could feel the jump of his pulse. I squeezed tightly.

"Are you still in?" I asked. He nodded, his eyes soft and unfocused. "We have to hurry." I hopped down and yanked off the nearest tarp. Toolboxes, circular saw, PVC piping. An old sink, broken towel bars, the cracked lid of a toilet. Kai hopped down beside me and pulled up the next tarp. Paint cans. At least fifteen. Kai put his hands on his hips. "What now?"

"Okay, so I know she's using one color—it's a greige, and it's not allowed. It's called Silver something." I turned the cans—some empty, some full—looking for their little white labels with the paint droplet. "It'll be an eggshell finish, like this," I pointed to a can. "Exterior eggshell finish."

Outside, car doors slammed, and I heard my mom's voice. Then Charlie's. They were both home. For a moment, there was nothing but the spin and clunk of paint cans twirling on plank floors. "Is this it? Silver Cloud?" Kai had his hands around a half-used can.

"Yes!"

He pointed to more beside it. "Three of them." He picked up two, and I grabbed the third and we rushed downstairs.

We stopped at the landing. "What do we do with them?" Kai asked, and his voice carried across the open hallway. I pressed my finger to my lips, and we stood very still. Below us, keys hit a counter and the side door slammed closed. Charlie called out in Spanish to the project manager.

"Follow me," I whispered. Kai followed me down the stairs, both of us creeping close to the walls. I stopped at the bottom, listening. They were in the dining room. We hurried around the corner into the foyer, where framing wood had recently been cut and stacked. We placed our paint cans beneath the stack, where no one would see if they were just walking by, but the paint would be obvious to someone who walked through the front door.

While Kai kept a lookout, I pushed the newly hung curtains aside to reveal where my mom had tested paint colors on the bare, original woodwork. Then we hurried back into the foyer and grabbed our backpacks from the kitchen. We were brushing the dust off our clothes as Charlie and the project manager walked in, both speaking in rapid Spanish.

"Oh, Sabine. And Mr. Thompson." Charlie finished his conversation quickly.

"I was just showing Kai how nice the . . ." I glanced around for anything that could be called "nice" looking. "How nice the new windows look."

"An improvement, it's true." Charlie reintroduced himself, and he and Kai shook hands. It was so *dad*-like, I cringed. My dad would never meet Kai; he'd never shake his hand. "Would you like to see the other changes? I'm sure you appreciate houses in your profession."

I shot Kai a glance and said: "We need to study."

Just as he said: "I have soccer practice."

Then we both said: "We should go." We smiled at each other and were turning away from Charlie when a persistent knock came from the side door. From somewhere in the house, my mom yelled for Charlie to answer it.

"Excuse me," Charlie said, and headed toward the side door.

Kai and I locked eyes. I grabbed the straps of my backpack tightly. "I thought she'd come through the front!"

I bit my lip and followed Charlie. We didn't have to go far; Mrs. McMichaels was trying to push her way through the side door and into the hallway.

"Mr. Parker, I said step out of the way." She swung her tote bag in a small arc around her carrot stick of a body, forcing him to step back. "I have an inspection to complete."

Charlie had both hands up, like she was placing him under arrest and planning to secure him with her canvas bag. "You can't just waltz in here. You can only fox-trot, and only if you're dancing with your lawyer—"

Mrs. McMichaels swung the bag again. "The city of Thornewood allows surprise inspections to ascertain historical accuracy. We take history seriously. It's essential the city is fully aware of the historical accuracy of your repairs!"

Charlie threw his hands in the air and turned, almost falling over me and Kai.

He ground his teeth, balling his hands into fists. Then he smiled in that toothy Southern way that says: *I'm smiling, but it's only because I'm considering cannibalism and you look delicious.* "Where's your mother?" I shrugged, and he muttered an expletive under his breath. He jerked his thumb at Mrs. McMichaels. "Tell that woman I'll be right back."

Kai and I exchanged a glance then stepped up to stand

in the doorway between Mrs. McMichaels and the evidence of historical misrepresentation we'd strewn in the entryway. Just as I was about to ask her inside, offer her tea, then point out the attractive paint colors my mom was planning to paint the woodwork, Charlie hollered: "And for God's sake, keep her out of the house!"

"Okay!" I hollered back, and then smiled at Mrs. McMichaels *way* too wide, the nervous energy of perfect kisses still buzzing through my body.

"Hi, Mrs. McMichaels," Kai said. Then he cleared his throat. "Nice day. And such nice new brick, right?" He tapped his foot on the new, shiny red brick. Where once were crumbling stone and broken concrete pieces was now perfectly aligned brick. Charlie said foundations are important, or something.

"New brick?" She peered over her glasses at her feet.

I nodded. "Yeah. It's so . . . uncrumbly." I glanced at Kai, who nodded for me to go on. "And speaking of uncrumbly, have you seen the garage apartment? It's gorgeous."

"Apartment?" Her eyebrows rose like shoulder spikes on a Vivienne Westwood gown.

"Yeah." I looked up the driveway and realized that the garage apartment wasn't visible from the street. Even on an interactive map, it probably looked like just a garage. She followed my gaze and took a few steps up the driveway.

The clatter and clack of high heels sounded behind us, and my mom's best Maryann Interiors voice drifted out. "My deepest apologies for the wait, Mrs. McMichaels." She touched my shoulder and I let her pass. "Something cool to drink?"

"You've stalled long enough," Mrs. McMichaels said,

brandishing her inspection clipboard. She barreled straight for us, forcing us to step aside. I stumbled down onto the brick beside Kai, while my mom stepped backward, looking as if she'd invited Mrs. McMichaels inside.

My mom turned to follow Mrs. McMichaels as she stalked into the house, but glanced from Kai to me, and back to Kai. "You're Mr. Thompson's son, aren't you?"

"Yes, ma'am," Kai said, and shook my mom's hand. She looked from him to me, as if she could see our crimes—dusty-attic kissing, unauthorized paint-can movement, new-brick confessions.

"We're studying. For French," I said. Her eyes went vague as she listened not to me, but to voices from inside. Mrs. McMichaels was muttering about esteem and history and incompetence.

"Maybe go to the library," my mom said, and shut the door in our faces. I let out a breath and slumped against the closed door. I gave Kai a *let's get out of here* look, and we headed down the driveway, toward the sidewalk.

"I was sure we were busted," Kai said when we stopped at the curb. "It was like she could see inside our souls."

"She's always been like that," I said. "But she usually uses that power to look inside her clients' souls, not mine."

Kai glanced to the house. "I hope what we did works." I pressed my lips together, too aware of him standing there on the sidewalk beside me, his head bent toward mine.

"Me, too." I took a step closer to him. "It's not too much to ask for, is it? A place in the world that feels like mine?" He shook his head, then pulled me to him and kissed my cheek, then my lips, right there on the sidewalk. It was sweet and breathy and over too quickly. His pocket was buzzing.

He pulled out his phone, frowning. "Sabine, I'm sorry. I've got to go."

I remembered his soccer practice. "If you're late, I can ask Charlie to give you a ride." But he shook his head, still looking at his phone.

"That's okay. I've got to call my brother. And my coach." He rubbed the back of his neck, squinting at the phone like it might change its message to something he'd rather see.

A little flutter of fear winged in my heart. "Can I do anything?" He pulled his eyes from his phone and put it in his pocket.

"Yeah." He took my hand and kissed the inside of my wrist. My hope bird just about tried to punch through my chest and fly away. "Keanu's having a party tomorrow night at our place. Come." I'd barely nodded before he was off, jogging down the block. I watched until I couldn't see him anymore. My face had gone numb from smiling.

I sat down on the front steps, pulled an old box of Red Vines from my backpack, and nervously chewed through three of them until my heart settled. Then I pulled out my homework, since I wasn't about to make it to the library now. I had finished a paragraph for French when Blythe walked up.

"Where did you go after school?" she asked, sitting down beside me. It was on the tip of my tongue to blurt it all out: city hall, the punch list, the paint cans, and kissing Kai. To tell her how Mrs. McMichaels was in there now, probably fining us within an inch of our house. To tell her that I was saving us from this place, even if she wouldn't.

But Mrs. McMichaels's voice echoed down the driveway, followed by Charlie's.

A door slammed, and we both stood up to see the

commotion. "I *assure* you there's no limit to the number of fines I'm authorized to levy!" Mrs. McMichaels lifted her voice over echo of the slam. "I might as well *be* city hall as far as you're concerned."

"Oh, for pity's sake." Charlie's voice rose as he followed her down the driveway. "You can't stop every single project in Thornewood just to spite us!"

My mom hurried out, hands wide in appeal. "Mrs. McMichaels. There must be some course of action." She was using her displeased-client voice. "A committee we can speak with?"

"I *am* the committee. The neighborhood vote was denied. You can put in permit requests every day for the next fifty years, but they won't be granted." Mrs. McMichaels swung her tote across her shoulder, gripped her clipboard to her chest, and planted both feet. "You have no choice but to stop these so-called renovations and sell Magnolia Blossom to the city. Good day." She spun on her heel and headed toward a white Tesla decorated with the Thornewood crest: a tree that looked more like a brain.

Sell to the city. The relief I felt in that moment sagged my shoulders. We could leave. We could go home.

"What's going on?" Blythe asked. Charlie and Mom were exchanging nasty looks worthy of their ten-year history. My mom flattened her lips into a line, giving Charlie a long look before she turned to us.

"You know what?" Her voice was suspiciously sweet, like it got when she talked to resellers who were trying to raise their prices on her. "I need you two to go next door and pick up our misdirected mail. The house with the big hedge. Mrs. Costello is waiting."

"But what about the—" Mom cut me off with a hand, then

135

pointed down the block. As we walked a few houses down to number six Highland, which sometimes got our mail, I opened my mouth to tell Blythe everything—especially now that my plan had *worked*. But she spoke first.

"Did I hear that right?" She glanced back at the house, where Mom and Charlie were walking back up the driveway, bickering. "We have to sell the house?" She shook her head. "I'm so sick of all this *change*." She stopped on the sidewalk outside Mrs. Costello's house and let her backpack drop to the ground. "I don't want to move again. I finally found a school that works as hard as I do."

The nervous flutter of my hope bird's wings made me feel a little queasy. I chewed my lip as she kicked her backpack half-heartedly.

"We could move someplace here, in Thornewood." I glanced around at all the sameness—big green boxwood and big white houses. It wasn't what I'd had in mind. "There's probably another place here for us. Just you, me, and Mom."

Blythe kept her eyes on the ground. "Thornewood is expensive. We can't afford another house here."

I swallowed over that truth. "Kai lives in an apartment." Blythe seemed to consider that, then shook her head, toeing her backpack. "But what's the likelihood of us getting one? No. We can't move. We need to figure out a way to stay."

"What?" I tried to stop my face from showing how pissed off that made me, but I couldn't. I'd just spent hours upon hours reading forms of tiny print and weirdly worded fifty-year-old Thornewood Historic District rules to make sure we *could* move. How did she not see that as long as we stayed here, every day would remind us that our lives were lies? "No."

"What do you mean, *no?*" Blythe curled her lip, unused to me disagreeing with her. "Do you have any idea how hard it is to get into MIT? Rolly is a top-ranked school. If I do well, I'll be a serious candidate."

I just wanted a place that felt like mine. Why didn't Blythe want that, too? Why was she so focused on two-point-seven years from now that she couldn't see how bad *now* was? I had to keep it together and convince her to be on my side. "So in the meantime, we live in a construction zone, then share a room with strangers?"

She shrugged. "You heard Mrs. McMichaels. They can't get their permit, so there won't be any bunk sharing. Just get over it."

I suddenly wished for the scent of my dad's study—that smoky, cracked-leather smell. Manila folders and musty books. And I wanted the *Handbags: A Love Story* book he always kept open on a side table, in case I wanted to flip through it. I wanted a home for my family. Without that— without a true place that looked and felt like me—who was I? *Nobody.*

I swept my thumbnail across my lower lip. "I'm nobody, who are you? Are you nobody, too? Nobody, no body." Blythe had turned to Mrs. Costello's door, thinking the conversation was over. Now she turned back to me, hissing.

"Can't you control the weird?"

I didn't like to stop midphrase. "I'm nobody, who the heck are you? Shhh. Don't tell. Never tell." She yanked my hand away from my face. "You have a compulsion, you know that? This is a compulsion." I swallowed until the words went back where they'd come from. "Can you try not to quote poetry at school anymore? Unless it's for a class or something?"

I looked at Blythe's drawn-on sleeve. Talk about *compulsions*.

Probably hearing us on her front porch, Mrs. Costello opened the door, her long brown hair swinging. Her house smelled of gingerbread, and pictures covered the entryway and living room walls—family photos thrown in with art—some in mismatched frames, some tacked up without any frame at all. Maryann Interiors would never approve, but I loved it. On a sofa, there were tamped-down throw pillows, and the softwood floors were covered with scuffs. We'd never been allowed to put up family photos or art on the walls unless they were in matching frames, but still—something about Mrs. Costello's home reminded me of our cottage in Dana Point.

"Wait a minute, okay?" Mrs. Costello said. "I have mail and ginger cookies for you." When she walked into the house, flipping on warm yellow lights as she went, I turned on Blythe.

It was on the tip of my tongue to tell her that her clothing-drawing thing was just as weird as my poeting thing and that everyone knew she had a crush on Nate and that she should just go for it already because she may never find another guy who liked Sharpie as much as she did. But if I wanted to get out of number six Magnolia and into a home like Mrs. Costello's, I needed Blythe. If I wanted to keep the memory of my mom's head on my dad's shoulder each night at the kitchen sink, then I had to get Blythe on my side. Because if we left this place, if we never had to see Charlie again, my parents could still be two people who were truly in love, and they could stay that way forever.

I took a deep breath. "Don't you want a home like Mrs. Costello's? All lived-in and comfortable?"

Her face was in her phone, and she didn't look at me. "I want to get into MIT."

I needed a new tack. Mrs. Costello was coming back, a plate of steaming gingersnaps in one hand and a pile of mail in the other. I had the overwhelming compulsion to ask her if I could live here, with her and her funky art-covered walls. I pinched my eyes closed tightly for one moment. Then I had an idea:

"Do you want to go to a party tomorrow night?"

17

WE NEVER KNOW HOW HIGH
OUR HEARTS CAN FLY

The next night, Blythe and I stood in the parking lot beside Kai's building, sweater-lint removing and teeth checking. Blythe patted her hair, which she had straightened and worn down, for once. I gave her a thumbs-up, and we followed the sound of rap music up to the exterior stairs to the second floor. At Kai's apartment, the door opened, and two college guys stepped out, beer cans in hand.

Blythe raised her eyebrows. Neither of us fell into the prude category, but neither of us drank. In eighth grade at a sleepover, we'd gotten sick off of a bottle of my mom's red wine, and I'd vomited burgundy onto our white shag rug. That was it for us and alcohol.

"They're in college," I told her. "Berkeley." She gave a nod, like this made their drinking okay with her, and we walked in.

Inside, the music was booming, and people were everywhere. The crowd skewed white and Asian, but, like the Bay Area itself, there were people of all colors and all hairstyles and—what I liked to see best—people with some seriously great fashion sense. But I didn't see anyone I recognized. I squinted through the dark, looking for Kai. Just the thought of seeing him sent flutters across my skin. I was having trouble stopping thoughts of me and Kai, Kai and me. When I thought of that kiss in the attic, which I did during most waking hours, my cheeks got hot, and I couldn't help but wonder what would happen next. Would he be my boyfriend now? Was that how this worked? I tried not to think of the selfies we'd post together as I looked into the darkness for Kai's now-familiar face.

But it was Nate, hair down and wearing a purple headband, who popped out of the crowd. He pulled us into the more well-lit dining room, where a group of people were playing beer pong. When we came in, they offered us cups. Nate grabbed a cup to play, and Blythe reached up and snaked his hairband off and put it on herself.

"Hey! That's my beautification device." He handed her the cup, as if in exchange for the hairband, but when he reached for it, she ducked away.

"Purple's more my color," Blythe said.

Nate threw his hands up in exaggerated frustration. "But you don't need beautifying. You look great." It took him a minute to follow that with: "You both look great." But I didn't mind that he was only looking at her. I'd convinced Blythe to wear a plain black V-neck, and when she'd tried to bring her hoodie, I'd thrown it back on its hook. If all was to go accordingly, and Blythe was to be wooed back to my side, I would not be needed for beer pong. So I stepped back to give them space and caught a glimpse of Emma in the kitchen. I heaved a sigh of relief. At least there was one person I knew here.

I made my way toward her, ducking around couples dancing and a huge coffee table littered with red Solo cups. Emma looked gorgeous, and I couldn't wait to see her dress up close—the hem had an asymmetrical line and no ruffles for once, just a little fringe on the hem and seams. It really flattered her narrow figure. I was so glad I'd gone ahead and worn my crazy thigh-high boots and red knit minidress. I could never compete with Emma for fabulousness, but at least my boots were awesome.

I finally got around the table and tried to wave to Emma, but people moved between us. I craned my neck and stepped into the doorway. That's when I saw the guy she was with. He was leaning back against a cabinet, one arm loosely propped on her shoulder. I watched as she wrapped herself around his waist and nestled into his chest. Then she lifted her face and kissed his neck. Right in the muscled sweep beside his shoulder. My face fell off my body. I'd have to come back for it later.

Because . . . it was Kai. Emma and Kai. Kai and Emma. Emmai. Kaima. *Karma*.

I pressed my fingertips to my lips. I touched the side of my neck. Just yesterday, his hands were there, his lips were there. I could still feel the warmth of him. I could still taste his mouth, tingling like cinnamon. But he was standing there, letting her kiss his *neck*. Letting her run her finger around his *collar*. And down to his *heart*. I could still feel his heartbeat beneath *my* fingertips. But—she was blond and beautiful and great. Of course she would get the guy. Who was I, with my curls prone to random frizz and my brain prone to insane poetry? It wasn't like Emma hadn't warned me. I just hadn't listened.

I closed my eyes and started to turn away. But it was too late. Emma was already waving me over. I lifted one hand in a pathetic wave and took three wooden steps into the kitchen, which was even more busy and full than the rest of the apartment, because it was where the keg was.

"Get a drink!" Emma pulled away from Kai for a single moment to do a little crazy dance, holding her red Solo cup high. When I shook my head—*no thanks*—she pushed the cup at me and said, "you need a drink!"

I could feel Kai watching me as I stood there, her cup waving toward my face, my face likely as red as my dress. I took a step back and grabbed a Pepsi can from the countertop. "I'm good," I said, and held it to my lips. It was empty, so I pretended to take a drink. And that's when the cigarette butt someone put out in the dregs of the can went right into my mouth.

I pressed my lips together to keep from vomiting and pushed past Kai and Emma toward the balcony beyond the kitchen. I shoved open the sliding glass door and hurried to the edge to spit the butt into the shrubs below. I stood there for a long time, spitting the taste of tobacco off my tongue and wondering how my day had gone from dreamy and perfect to a nightmare of ruffles and cigarette butts.

"Sabine?" I didn't turn. I didn't look. I didn't have to. He was beside me. Something caught in my throat: a feather. And I knew how much I'd hoped. How high my heart had flown. I saw the view from the sky; I saw it all. I saw my life from a thousand feet in the air, and then my hope bird plunged to the ground.

I swept my thumbnail over my lower lip. "We never know how high we are." I swept my thumb harder and harder. "We never know how high—how high our hearts can fly. Fly and touch the sky. How high."

"Hi." Kai came up to the balcony railing and leaned against it. Inside, someone closed the sliding glass door, hollering about how someone would call the cops with a noise complaint. I didn't look back at them, and I didn't look over at Kai. I kept my eyes on the night sky.

I wondered: Would he be casual, like, *It turns out that I'm with someone*? Would he act as if our kiss was no big deal? Maybe it wasn't. We'd spent a few lunches together. We'd held hands in a garden. We'd kissed. It wasn't a life commitment.

"I'm really glad you came," he said. I glanced at him just once, quickly. His hair hung in damp waves, like he was just out of the shower. He smelled like cinnamon and cardamom—like he'd be good to eat. It turned my stomach.

I didn't say anything. My lips were covered in sadness glue.

"Can I show you my room?" He offered his hand, palm up, on the balcony railing.

"I . . ." I had to say something. "I'm leaving."

"But you just got here," he said. I wanted so much to look at him. But if I did, I was afraid I'd cry. Or worse, that I'd poet. "Didn't you just walk in?"

I was having the worst kind of heart canal. I needed to get out of there. So I turned and, trying to smile, went to open the sliding door.

"Wait. Waitwaitwait." His hand found my elbow, and I stopped, hand on the door.

I was just steps from the kitchen. If I could get inside and through the house, I would not make a fool of myself in any number of ways I was currently considering: crying fit, screaming fit, kicking fit, biting fit, or tearing-my-curls-out fit.

"Did you . . . you didn't see . . . you did see." I didn't turn from the door. Inside, Emma was talking to someone I didn't recognize. He took her glasses off and put them on himself.

She snatched them back and twirled around, her hair flying around her face in a playful mess. How was she so cool, so confident, so easy? I was nothing like her. I was panicky and terrified and as hard as glass slippers.

"See what?" I asked. I wasn't going to make this easy on him. No way. He might think a kiss was nothing, but the way he'd made me feel was *something*. I turned toward him and raised my eyebrows in my best Maryann Interiors imitation.

"Okay, so you saw Emma do that thing. To my neck, and you probably—"

"So, she was doing *what* to your neck? Because it kind of looked like she was making out with it. And you were just standing there, like she and your neck make out all the time. Which is fine. But I'm out."

He dropped my arm and laughed sardonically. "Who am I kidding? That looked really bad, didn't it?"

"Only if us kissing yesterday wasn't in my imagination." For a second, I wondered: Was it my imagination? This whole conversation felt like it might be happening in a dream. A very bad, very realistic dream that smelled of pine trees, cheap beer, and cigarette butts.

"It was not in your imagination. It was pretty awesome. I was hoping to make a habit of it." He touched his heart, then dropped his hand. "If you felt what I felt yesterday, please let me explain." I tried to pretend he wasn't pumping my heart full of adrenaline, that I wasn't *hoping* again.

"Give me a reason," I said, sounding more confident than I felt that I really could walk away from him.

He licked his lips. "I have one good reason: I promise if you hear me out, you'll forgive me." I looked at him for a long time. My eyes dipped to where Emma's lips had touched the curve of his neck. In what scenario would her kissing him make sense? What could he say that would give me back the feeling I had when I walked in here tonight? I tried to turn away. But I *wanted* him to explain. I wanted him to make sense of this moment. I wanted to stop feeling like my hope bird was a sick little pile of feathers and hollow bones and go back to feeling like she was soaring through the sky.

So I nodded.

"Okay." He let out a breath and sagged against the balcony railing. "It's cold out here. Will you come inside?" I nodded again but crossed my arms over my chest when he reached for my hand. I followed as he led me through the apartment and halfway down a hall I hadn't seen before. Kai opened a door, and we were about to slip through when someone called Kai's name.

"Please tell me you're not going to study." Keanu was there, a beer in hand. Kai stepped aside so his brother could see me, then took my elbow and led me through the door as his brother called over his shoulder, "Oh, Sa-*bean*, I see what you *mean*. Don't forget to think safety!" Kai closed the door, shutting out the noise of the party. He spoke in the dark, closer to me than I thought he was. "Sorry about that. It's what our dad always says. *Think safety.* Mover motto." He sighed, and I could feel his breath on my bare shoulder. "I hope he didn't offend you."

I stepped away from him, shaking my head to dispel the heat in my cheeks. I didn't dare open my mouth, afraid of what would come out.

Kai hit the light switch, and an ethereal Tiffany lamp illuminated the large space. It would have been the master bedroom if it hadn't been converted into what looked like the Lost

Boys dormitory. I fidgeted, running my hands up and down my arms. "People are weird about my name because they don't meet many Sabines." How could it feel so awkward to be alone with Kai? "But my dad grew up in Louisiana. French names are common there." Just a day ago, being with Kai felt like falling into a faux-fur coat. And now? I thought of Anna Sui's spike-adorned peacoat—this was more like that; I was afraid I'd cut myself.

"I love your name," Kai said. He walked to one of the oversized built-in bunk beds that sat on opposite walls. On either side of the far window was an arcade-style *Donkey Kong*, and a foosball table. The bottom bunks were desks, so instead of mattresses, they were covered with stacks of papers, piled books, and humming laptops. Two fat black beanbag chairs patched up with silver duct tape acted as desk chairs. Kai's beanbag had his soccer sweatshirt thrown over it. The room should have smelled dank and gymnasium-y, like boys, but it didn't. It had that same night-air smell that Kai did, and beneath everything was the smell of just-cut oak. I breathed in deeply, hating myself.

I wanted to tell him that I loved his name, too, but I couldn't bring myself to. Instead, I nodded to the bunks. "Did your dad build these?"

"My dad made one for each of us and one just in case. Kind of a family joke." He blushed, his eyes skittering away from mine. "I guess I wasn't planned." I swallowed, wondering if Blythe and I were planned, or if we were the reason that this whole mixed-up marriage began. I didn't want to think about it. Instead, I focused on Kai's bunk—on the unexpected third boy of the family. A scrap of paper was tacked up beside a map and a few other keepsakes. It said, *S— Want desperately need a Rolly tour guide? —K"* I walked over to it. It looked like it'd been there awhile. Whatever we were, at least we weren't a joke.

I gathered every piece of bravery I had. "Make me forgive you." He took a step toward me and let out a long breath.

His throat bobbed. "I'm not supposed to tell anybody this."

18

THEY SAY THAT "TIME ASSUAGES"—BUT

Kai snatched his sweatshirt off the beanbag chair and gestured for me to sit. I shook my head. This dress did not allow for . . . beanbag chairs. Instead, I perched on the edge of his desk in front of a world map covered in red tacks and a *Médecins Sans Frontières* (Doctors Without Borders) trifold hanging.

"Okay," he said and sank into the beanbag chair. "Emma would kill me for telling you this, but . . ." He rubbed the back of his neck. When he looked up, I made the mistake of looking right back. His eyes were hooks, and I was the dumb fish. "You know the messages I got yesterday? I had to pick Emma up from the police station."

The police station? "What happened?"

Kai covered his mouth with one hand. "Her dad was arrested," he said. Then he started at the beginning. "Emma's mom died in sixth grade, and her dad moved them in downstairs. That was the first secret I ever kept for her—where she lived. I guess they weren't welcome in the McMichaels estate anymore, but Emma didn't want anyone to know where she lived." He looked up at me. "And I swear I've never told anyone until today."

I didn't even know about her mom. I dug my nails into the raw wood edge of the bunk, ashamed of my jealousy.

"And her dad started drinking." Kai ran a hand through his hair, turning it punk. "We never heard any . . . disturbances. And Emma never complained. But this past summer, they moved out, and she didn't tell me where. I should have asked. I should have found out." He shook his head and sank lower in the beanbag. I shifted closer to him, listening. "Yesterday afternoon, Emma's dad was pulled over and he was found to be over the legal limit. It wasn't his first DUI, and they arrested him and took their minivan to impound. Now he's in a court-mandated rehab center, and all Emma's stuff is gone and she has nowhere to go."

I frowned. Her stuff? "What do you mean?"

He cleared his throat. "I guess they were living in the van." I pressed a hand to my stomach. I'd been complaining about living in a run-down mansion while she'd been living in a minivan.

"I have to talk to her." I stood up, already thinking how I had to find Blythe so she could get Red Vines and fancy soda with straws. We needed to get home to our construction site so she could safely talk/cry/scream it out. Then we'd just keep her with us for as long as we could.

"Whoa." Kai shot up. "This is a secret. Especially from Emma."

"Wait. Why?" I dropped back down, thinking of her racks of clothes in the costume closet. Is it possible that the costume room wasn't just for costumes—but that it was her closet? "She needs friends right now."

Kai held up his hands in supplication. "I know. And I'm here for her. But Emma's afraid if Mrs. McMichaels finds out her dad got another DUI, she'll file for custody. Or get a restraining order."

"A *restraining* order?" I shifted on the hardwood. I did not feel okay with this secret. "On her own son?"

"Son-in-*law*. He took his wife's name." I started to argue, but Kai held up his hands again, then dropped them into my own, and I froze. "Listen. I *tried* to get Emma to talk to her grandmother. I really tried." He let out a snort of laughter. "My mom's not too happy about a girl living here."

I pulled my hands from his. "Emma's living here? In this *house*?" I could swear my boots were crawling up my legs.

"Well not *here*." Kai gestured around the room, pointing at *Donkey Kong*. "Her things are in the van and in my parents' room. She's sleeping on the living room pull-out couch."

I dropped my head into my hands. These were more problems than I knew what to do with. But—I wished she'd called me, instead of Kai. I understood wanting to keep a secret. I did. But . . .

"It's just for a month." Kai said, shrugging. *Just for a month*. All of my righteous indignation returned, flooding my face with heat.

"Excuse me . . ." I looked at him, leveling him with a gaze I hoped would chop down a redwood tree someday. "How does Emma living in your house give her the right to hook up with your neck?"

"Oh." He looked away, and his hands were in his hair again. "She moped around all day so Keanu gave her a pack of wine coolers. What with everything, I couldn't just push her away. I figured tomorrow I'd pretend nothing happened."

I stood up, completely done with this conversation. "Do you know how ridiculous that sounds?" I put my hands on my hips and pinched so hard I dug into my ribs. "If this were my party and you'd walked in to find a guy kissing my neck, would you even be talking to me right now?"

Kai looked green. "I . . ." His Adam's apple bobbed. "If that had happened, I'd probably be in a fight right now."

"Yeah," I said. At least yesterday had meant something to him, too. "Well, I might not beat her up."

Kai watched me from lowered brows. "Do you hate her? Do you hate me?"

I started to speak, but my tongue tripped on all the words. I swallowed hard. "Of course not." I couldn't hate Emma. I knew what she saw in Kai, and I knew what it was like to lose one parent and have the other seem like a stranger. And I knew what it was like not to have friends to talk to. I swept my thumbnail over my lower lip, tracing my scar with my shiny, soft nail bed. "I had no time to hate—no time to hate. No time to hate. No hate."

He lowered his lashes. "I had no time to hate, for the grave would hinder me." My heart split in two. He was *poeting*.

"It's *because*." I smiled. "Because the grave would hinder me." The words were still running over my tongue—*I had no time to hate because the grave would hinder me.*

Kai leaned forward in the beanbag until his chest met my knees where I sat on the desk. "You're amazing." He picked up my hand and turned it over, tracing my thumbnail.

"They're just words." But my hope bird hopped inside my chest. My body felt like a hundred magnets, each one pulsing toward him. I shivered. "So you're memorizing Emily now, huh? She cure you of the Cure?"

He laughed. "No way. In fact . . ." He pulled his phone from his pocket and put on a song. "This is called 'High.'"

I listened. It felt like someone eating candy through tears. "What do you like about them?"

He pressed his lips together, thinking. Then he smiled. "Robert Smith, the lead singer, has this completely nontraditional voice that's almost part of the music. And he did some of his best writing when he was insanely down, just completely depressed. Even when we're hurting, we can still be great. And those lyrics, especially on *Disintegration*, are poetry." His words were mending something inside me.

I pressed my lips together in a smile. "They're *lyrics*."

"Oh, but let me remind you of my premise. Lyrics *are* poetry." I felt the room changing, our sparkling energy converging. "I didn't have poetry, like you did. I had song lyrics. Hanging out in bars will give you lyrics galore."

"Bars?" I sat back, feeling like I needed to get my feet beneath me again.

"Yeah." Kai cleared his throat. "My dad used to take us to bars while our mom worked nights at the hospital. My brothers would play foosball and order Cokes. I stole the cherries out of those little plastic bins. If we hadn't had dinner, I'd steal the olives, too. And I memorized a lot of lyrics." His eyes grew unfocused. "That sounds weird, doesn't it?"

"No." I leaned forward until he was looking at me again. "It sounds like you were hungry a lot."

The corner of his mouth quirked. "Yeah. My dad finally got us this foosball table." He threw a thumb over his shoulder. "That was a couple years ago. It was a message to himself: no more bars. Or maybe that message was from my mom." He laughed. "Why am I talking so much?"

I grinned and tucked my legs beneath me, leaning toward him. "That's usually my thing."

Kai reached for a Hacky Sack from a row on the floor. He tossed the ball in the air, then threw it to me. "And now you know my secrets."

I caught the ball. "And you know my secrets. All one million of them." I placed the Hacky Sack on the desk. Kai reached for the Hacky Sack and placed it back in its ordered line. I looked at the foosball table. "Maybe it's better not to have secrets at all."

Kai's hands hovered beside my knees. "When everything went down with my dad, my mom said people lie to protect the people they love."

Would we tell Emma about us? How could we do that? I swallowed. "You know how much Emma likes you. Like, *really* likes you." It was the worst infraction against friendship, and I couldn't take it back. But he must know. It's not like she was hiding it.

"It's not like that. She's a sister to me." His eyes followed the line of Hacky Sacks, and I couldn't tell if he was avoiding my eyes. "She was just drunk and lonely. It didn't mean anything."

"It might be different for her, though." I knew how Emma felt. She'd made it plain. What I didn't know was whether he knew and was ignoring it, or whether he really didn't get it. "And if it is, how can we tell her that we're . . . anything special to each other?"

"We'll figure it out." He traced the top edge of my boot where it met my knee. I closed my eyes. My resistance was fading. I inched my hand toward his, and he pulled me, slowly, to my feet, then into the beanbag beside him. He kept my hand in his and held our linked hands to his chest. "We'll find a way to tell her. Soon." I relaxed against his side. I could feel his heart pounding. "Will you go somewhere with me next Saturday?" he asked. "Just you and me."

I was afraid to speak. My heart might fall out of my mouth or something. So I nodded. He let out a breath and smiled that open, lopsided smile. I looped my wrists around his neck and settled against his chest. Slowly, his head dipped to mine. I closed my eyes as our lips met.

The clean smell of him was in my nose and the coarse thickness of his hair was in my hands, and the cinnamony taste of him was in my mouth. The noise of the party and the memory of the kitchen disappeared into nothing, until we were the only two people in the world, our hearts the only two beating, filling up all the space here and everywhere. When we broke apart, I placed my hand against his chest. It was like something was about to break out of a cage. I wondered if he knew about my hope bird, blinking at this amazing turn of events, at this new person growing grass where there had only been ashes. He twirled one of my curls then lifted a few pieces of my hair.

"Your hair is softer than I thought it would be." He rubbed the strands together. I took it as permission to touch him back. I traced the line of one eyebrow, but lost myself in the blue of his eyes. Close-up, I could see his eyes were surrounded by a deep, dark blue, and shot through with lighter blues and dark green. "No poetry," he said. "A good sign."

I blushed, but before I could ruin the moment by stuttering, he kissed me again. Then he lifted me onto his lap so we pressed together, our mouths, our chests, our stomachs meeting perfectly. I could feel the planes of his chest beneath his shirt, the glide of his muscles as he pulled me closer, the thump of his heart pulsing against mine. My mind drifted into patterns and colors as tingles scattered down my spine. My hand drifted to where Kai's shirt had come untucked, and I touched the smooth skin of his stomach. He sucked in a breath, and I was about to pull away, but he covered my hand with his, keeping it where it was. That's when someone started pounding on the door.

I scurried off Kai's lap as Nate ducked through the doorway. I folded my legs beneath me and crossed my hands as Blythe and Emma stepped in behind him. Emma looked from him to me and back to him. I wiped the back of my hand across my mouth, hoping I didn't look thrown around a beanbag chair and kissed.

"*There* you are." Emma flopped onto the opposite beanbag. She was a little droopy-eyed and unsteady. She grabbed a Hacky Sack from the row of colorful bags, and Kai stood and walked to the window. I settled into the warm spot his body had left, wishing we were still curled up together. I took a deep breath, trying to settle my pounding heart. I glanced at him, and saw he was retucking his shirt and straightening his collar. He met my eyes with a shy smile.

"This is what I wanted to show you," Nate said, and pointed to the *Donkey Kong* arcade game. "Old-school cool." Blythe lifted her brows. She was very into video games, true, but she was also extremely selective. She started to reach for the joystick, but Emma leapt up and grabbed it first. Nate slipped two quarters into the machine, and Emma squealed when the screen lit up. She was definitely not herself. Maybe Kai was right, and she wouldn't remember this tomorrow.

As Emma slammed the game around, Blythe sat down

across from me, looking either very bored or very tolerant, and tossed me a Hacky Sack. Nate intercepted it, then tossed it on.

"I said *right*, you stupid monkey!" Emma's blond hair turned all flyaway as she leapt up and down. I glanced up at Kai, who was watching me, gently biting his lower lip and smiling. My heart lurched, and I couldn't stop myself from smiling back. I looked too long and the Hacky Sack hit me square in the nose. It fell to my lap. I glared at Blythe, who was laughing.

"Sorry!" she said, and I looked down as a drop of blood fell into my hand. "Oh no," she said as she saw what was happening. A bloody nose. At a party. With the guy who I wanted to keep kissing. Perfect. *Donkey Kong* made that spirally *zero-zero-zero* noise that means: *You lose.*

"You're hurt," Kai crossed the room, reaching toward me.

"Stop." Blythe put up a hand. "Taking care of Sabine is *my* job." Kai opened his mouth to argue, but Blythe elbowed him out of the way. She helped me up and hustled me out of the room before my nose became so bad, I'd have a blood-splattered dress. We stumbled down the hall until we found the bathroom, and cut the line.

Inside, I rinsed my hands, letting my nose drip into the sink, trying not to swallow too much blood and humiliation. I gulped a handful of water then pinched the bridge of my nose closed. I didn't get bloody noses often—not since sixth-grade volleyball. But when I did, I got them good. "That was embarrassing," I said.

She offered me a decorative pumpkin towel, the kind that my mom would never allow in our house, but I didn't want to stain it, so I used toilet paper to soak up the blood. "I'm sorry about your nose," Blythe said. "I didn't mean to throw while you were ogling." Her eyes shone catlike under the fluorescent lights.

I glared at her as I stuffed TP in my nostrils. "I wasn't *ogling*. I was using nonverbal communication." She gave me a flat look that said: *Have you forgotten I'm your twin?* So I changed the topic. "Seems like Nate is pretty into you." She was still wearing his headband.

She fiddled with the towel, folding and refolding it. Then she picked up another one and refolded it. "I'm not sure he likes me when I'm really me-ish."

I rolled my eyes, stuffing more TP up my nose. "You're very *you-ish* all the time."

She shook her head and grabbed another towel. "I let him answer a question in class the other day." I tried to catch her gaze, but her eyes were on the towels.

"That you knew the answer to?" I asked. She glanced at me like: *Duh.* I made a face, and she carefully hung the towel on the rack. "So you do like him." She shrugged noncommittally and handed me a new wad of toilet paper.

"I don't want to talk about Nate. He's confusing." I tried to look away, but her eyes found mine in the mirror. "We need to talk about Charlie."

I coughed, and blood splattered across the sink. "What? No." If this nosebleed wasn't going to ruin the night like a model falling off a runway ruins a fashion show, talking about Charlie 100 percent would.

"You should ask him about the Mission Project. It's pretty interesting."

"Interesting *how*?" I didn't want to talk about this. I just wanted to get back to Kai. I sniffed. I tested my nose again.

It was drying up. "Don't answer that." I stepped toward the door, but Blythe caught my arm.

"Bean." She opened her mouth but hesitated. "I want to try to forgive him. And forgive Dad." My hope bird got very still. My dad was dead. Forgiving him wasn't even an option. And forgiving Charlie? Much less plausible.

"Dad lied to us, and didn't want us," I said, pulling her fingers off my elbow. "*Dad* was planning to leave us." Why was she bringing this up now? Bringing her here tonight was supposed to get me on her good side so she'd decide to help me sabotage the house—and we could feel like sisters again. I searched around for a way to bring the conversation back to Nate, but Blythe was gathering her hair up in a ponytail, her eyes shifting back and forth, like she was thinking.

"I . . . read an article in *Psychology Today*." She pulled it up on her phone and sent it to me. "It says that in the grieving process, forgiveness is the first step."

I shook my head. "The first step to where, Blythe?" When our dad was alive, he was the mediator. Literally, he was a mediator by profession, but his skills came in handy with us. Whatever had gone wrong between us, wherever we were, he would come over and stand between us to work it out. I remembered him wading into the shallow end of the pool once, still wearing a pair of gardening shorts and a T-shirt, holding his grimy hands above the water as he said, "Let's identify what's at issue."

But what happened now that *he* was the issue? "I don't want to forgive, Blythe. And I don't want to live with Charlie. And I don't want to live in a house that's not a home. And if you can't see how crappy this situation is and help me try to change it because you're so ready to forgive everyone, then you're one more person I can't forgive."

I felt as if I had a Manolo stuck in my throat. I should *not* have told off Blythe, who I loved, and who I needed to be on my side. But it was too late. I unlocked the door and pushed through the hallway toward Kai's room. Inside, it was now standing-room-only video-game central. I kept walking through the house, into the kitchen, and out onto the balcony. I leaned against the railing, sucking in the cool night air, feeling dizzy. I swept my thumbnail over my lower lip. "They say that time assuages." I breathed words, in then out. Someday, my heart would feel like a closed wound, instead of an open, seeping one. "Time assuages. Time assuages. Time. Time. Just time."

I walked back and forth, poeting beneath my breath. Through one of the house windows, I saw a slice of bunk bed. I stepped closer as Kai walked by. I stopped poeting and took a deep breath. I didn't want my grief and anger to stop me from a good time. But just as I was about to walk back in, Emma danced past the window, trying to balance a red Solo cup on her nose. Beside her, Kai did the same. They laughed and downed their drinks. And her head fell to his shoulder. That's when I remembered the second line of the poem: *Time never did assuage.*

I wanted to leave, to give up, to give in. But I swallowed it down and walked back into the party.

19

TEXT MESSAGES
REALLY CAN ASSUAGE—

The next morning, I did all my homework, caught up on my favorite fashion blog, dipped into Charlie's stash of bologna, and drank two of the fancy sodas labeled PLEASE ASK BEFORE DRINKING without asking before drinking. But by noon, I couldn't stand it anymore and checked my phone for texts from Kai. Three messages. I sighed in relief, slumping against the kitchen island.

After the nosebleed incident, we'd hung out and played video games, but we hadn't been alone again the entire night, so when I left, it was with a wave and nothing more. That wave goodbye made me think I might have hallucinated the beanbag hookup, but *it had really happened.*

I replied to him, telling him I would be happy to visit his boy cave again soon, then put my phone away so I wouldn't be tempted to over-message and went back to the second of the two stolen sodas. My pocket buzzed. I bit my lip, wondering if Kai was done working for the day. I pulled out my phone just as Blythe tapped my shoulder and said: "Don't run!"

I screamed and dropped my phone. It wasn't broken, but I glared at her anyhow. "What are we? Playing hide-and-seek?"

She was frowning like she'd just seen someone insult

mathematics. "I know you're mad at me," she said. "But I need your help." I ignored her, my eyes on my phone, rereading Kai's text. Kai was thinking about me. He wondered if I could come to his soccer game. I smiled.

"Bean," she said. I was *not* talking about Charlie again. Or forgiveness. Or anything else. I downed the dregs of my mandarin soda. Blythe covered my phone with a wrinkled and red-marked paper. At the top was a huge C+.

I stared at the paper. "What is this?" Had she picked up one of my assignments for me? But why? I took it from her and put my phone away. When I looked more closely, I saw it wasn't mine—it was Blythe's. It was her poetic mash-up, and it was *terrible*. The teacher hadn't been kind. She called Blythe and Nate's poetic choices "unhinged." And she wasn't wrong. A mash-up of Dr. Seuss and John Donne made no sense. And I was a big Dr. Seuss fan.

"Sorry? Pretty harsh." I handed it back to her, but she just shook her head and shoved it back into my hands.

"Fix it." She fiddled with the edge of the rumpled and ripped assignment. "Please." I looked at the mess of a poem in my hands. "Green Eggs and Death." I was not touching this, not even wearing Gucci elbow-length black leather gloves. I handed it back to her.

"Kai has a soccer game, and since I'm done with my homework, I'm going to head over there."

"Bean, wait." Blythe rubbed the back of her hand beneath her nose, like she might be having . . . feelings. "MIT only takes the top one percent of any school. That means I have to be perfect. Please." I just stared at her. "I'm sorry I told you not to poet at school. And sorry I don't agree with you about Charlie and the house, but—"

I grabbed the sheet from her and squeezed it between my palms. "Where do we go for holidays? For birthdays? What if there was an emergency, and we had to come home from college? What if we get sick? Where do we go? Where will Mom live?"

"I don't know." Her eyes were on the sheet in my hands. "I didn't think about that."

"Maybe you should have." I started to walk away, continuing to crunch the paper.

"Wait! Okay," Blythe said, and I turned back to her. "If you help me with this, I'll . . . I'll . . . I'll help you talk to Mom and Charlie. Or something."

"Or something?"

"I'll tell them we need our own house." She looked as deflated as an evening gown at the end of a dance. She put her hand out for the "Green Eggs and Death," but it wasn't worth saving. I asked her for the assignment instead.

THE ROLLS EDWARD ANNUAL
POETIC MASH-UP CONTEST

Nineteen appearances on nationally syndicated talk shows!

Authenticity

The judges will act as experts to certify verbiage authenticity. A written submission must accompany the mash-up for certification purposes.

Poise and Delivery

Students must have stage presence, poise, and smooth delivery. The beauty and singularity of the mashing are essential to success.

Content

Contestants should include all pertinent information about their two poets, including origin, inspiration, and influences. The information should be organized, composed, and in excellent taste. The meter must remain the same, and at least 75 percent of the original piece should be included.

Humor may be a positive influence if it has propriety.

"Okay," I said, looking from her to the assignment and back. "I don't get it. How are you supposed to stage this?" She didn't explain. Instead, she pulled up a video of last year's contest winners performing on the Rolly playhouse stage. Mother Goose and Mary Oliver, goose costumes and feathers flying. But it worked, and it was really funny.

"This barely sounds like a poetry contest. It's more like . . ." I licked my lips. It really wasn't *poetry*. It was more like costumed performance. And if I'd learned anything from watching runway shows all my life, it was performance. "Can you use song lyrics?"

"Sure. Whatever we want. Obviously. We can use chicken costumes." She almost smiled, and I almost smiled, but I was still too mad at her for wanting to forgive Charlie and live in a construction site to really smile. "Do you have an idea?" she asked, lifting her eyes hopefully.

"Maybe. Let me think about it some more." My phone buzzed in my pocket, and I remembered that I wanted to be someplace else. With someone else.

"You have a week to figure it out. Next Saturday is when Nate and I are rehearsing."

My phone buzzed again, and my heart itched to pull it out. "I can't help you Saturday." I smiled, thinking of how Kai had said *just the two of us.* "I have plans."

"But that's the only day we have a chunk of time," Blythe said. I looked at her, then took out my phone and looked at Kai's message: *Got slide-tackled and I'm out for the rest of the game. Not worth coming by. But see you Monday. And next Saturday?* Then a kissy emoji. *A kissy emoji.* My stomach flip-flopped.

I looked up at Blythe. I had to have her on my side. But I wasn't giving up a date with Kai. I could help Blythe and go on a date with Kai.

"No problem," I said.

20

THIS QUIET DUST
WAS LIGHT AND LOVE

At nine forty-five the next Saturday morning, Kai and I were in San Francisco. But instead of Kai showing me his favorite places, we were standing outside a glass-and-chrome building that was wearing a colorful sign like a necklace: THE MISSION PROJECT. I pinched my eyes closed so as to avoid looking at what I'd agreed to in order to spend the day with Kai. I glanced over at him, hunched into his fleece, the wind whipping his dark curls around his face. His bright eyes took in the building, then, so quickly I didn't have time to pretend I wasn't staring, they were on me. I told myself spending the day with him was worth it.

On Friday night, after a week of failing to tell Blythe about my date, and failing to ask Kai to reschedule, I figured I could count on my mom to help. But when I got home, there was a note on the kitchen island: *Popped to Vegas for an interior design fair. Bring you home a scarf.* I glared at the note. That scarf had better be Hermès. What was I going to do? Cancel my first-ever official date with the most perfect boy ever? Or tell Blythe and lose her help finding our forever home? I dropped my head to my hands.

Just then, Charlie walked into the kitchen, whistling and spinning his car keys. "I'm making Blythe a hot cocoa. Want one?" He tossed the keys on the island and grabbed the milk from the fridge. No wonder they were close: sustenance bribery.

I realized, as he continued his infernal whistling, that I had a third option: Charlie. I just needed to . . . ask for help. Somehow.

"So . . ." I bit my lip. "I overcommitted this weekend. I'm supposed to help Blythe with her poetic mash-up. But I have plans to visit San Francisco with Kai. If I show you my idea for the Mash-Up, would you help Blythe practice?"

"Kai's a nice young man." His Southern drawl always made me think of my dad. Always. I pressed my fingers into my temples. This conversation would be worth it if I ended up alone with Kai. For a whole day. "All right," Charlie said. He tapped cocoa into two mugs. Our eyes met across the kitchen island. I was about to say *thank you* and run, but he held up a hand. "Don't light yourself on fire. I have conditions. First, tell me why you're not telling Blythe. A date is a good thing, right?"

I dug my thumbs into the kitchen island's butcher block to stop myself from poeting, but instead, everything else came spilling out like I'd opened a too-full closet. I told him about Emma's Kai crush and how much I adored her. And that because of that, I hadn't exactly 100 percent told Blythe.

"You should tell your friend Emma. You may think it's better to ask for forgiveness, but . . ." He'd shaken his head. He hadn't needed to say more. I knew what he meant then, and I knew now. When he gave me this package to deliver, I knew it was because he wanted me to see whatever was inside the Mission Project. Because he thought it would help me forgive him.

Now I held out the package. "Let's drop the envelope here and run."

Kai took the package, and then my hand. "The first rule of battle is: know your enemy. We're going in."

I steeled myself as Kai pull me through the tall glass doors and into a narrow, high-ceilinged foyer filled with life-sized black-and-white photographs. It looked like a gallery. At the back of the deep entry below a set of chrome double stair-cases was the reception area: where I was supposed to drop this package off. It looked very far away.

I took a single step inside, trying to keep my eyes on the reception desk. But the pictures—they were huge. Unavoidable. I glanced over, feeling the squeeze of Kai's hand in mine. He'd already seen.

Black lettering on the bright white walls announced: THE FACES OF AIDS. In front of me was a candid close-up of an African-American woman with long beaded hair and an impossibly bright smile. She was so *there* I almost expected her to say hello. I stopped walking. I didn't want to be linked to HIV/AIDS, but I was. I was linked to my dad, and he'd died because of HIV. So I was linked to all of these people, even in an infinitesimal way. I tried to turn away from the faces along the wall. I tried. But it was like watching a runway show with way too much camo and threaded cuffs that looked unfinished instead of intentional: I couldn't look away from the scene.

The next image was of two middle-aged men, framed where their arms wrapped around each other. They were looking at the camera, but somehow it felt like they were also looking at each other—like they were sharing their love for each other with the audience. I wondered who they were. The next image was of a young, handsome, shirtless, and very well-inked guy sitting in lotus. His eyes were closed, and in the backdrop was a gorgeous motorcycle. He wore a small smile, and at his throat glinted a necklace—a name? I squinted. It said: HOPE.

Did Charlie expect me to connect to the people in the photographs? To want to share a house with them? And I wondered, were these the people who'd stay at number six if it became part of the Mission Project? Suddenly, I hated Charlie for making me come here, for making me see this. I pulled away from Kai and hurried the few steps toward the receptionist's desk. With a thunk, I gave her the package. I was about to turn away when she looked up and said: "You have to sign."

I scribbled my name and handed her back the pen. She took the sheet and said: "Oh." Her eyes traveled to the image closest to the desk, at the base of the right-hand-side stairway. My gaze followed hers.

The photo was of a man beneath a willow tree, smiling as he looked up into its branches. I knew that tree. I knew that man. That was my dad. That was my *dad*. I turned and looked at all the other pictures. Were they all dead? They all had HIV/AIDS, but like Blythe said, people lived long lives, healthy lives, with HIV. I turned back to the photo of my dad. That's when I saw a tiny plaque on the wall. ARTIST: CHARLES PARKER.

The camera equipment in his car. The photos on the walls of his apartment. Charlie. Charlie was a photographer. And he'd wanted me to see this. Why? So that I would forgive him? So that I would care about him? Was he showing me that the people who would come through number six were like my dad? That I should care about them, even if I didn't know them? I shook my head. This didn't make me love these people like I'd loved my dad. It made me wonder if the love I'd felt for my dad was ever real.

"I need to get out of here," I said, and I rushed out to the street and turned toward where we'd come from, and I knew we'd be heading back to: the brick stairs of the Sixteenth Street Muni station. I didn't even realize how fast I was going until I heard Kai call from behind me. "Sabine! Wait up!" But I couldn't. My vision blurred as I clicked my card and pushed through the turnstile. I just needed a minute to get it together, to feel like I knew my life and I knew myself and I knew my dad. But maybe that would never happen.

Since we'd moved, my memories of my dad had dimmed— as if they were dependent on our garden and his office and the bagel shop on the corner to exist. Those were the places where I could picture him. But now, thanks to Charlie, where I pictured him was in his other life. Maybe Charlie had thought it would help. But it didn't help. It *hurt*.

"I should recruit you." Kai stood with his hands on his hips, breathing hard. "Played soccer before?" I looked up, and Kai's bright blue eyes filled my vision. I breathed in as deeply as I could, but it was a jagged thing. I shook my head.

It looked like Kai would say more, but I held up a hand. "Let's go to the park, okay?"

He nodded and took my hand, and he didn't let go. Not as we ran up and over to another platform or as we boarded then held on through the roar of the tunnel. Not even when we rose into a colorful neighborhood of Victorian homes and the train came to a sudden halt.

Kai slammed his boot on the release lever and we hopped off the train. We walked through a foggy, quiet neighborhood, turning onto Ninth Avenue. Mist hung in the air. In the distance, a modern cement building rose from redwoods into the sky.

Golden Gate Park.

We walked from city into park, and after a few blocks of trees, Kai ducked onto a dirt trail. He held aside a branch and gestured for me to follow. I followed him into a garden so civilized it could have been on an estate in England. Yellow-leafed plum trees and stone benches lined the grass and redwoods rose all around. In the middle of the garden was a tall brick wall etched with quotes, and in the center of the wall was a bust of Shakespeare. "The Shakespeare garden?" I asked. Kai threw a grin over his shoulder and nodded.

He walked to the *Romeo and Juliet* plaque and read aloud: "'My only love sprung from my only hate.' I love all the fighting in this play, but I can't get behind the dual-suicide thing. What were they thinking?"

I shrugged. "The Heart is the Capital of the Mind." I glanced over to find Kai's eyes bright against the gray sky.

He pressed his lips together and his hands deep in his pockets, as if looking for a Hacky that wasn't there. "I looked that up the day we met. What's so special about Dickinson?"

I bit my lip. Did I even know? I was afraid if I opened my mouth I would poet, but I did it anyway. "It was what my dad read to us when we were little. Emily Dickinson. I kept the books, but I didn't know how well I knew them until he died and I opened one. I didn't read them. I already knew them. Opening that book was like finding words my dad hid inside my mind a long time ago. I let them out. And I can't put them back in."

"You don't need to," he said, then squinted at me. "Stay still." He held up his phone to take a picture, but I turned away. "Okay," he said, laughing. "Both of us." I handed him my phone, and we took a picture together—neither of us was really smiling, but our heads were together, and we looked . . . content. I felt content, to be with him.

We left the Shakespeare garden and walked past tourists trailing cameras and children and locals trailing dogs. We wandered through the Music Concourse, then stopped for lunch at a hot dog cart across from the de Young Museum. After eating, we snuck past a guard to walk through the museum's sculpture garden. Then as we headed back toward Ninth, we stepped off the sidewalk and followed a path that dropped down a set of wood-and-gravel stairs to a grassy dell. Below street level, the trees rose up, and birdsong replaced the buzz of traffic. My hope bird stretched its wings in answer.

"I did a Boy Scout project here with my brothers a few years ago." Kai jogged to a bench and pointed out an area of new planting. "Pretty nice, right?"

"Goody Two-shoes," I said, and poked his side.

He pointed at me in mock surprise. "That's what it said on the merit badge." He gave me that lopsided smile as we walked over a crushed granite trail to a small copse of trees.

It was like a tiny enchanted forest, complete with babbling brook and oversized boulders. It was man-made, but in the middle of the trees it felt like it had always been there. We sat down, and I pulled my legs beneath me, staring up at the dizzying height of the trees. I breathed in the woody air. There was something about the whole place, how you dropped down into a little valley, and this forest sprang up out of nowhere. The word *reverence* came to mind. We sat for a few moments, listening and looking.

"That was your dad, wasn't it? In the photograph with

the tree? You look like him." I shook my head, but I didn't disagree. "You have his eyes." He touched my cheek. "You have his same bones. All angly. And beautiful."

I tried to smile, but thinking of my dad was as painful as stitching my fingers with a sewing machine. "Thanks," I got out, but didn't trust myself to say more.

"I want you to know I didn't think about this before—I mean, I didn't know. About your dad. About how he died. I mean . . ."

I turned to Kai, facing him on the bench. "What are you talking about?"

"This is the de Laveaga Dell. It's the National AIDS Memorial Grove." The trees suddenly looked too tall. Too branchy and scratchy. Too close. I took a deep breath and felt a little tugging in my heart.

"It's okay," I said, because I wanted to be with him, and I wanted to be happy. I wanted not to care that everywhere we went reminded me of my dad. "Show me around."

He nodded but gave me a long look before pulling me to my feet. I followed him to the main pathway, where the gravel was lined with stone benches bearing name plaques. Now I looked at them differently. Was each one a grave marker? I thought of my dad's Little League trophy plaque and wished, for just a split second, that his name was in a garden, near a flowering plant, and not on a drawer. We kept walking, and the path opened into a circle. It was like a meditation labyrinth, but instead of the marks of a maze, there were names engraved in the stone. Hundreds of names. Kai started to walk across it, but I stopped him. "What is this?"

"It's the Circle of Friends." He tugged my hand. "It's okay to walk on it." I looked at the ground. Kai tugged on my arm, but I kept staring. All these people. All these lives. There were *so many names*. I rubbed my thumbnail over my lower lip.

"This quiet dust was gentlemen and ladies. Light and love and girls and boys. " The poem floated through my mind, and I imagined them, the people laughing and sighing. And then no more. "Light and love and life and curls." I was made of words. Wordswordswords. I was still poeting, and I couldn't stop. I felt Kai's hands on my arms. When I met his eyes, the words dropped from my lips back into the stone. I said: "I can't walk on them."

"No problem," he said. We edged around the names until we were on the other side where a path led up and out of the garden. Then we walked and walked, through the Conservatory of Flowers and then the Rhododendron Dell, until the sun began to peek through the clouds. We were quiet, but it wasn't a sad silence, or an awkward one. It was just quiet. As we were leaving, we slid down a cement slide behind a carousel that chimed a tinny version of "Bicycle Built for Two." Even that reminded me of my dad—and his darn whistling.

I tasted that particular tang of sadness—like the scent of thunder—and tried to swallow it away. But it was there, filling the air around us, so that it wasn't companionable silence anymore. We boarded the train at Sixth Avenue and found a place to stand together, then watched in silence as the houses disappeared, and the train rumbled into a tunnel. We got out to change trains, and sat down on one of the round stone benches in the middle of the station, no longer distracted by scenery, or houses, or foggy parks.

Kai pulled his legs up in crisscross applesauce so we faced each other. "Was it seeing your dad's photo? Why you're sad?" Kai's eyes were drawn, and they'd gone darker, like the fog. "Did Charlie warn you?"

I shook my head. "I think Charlie wanted me to connect to the Mission Project. He wants me to stop fighting them about number six." Kai went to take my hands, but I buried them in my lap. This wasn't how I wanted this date to go—and it really wasn't how I wanted it to end. There was that far-off rumble of an approaching train, and we stood. "Let's talk about something else."

"It's okay to be sad, Sabine," Kai said, his hands in his pockets. "We get all this pressure to pretend we're perfect and happy all the time. I'm sore all the time, but I have to pretend I'm happy to help my dad on weekends, and that I want to go to soccer practice every day. I hate it. It should be okay *not* to be okay." He hesitated, then gave me a little smile. "At least, when you're with me."

I pressed my lips together, thinking about how hard it had been to see that picture of my dad in a public place, where people walked by him every day. It was like he was plastered here, in a BART station, for everyone to see, and there was nothing left of him for me.

"It's like I didn't even know him," I said, swallowing hard. That intimacy I'd felt with the other photos—it was as if the photo of my dad had the opposite effect. It was confirmation that we had *no* intimacy. Kai reached out a hand, and I took it, stepping closer to him. When I looked up, his eyes turned down, his lashes long and spiked against his cheeks, and I realized he looked the way I felt—*bereft*. And then I started to cry right there in the middle of the stranger-filled BART station. I pinched my eyes shut and willed the tears away, but it was too late.

Kai pulled me to him, and I held on tight. The rumble of the incoming train shook the floor, and a whoosh of air pushed through the station. Kai held me tighter. The tears came, and I burrowed into Kai's fleece. I took a breath, listening to the rumble of the train. Beneath was Kai's steady heartbeat. I pressed close and listened, letting the sound soothe me, letting it bring me back from where I'd gone. I took another breath and dried my cheeks. I lifted my face, grateful for his calm when I felt so crazy.

"Thank you for . . ." Our eyes met, and I lost whatever words I had.

"There's not enough said about hugs, is there?" He held me tightly. Then he nudged my nose with his, and when I leaned into him, he kissed me.

I was so aware of every place we touched—our hips and bellies. Our knees. Our toes. The shaking ground was joined by the careening screech of the train, and suddenly it wasn't a sweet kiss like we'd shared before, but a deep and hungry kiss, fueled by adrenaline and tears and noise and vibration. And a touch of insanity. When we broke apart, I didn't feel normal or whole. But I felt on solid ground. I took a deep breath, and I started toward the train, but Kai pulled me back.

"Nope. That train's going to the airport," he said. I turned back to Kai and laughed, and it was loud enough to hold all my pain and all my joy together.

We didn't move more than a few inches apart all the way back to number six Magnolia. And when we got there as the sun began to set, I knew I didn't want to say goodbye. Maybe ever. I put my hands on his shoulders and kissed his cheek, then the corner of his mouth.

"Thank you," I said. "I had a great time being not okay. With you."

"Me, too," he said, and turned his head, and then we were really *kissing*, and I wondered why we'd been doing anything *else* all day.

That's when I heard a sound, a scratching, like branches in the wind. I looked up, but the trees were still. I pulled away and looked to the house.

A light was visible on the second floor. And there was a silhouette in the window, watching us.

NOT WITH A CLUB,
THE HEART IS SMASHED

Inside, the house was still and quiet, as if all the breath had been sucked out of it. I listened for a few moments, shutting the door as quietly as I could, wishing Kai were still beside me. Who was at the window? It hadn't been Blythe . . . I knew my sister.

I started to call out, for Blythe, or Charlie, or anyone, but the silhouette in the window stopped me. Instead, I crept through the house, walking around the plastic and piled materials to the main staircase. There was a light on upstairs, and I heard a sudden noise, the clatter of a machine. Was that . . . a sewing machine?

I held my breath as I continued up, listening as carefully as I could. I paused and the noise stopped. I kept going and hit a creak.

"Bean?" Blythe's voice slid through the thick air inside number six, and I let out a long breath. "We're upstairs!"

We? Was Charlie with her? I took the stairs two at a time, moving toward her voice. I knew Charlie was staying in the house this weekend with us, but did that mean he had to babysit her every minute? I turned the corner on the landing to find a little room at the front of the house all lit up.

I caught myself on the door frame and peered in. The walls were a deep green, and I thought it might have once been a nursery. The white curtains were lacy and had the feel of whimsy even in their yellowed disrepair. The mess that was left had been cleared to one side, and now a big table occupied the space. The table was piled with fabric and a sewing machine, and at two chairs were Blythe and Emma.

"What did . . . how are . . ." I looked from Blythe to Emma. Had one of them been at the window? "What's going on?"

"When you bailed on your sister," Emma said, and pumped the foot of the sewing machine, sending a tinny snap-snap-snap sound through the echoing room, "she called me to help."

"I didn't *bail* on her." I looked at Blythe, whose eyes were on her phone. "I wrote your mash-up, Blythe. I just couldn't rehearse because . . ." I tried to say something, but all the things I could say seemed like the wrong things.

"Because?" Emma blinked at me in the hard glare of the overhead light. I swallowed, wanting to take a step back out of the doorway and run to my room and slam the door closed. When I stayed silent, Blythe put her phone down on the table and twisted her lips.

"Who *was* that she was kissing outside, anyhow?" Blythe looked at me, not blinking. "Whoever it was, I guess they're more important than I am."

"Blythe." I stepped inside the room. "Come on. You know no one is more important than you are."

"And yet," she said, and stood up. Blythe turned, and the light caught her eyes. They were bright green. "From what we just saw, it didn't seem like your first kiss." It wasn't jealousy in her voice. It was something worse. Mistrust. I opened my mouth, searching for words, but I gulped air and humiliation and, worst of all, *desire* for Kai.

She pushed past me out the door. "I was going to tell you about Kai!" I called after her down the hall.

She shouted back: "Like you were going to help with the mash-up?" Our door slammed at the end of the hall.

I shifted from foot to foot, watching as Emma focused on her sewing, turning the fabric this way and that before placing it back beneath the foot of the machine and tapping the pedal until it hummed again. When she paused, she met my eyes over her glasses. "You know he missed soccer to do . . . whatever you did today. I went to practice, but he wasn't there. So if he doesn't get a scholarship, I can blame *that* on you, too."

He hadn't told me that. "What about an academic scholarship? He could—"

"Be realistic." She shook her head, gathering up her sewing. "I hope it's okay if I leave this here. When I told Blythe my situation, she said that since I didn't have a sewing room anymore, well . . . you understand." I thought of her staying on Kai's pull-out sofa and flushed with shame. Of course there wasn't space for anything of hers there. I imagined her going to the impound lot and hauling this sewing machine and her fabric bags out of the van by herself. My cheeks flamed.

"Emma, I'm sorry about . . ." I tried to find words to exonerate myself. To blame my hope bird. Or fountains. Anything.

"I'm doing their costumes. So it all worked out. Nate's paying me. So now we have a business relationship." She set her work down, snipped the ends of the threads, and closed the top of the sewing machine before turning it off. She dropped her sewing shears with a clunk. "And that's all."

Her chair made a loud scrape as she pushed it back, picked up her coat, and walked toward me. I stepped into the hall, making way for her to leave.

"Emma, please know that I—"

"That you pretended to be my friend to get close to Kai? Don't worry. You're not the first." She pushed her glasses up her nose. "You're just the first for whom that's actually *worked*."

I opened my mouth to tell her that I met Kai *before* I ever met her, and that there was no way I was her friend because of him—but she was already whipping down the stairs, her heels clattering on the new hardwood.

"I told you to tell her . . ." Charlie's Southern drawl sounded so much like my dad's, I wasn't sure if I leapt a foot in the air because he'd snuck up on me in the dark or if it was because, for a moment, I'd thought he was my dad. "Sorry. Didn't mean to scare you. But I did tell you—"

"I know. I know." I looked over at Charlie. When did I start having so much trouble with truth? "What is it y'all always say? No crying over spilled milk?"

"I think it's cat's milk, but you're getting the gist of the thing." He crossed his arms and leaned against the doorway to the sewing room. "I'm afraid I owe you an apology. Your sister's more astute than I thought."

"What do you mean?" I glanced down the hallway to where pink light shone from under our door. "She knew I was on a *date*?"

"Well, she knew you weren't doing charity work." He crossed and uncrossed his arms. "Maybe you could tell Blythe the truth next time." I couldn't believe him. If he thought he was teaching me a lesson about honesty, he was totally wrong. If he wanted to teach me about honesty, maybe he could have kept his word and helped me out.

"You know what? We don't need you babysitting us. Go back to your million-dollar apartment." I pointed in the direction I was pretty sure was the backyard. "And all your *photographs.*"

"So you're angry. You want me to leave because of the photographs?" He looked down and tapped his Ferragamos against the new floor. "The photograph of your father?"

"That's what you wanted me to see, wasn't it? To know that my dad was a total stranger to me? That he was never mine, but *yours?*" I felt the pinch of tears and pushed through it. "But *we're* not. We will *never* be yours. And I'm going to get us out of here and into a home *of our own.*"

"Go ahead and try." He brushed his hand beneath his nose then turned on his heel and left. When I couldn't hear him anymore, I leaned my head against the doorjamb, rolling my forehead back and forth against the cool, painted wood. How could I have messed things up so badly? Charlie had said he would help—but what had come of it?

I'd stepped on Blythe's heart.

I'd kicked in Emma's heart.

And now I'd twisted Charlie's heart. I swept my thumbnail over my lower lip, pressing hard into my scar. "Not with a Club, the Heart is broken. Broken. Broken. Slivered. Splintered. Smashed, pierced, taken apart. Slivered, slivers." I reached for the fabrics to give myself something else to touch, breaking the poeting. I ran my hands over one beautiful textile after another until I'd let go of the words that kept intruding into my mind.

I walked to the sewing room's front window, looking out through the curtain I'd seen pushed aside before. Out front, I saw a brother and sister racing their bikes in the twilight. The wind picked up, and through the glass I heard the threat of rain, a wet whistling from the edge of the sky. I wrapped my arms around myself.

It wasn't until the tears came that I knew. It wasn't their hearts I'd broken.

It was mine.

22   SO FAR FROM CHILDHOOD

At lunch on Monday, there were only a few students in the quad because of midterm conferences, so I spotted Kai and Emma right away. They were sitting at a picnic table opposite from where we usually sat. I hesitated to join them, but the worst was already over: she knew everything. Now all that was left was to live with it. So I headed toward them. In French, we'd had a test, so all Kai and I had exchanged were tense smiles. I had no idea what he'd told Emma. But when she saw me, she grabbed her bag and stalked off in the direction of fine arts.

I sat down and pulled out the lunch Charlie had packed. "And you thought she wouldn't care. She's not speaking to me now." Kai wrinkled his nose. I met his eyes and said: "Did she tell you she was at number six Saturday?"

Kai shook his head slowly, dropping his sandwich crusts onto a plastic bag. "Saturday? She said she was working." I frowned at him. "Why would you think she's not talking to you? She told me she knows about you and me and that she's happy for us."

Wait—*what?* While I'd been living with a silent, glaring sister and zero messages from Emma, he'd been going about life as usual? I glanced to where Emma had disappeared, wondering what she was playing at. I didn't want to say anything to him until I knew. "So what were you talking about, then?"

"Our Halloween costumes." He stared into my eyes for a beat, looking a little like he thought I was acting jealous. "It's her favorite holiday." I glanced around at the posters advertising a Halloween dance. They were everywhere, but I hadn't really noticed. I didn't want to know about Halloween and dancing when Blythe and I weren't speaking, Emma hated me, and now Kai was giving me the side-eye.

"Oh." I wanted to question him—had they been talking about Halloween, or the dance? Had she told him she'd seen us kissing, or had she just said she knew? To stop myself from becoming a prosecutor, I shoved half my bologna sandwich in my mouth.

Kai pulled his Hacky out and tossed it in the air. "Have you ever had a habit?" He squinted at the overcast sky. "Something that you just did, and never thought about?"

I couldn't speak around my mayonnaise-y bite, so I nodded.

"I just got my first B-plus." He tossed his Hacky Sack halfheartedly. "Emma doesn't think I should quit soccer because it's a strong chance at a scholarship. But I have two jobs and night practice and six hours a day of homework. And I can't quit either of my jobs. Something has to go. I don't know what to do." He leaned closer, his knees just touching mine under the table. On the table, he squeezed the Hacky Sack between his hands.

I thought of what my dad would say. "What's your gut?"

He pressed his lips together, looking up again. "That this is only going to get harder. If it's this hard to keep my grades up now, at Rolly, what will happen at college? I'll have to work there, too, and train. And you have to maintain a certain GPA as an athlete. What if I can't do it?"

"I bet you can do it," I said, finishing my sandwich. It seemed like he could do anything and everything. But . . . if he had to skip practice just to get one day off, maybe he was overcommitted. "What do you wish you *didn't* have to do?" He didn't say anything for a long moment, his eyes on the ball in his hands. I wondered how much of himself he saw as "soccer player" and how much was other things, like mover, or natty dresser, or future physician, or lyrics lover.

"I love soccer," he said. A group of students came milling through the quad, blinking sleepily at the overcast sky, in midterm dazes. "I just wish I didn't have to treat it like another job."

"Can you play just for fun?" I asked. I had never thought of fashion as a job—it was always just for fun. But . . . maybe it could be a job? Maybe almost anything could be.

"I need at least a partial scholarship to school." He bit his lower lip, drawing my eyes to his mouth. I took a deep breath, got up, and walked around to sit beside him.

"There are academic scholarships," I said. "Blythe knows a lot about it. Some are for specific regions, and some are for specific groups—maybe there's one for people of Hawaiian descent?" If this was his first B+, he should be able to qualify for an academic scholarship, as long as he kept his grades strong.

"Maybe." He straddled the bench and scooted closer to me. "I'll find out." He grinned, and my hope bird fluttered around in my chest. He closed the space between us and kissed my cheek. One of my curls fell on his nose, and he caught it with two fingers. "So, about this Halloween dance," he said.

He twirled my curl between his fingers, his mouth just inches from mine. My heart leapt in my chest, but caught, as if it had leapt too high and snagged on a branch.

"What about Emma?" I tried to keep my voice steady. "You two were talking about costumes?"

He sat back a little. "Yeah. We've won the Halloween costume contest every year since first grade. Our first costume was Breakfast. I wore a big box of Cheerios my mom painted, and Emma was bacon and eggs. Her idea." He laughed, his cheeks going pink.

"Wait, so you and Emma always dress up together?" I imagined little Emma, face scrunched as she hand-stitched felt bacon. "And you've been *winning* since you were six?" Winning a costume contest for ten years in a row—that was fashion school application–worthy. "So what about this year?"

"I don't know," he said, leaning in again. "I think this other girl might be mad if I didn't take *her* to the dance."

"Really?" I looked around. "Who is this girl?"

"Oh, you've seen her around." He grinned and tugged on another one of my curls, popping it so it flipped in my face. "She's got these wild curls big as the boots she wears. And she stomps around reciting poetry and pointing out injustice and speaking French like she was born in Paris."

I tried not to smile. "She sounds like a nut."

"Yeah. But a good one. Like a macadamia nut. With chocolate." He leaned in, and his nose brushed my cheekbone. "So . . . what do you think?" Kai was asking me to a dance. I was *being asked to a dance*. But I couldn't concentrate on the awesomeness of the moment. I looked across the quad toward the fine arts building. Did Emma become a designer while making their Halloween costumes? Was it all those years thinking of wild pairings that helped her imagine the life she wanted to lead? Her designs and her creativity were so much of what she was. I didn't want to take that away. And I wanted Kai, but I didn't want Emma to lose the part of him she'd always had.

I pulled back from Kai. "You should go with Emma."

"What? No way." He slipped his hand into my hair, and I marveled, for just a moment, at how quickly touching him had become comfortable, easy, *necessary*. I leaned into his hand.

It took every shred of humility I had to get the words out. "Go with Emma as friends. We'll meet there." But he still looked unconvinced. His hand lingered in my hair, and I gave him what I hoped was a lazy, happy smile. "We could meet there and I could say, 'You look so familiar,' and you could say, 'We met in a dream.'"

His eyes wandered over my face, then he sat back and laced our fingers together. He hummed a few bars of "Love Song," by the Cure. I pressed my lips together so I wouldn't poet over his humming, but inside I buzzed with words, thinking of what Emily wrote about how today is so far from child-hood—that growing up happens suddenly and it feels like childhood never really was. "Are you sure about this?" He asked.

I was in no way sure. "It's a costume, not a date. Right?"

"Right." He hopped up, scooping up his trash from the table. "Let's tell her together so she's not so bummed about the costume contest." I stood and took his hand and we headed across the quad. But as we got close to the fine arts building, I wondered if this peace offering would be enough for Emma to forgive me. I took a deep breath before we walked through the double doors into the costume room.

Inside, Emma pushed a bolt of shimmering gold fabric over the table. She looked up when we walked in, her glasses on her forehead. She was wearing a clingy white tank with a single tight red sleeve, and she looked ridiculously good. I wanted to take back my offer right then and there, because this was her not even trying.

She smiled at Kai, but looked away, not meeting my eyes. She was acting as if we'd never sat hunched together, analyzing how to save the school from fashion suicide. As if we'd never sewn together or shared Red Vines. I felt poetry rise in me but pinched a piece of the stretchy fabric between my fingers to stop it. "I heard you're the defending costume contest champs. Nine years running?" We all stood there looking down at the fabric for a moment. "You should make it ten."

Emma's eyes flashed up—not to me, but to Kai. "Really?" I glanced at him, but he was looking at the fabric on the table, wearing a tiny smile. I felt his hand on my hip and tried to tell myself that this was the right decision. Totally unselfish.

Kai finally looked up from the table and smiled at me. "Can we give her a hint?"

Emma spoke without meeting my eyes. "It's top secret for a reason." She looked at Kai shyly. "We've been talking about it for a while. I think it will be a hit." Emma pressed her lips together and flicked her eyes to the clock. "If I'm going to get this done after all, I need some photos, and we have to start measurements."

She gestured for me to take the photos, so I pulled out my phone and took photo after photo as she held different gold fabrics against her skin. I smiled uneasily through it, wondering whether we were cool, or if we never would be. She took my phone, scrolled through the photos, and sent herself one. But she never met my eyes. Maybe she just needed time. My hope bird flapped at my chest, constricting it. Being in the costume room made me realize how much I would miss it, and Emma, if she didn't forgive me.

"Is the gold for an evening gown?" I asked, but she didn't take the bait. Instead, she pulled out several black fabrics and started draping them over Kai's shoulders. I glanced at the clock. Ten minutes until class.

"Okay." Emma snapped the fabric tight and shooed me away. "You've seen enough." I glanced at Kai, but he was busy holding a bow tie under his chin. When he caught my eye in the mirror, he pointed his finger like a gun and winked.

"Sure." I hesitated at the door, but what did I expect? "Happy measuring." I was halfway down the hall when I realized I'd left my phone behind. I hurried back and slipped through the double doors of the costume room, already reaching for the table. I glanced up to find Kai with his back to me, shirtless. I froze.

My heart did a kind of wobbly, drunken dance, and I grabbed for my phone.

Emma had her arms around Kai as she positioned a measuring tape tight against his bronze skin. Her hands flattened over his back, then she slowly brought the measuring tape up to his shoulders, pausing at his biceps.

"I'm sorry." My voice was breathy, like I was the one caught in a compromising position. Emma looked up, and I looked back. I couldn't look away. She let the measuring tape drop and curled her hands over his shoulders.

"Oops," she said. Emma grinned at me over Kai's shoulder,

and in it was a challenge—a declaration of war. But I didn't want any part of it. Kai was mine or he wasn't, but I wasn't fighting her for him.

"I forgot my phone," I said, and this time Kai heard me. He whipped around, reaching for his shirt. I held the phone up and shook it a little as I backed away. My heart lurched as I watched him pull his shirt over his head. I pushed the door open, reminding myself I'd told him to do this. It had been *my idea.*

"Wait up." Kai grabbed his jacket. "I'll walk you to class." I shook my head, but he wasn't looking at me.

"We can finish later," Emma said. She stared at me, her glasses widening her already huge blue eyes. I almost laughed, because she could get to him night or day. *They lived together.* It suddenly seemed so unfair, I wanted to scream. I pushed through the swinging doors.

"Sabine." Kai's gravelly voice followed me. "Wait up." I didn't wait. I ran out of the building, my face smoldering. I couldn't look at him right now. I mean, couldn't she have measured him with a T-shirt on? *How could he think they were just friends?* I jogged to my next class, getting lost in the crowds of students hurrying to class. I was almost to my classroom when I glanced at my phone, hoping Kai had messaged me some kind of explanation. The screen flashed: PHOTO DELETED. I stopped walking in the middle of the breezeway as the other students streamed around me. I scrolled, thinking Emma must have chosen one photo then deleted the rest, but her dozen gold-fabric photos were all right there. What was deleted?

I scanned the photos slowly. There was an image of a book I wanted to read, and after that a sign for a Vivienne

Westwood exhibit that I'd seen in Golden Gate Park. Then the gold fabric. And suddenly I knew what was gone.

A picture of me and Kai in the Shakespeare Garden, our heads together. Not smiling, but happy. It was gone—deleted. As if that perfect moment had never been. I kept pressing buttons, but it wasn't in my recently deleted; it wasn't anywhere.

The bell rang, but I just stood in the now-empty breezeway, staring at the place where the photo should have been. There was no way that picture had been accidentally deleted. There was no way. And there was only one person who'd had my phone in the past few hours. Emma.

The first act of war. Maybe I cared more than I'd thought I did. Maybe I wasn't going to just roll over and let her mess things up between me and Kai. Maybe I needed to level the playing field.

I dialed the city hall directory.

"Mrs. McMichaels? Do you know where your granddaughter is living?"

23

I LIKE A LOOK OF
AGONY AND TERROR

That night, I couldn't sleep. It was almost midnight when my phone lit up beneath my covers. I stared at the screen, thinking of the words that had glowed that afternoon: PHOTO DELETED. Like you could delete a relationship with the push of a button.

It was Kai. *Mrs. McMichaels came by tonight.* Another message popped up. *Someone told her Emma was living here.*

I hesitated to answer him. I didn't need to; he'd think I was asleep. But I didn't want to hide anything from him. When we'd talked on the phone, Mrs. McMichaels told me I'd done the right thing. She said she'd take care of everything, that she'd take care of Emma. And that Emma should be with her family. And, of course, she *should* be with her family. I just wasn't sure Kai would see it that way. My thumbs hovered over the keypad. What could I say? I did it for her own good? That would be a lie. Instead, I wrote: *Is Emma at her grand-mother's now?*

Kai recorded a message and sent it to me. I played it softly, one eye on Blythe, where she slept holding one of our dad's old sweaters. "Dude, it was crazy. Mrs. McMichaels showed up at our door when we were cleaning up from dinner holding a bouquet like she was taking us on a date. She kept apologizing, as if Emma were squatting at our place instead of us inviting her to stay. Emma tried to say no, but it was obvious she had to go with her. She and my mom talked in the kitchen, and when Mrs. McMichaels dragged Emma out, she was yelling at her that she was going to file for sole custody of Emma in the morning."

I bit my lower lip. That wasn't supposed to happen. I wrote: *That is really crazy.* He wrote back: *I feel horrible. I can't sleep.* Then: *I wish you were here.* I hesitated, my thumbs over the keys. I should tell him it was me who called Mrs. McMichaels. But instead, I wrote: *Me, too.*

ON FRIDAY WHEN I CAME home, it wasn't to the sound of hammering and the rev of the circular saw, but to shouting. There was a slam, and the scuffle of gravel, then Charlie's voice, rising in pitch. I hurried up the driveway and into the garden, toward the voices. He was yelling: "No, absolutely not!"

"I advise you to take this immediately!" I turned the corner to see Mrs. McMichaels, her gardening hat in place, staring Charlie down. A pile of deadheaded roses was at his feet, and a pair of clippers in his hand. On the ground was a big bag of new gravel—maybe that was the slam I'd heard. When I got closer, I could see she was waving an envelope at him.

He shook his head, brandishing his clippers to keep her away. "Not without my attorney present. You turn right around and walk away."

"You *are* an attorney, Mr. Parker. You should have understood that November fifth wasn't a negotiable date." Mrs. McMichaels's tone was as sharp as Charlie's clippers, and I wondered if she used that tone with Emma.

"I didn't suggest it was, Bernie. But there are protocols

that must be followed. My attorney and the attorneys of the Mission Project must be here for me to accept any—"

"Don't try to talk fancy to me, young man." Mrs. McMichaels stamped her walking stick into the ground, and I realized that was the resounding thud I'd heard before. "Magnolia Blossom is the most illustrious, *oldest* house in Thornewood. This house *must* conform to neighborhood-approved dictates or you will not keep this house, not for longer than a single—"

"Keep the house?" The words were out before I thought them. Mrs. McMichaels whirled, faster than I'd expect a woman of her age to move. Charlie looked to me then back to Mrs. McMichaels, still clutching the shears.

"Is that a twin?" Mrs. McMichaels gave me a cursory glance. "Which one are you? The unkempt one? Or the one with the boots? Oh, I see. Boots. Well, Boots, the city takes taxes, fines, and shrubbery very seriously." She turned back to Charlie. "The fines stand, whether you take the letter or not."

"Sabine, go on inside and find your mother." Charlie kept his eyes on Mrs. McMichaels as he spoke. "Mrs. McMichaels was just leaving." But I didn't move. I was finding out what was going on.

"I'll have you know I've brought this to the council. We have serious doubts about the historical accuracy of your renovations, you've disregarded the stay order on your zoning, and there's no excuse for building a rental unit without approval, even if it wasn't on your watch. Now that the fines are in excess of the property value, you have—what is the expression? No leg to stand on? No house to live in is more like it." She turned, taking me in with a head-to-toe look before turning back to Charlie. "But rest assured, when the house belongs to me—to the *city*—it will be a tribute to Thornewood."

"Don't go shopping for wallpaper samples just yet," Charlie said. "There are banks to call and people to consult. We'll see where we are in a few weeks."

Mrs. McMichaels jabbed the envelope. "You don't have *weeks*. You have days. Next Wednesday you will vacate unless the fines are paid *in full*."

Charlie laughed, but it was high and pinched. "You can talk until your face is blue as your hair. But know this—if you don't give us more time and an interview with the council, I will tie this house up in so much legislation you'll die before it's so much as a dot on a Historic District map. Wrongful *eviction* is my specialization."

"My father is one hundred and eight, Mr. Parker." There was a long silence as Charlie eyed her, and she eyed him. I wondered if he might stab her with the clippers to speed along the process. I stepped out of the shade of the house and between them.

"Mrs. McMichaels?" I said. "What if we were ready to sell you the house?" Charlie narrowed his eyes at me, but I kept my eyes on Mrs. McMichaels. "Could we still make a deal?"

She turned to me and smiled like we had a secret. "Well, now that the fines are so high, a sale would no longer be in the financial interest of the city."

I glanced between them. "What do you mean? You said the fines would be forgiven if you bought the house." She shook her head and dropped the letter at my feet.

"This letter informs you that you are in violation of so

many Thornewood edicts that we practically own the house already. Why would we buy it now?" Mrs. McMichaels tapped her hat down.

The letter stared at me from the ground. I stepped back, stumbling over loose gravel. I'd wanted to leave from the moment we moved here. I'd wanted to put our family back the way it had been. To have a house that I could call home. But—one week's notice to move somewhere else? No money from a sale? I thought of Emma's dad's van and pull-out couches. I swept my thumbnail over my lower lip. "I like a look of agony. I like a look of agony—of agony, anger, agony, terror, mirror, terror, mirror." Charlie stared me down as if he knew whose agony I was talking about. As if he knew what mirror I was looking into.

"Happy eve of All Hallows' Eve." Mrs. McMichaels strode down the brick path and out the wrought iron gate. When she was gone, I looked back at Charlie, an apology on my lips.

"It's my fault," he said, and picked up the envelope. "Those Historic District rules were as long as the Bible and just as hard to interpret. I tried. Oh, Mick, I really tried." My chest tightened. Hearing my dad's name on his lips . . . I didn't know how it made me feel. Uncomfortable, but something else, too. What was it? Not angry, but . . . sad. So deeply sad.

"Can we pay the fines?" I stepped closer as Charlie opened the envelope. He held it up, flapping it in the air. Then he held it out, and we looked at it together.

Thornewood Historic District Violations. The first line item was *zoning infractions.* It was over two *hundred* thousand dollars. An Emily Dickinson manuscript—in quill ink. Wonder Woman's original boots. Blythe's MIT tuition.

Charlie shook his head and turned the paper over. He pointed to another figure. "You don't happen to have six hundred thousand dollars, do you?" I almost coughed my soul out.

"Charlie?" My mom's voice carried through the garden. "Charlie! Where are you? I got your message!" She hurried around the corner and almost knocked into us. She put a hand on my arm to steady herself. "Tell me it's not what I think."

He lifted the envelope. "She found out about the renovations on the garage apartment. Mick worked so hard to keep that quiet, but . . ." Charlie shook his head. "It's a few days' notice on the fines."

"It's my fault." She covered her face with her hands. "We should have approached the city council sooner. You told me we needed to, but I didn't listen." Way too much blame was being thrown around, and none of it mine. I tried to remind myself that it wasn't *me* who'd moved us here, and it wasn't me who bought number six in the first place. But . . .

My stomach heaved. "Mom, I have to tell you something—"

"It's going to be okay," Mom said, and pulled me into a fierce hug. I deserved comfort less than I ever had, but I took it. "We'll sort this out." She pulled away and pointed at Charlie. "Call our lawyer. Get him to city hall," she said. "Call the Mission Project. And I want to talk to the head of the neighborhood association. What's his name? Mr. Cade? Call him, too."

"Should I call the evening news as well?" Charlie asked. Maryann Interiors looked like she was considering it. "Don't answer that," he said. "Coffee first." He took her arm and they walked inside. I followed them out of the garden, but I didn't go inside. Instead, I sat on the warm brick steps and tried to breathe. The evening wind came up and found the open places in my clothes. I hugged my backpack to my chest.

I was still there ten minutes later, when Blythe walked up, hunching under the weight of her backpack. She stopped when she saw me. "Happy now?" I squinted up at her. She held her phone, lit with messages from Emma. "Emma said she helped you sabotage the house. You told Mrs. McMichaels about the illegal apartment?"

I swallowed. "I'm not the one who built an illegal apartment."

"Emma says her grandmother is planning to kick us out," Blythe said.

I dug my thumbs into my hips, poetry burbling in my mind. "It's not as if my plan was to get us kicked out." I stood up. "Mrs. McMichaels said she would buy the house from us. I thought we'd move and—"

"No, you didn't think." She glared at me. "Just like you didn't think when you hooked up with Kai." I wanted to tell Blythe that Kai and I were not just *hooking up*. I wanted to shout at her that he got me in a way that even she sometimes didn't. This past week, Emma had been leaning on Kai through the crisis of her grandmother's house, and I'd felt like I'd only gotten his full attention at night, when we messaged each other.

"Emma is fine," I snapped. "You haven't even heard my side. You promised to help me with the house, and you—"

"And I might have." She crossed her arms. "But you sabotaged it without even *talking* to me. Without thinking about our family."

The words were out of my mouth before I could think: "Charlie's not my family."

"But I am. Didn't you think about me?" She shook her head and started to walk inside. She stopped at the door and turned back to me. "You know, if you hate us so much, Sabine, maybe *you* should leave." She slammed the door so hard the glass rattled in its pane. I stared after her for a beat. I wasn't *wrong*. But I wasn't sure what I'd done was right, either. I picked up my backpack and heaved it over my shoulder.

Inside, I stepped as quietly as I could, wanting to take sanctuary someplace—anyplace. I got through the hallway and halfway up the stairs before—

"SABINE!" My mom sounded like she was about to send back a rug. She *hated* sending back rugs. I left my backpack on the stairs and followed the sound of anxious voices into the living room. Charlie was on two phones at once, and my mom was buried to her elbows in paperwork. When I walked in, my mom held up a finger to silence me and beckoned Charlie.

"What did he say?" she asked.

Charlie shook his head. "That it's all perfectly legal. We'll need to beg the city council for an audience and hope they grant one." She nodded, then flapped a hand, dismissing him. He walked off, already dialing again.

Blythe walked in with a fresh cup of coffee for Mom. "Maybe the Historic District neighbors would reconsider the vote?" She asked. I narrowed my eyes at Blythe. Suck up. Maybe she should go door to door and ask our neighbors for a recount.

"Sure," Mom said, but her eyes were on her phone. "Blythe, can you give me a minute with Sabine?" I glared at

Blythe as she floated away. She'd ratted me out. I could feel it in the air. I would have to tell Mom that I'd done it for the good of the family. "Sit." Maryann Interiors put her phone down, and I slumped onto one of the new divans, waiting for my punishment.

She set her mug down with a clunk. "Charlie says you're going on dates." All activity stopped, including my heartbeat. "With Mr. Thompson's son? Kai, is it?"

"Uh . . ." I looked at the paperwork, scrambling for new excuses. "Yes?"

"So you're seeing him . . . like a boyfriend?" When I nodded, unsure what else to do, Maryann Interiors's eyes went wide as if someone told her she'd missed a sale on Marimekko's new fabric line. "I wish you'd told me."

"I'm sorry?" I shifted on the divan. I felt prepared to talk about fines and neighborhood votes and why we needed our own place, but not about whether Kai and I were ready to update our relationship status.

Mom shook her head. "I have no idea what's going on with your lives. And I should." She picked up her mug again, took a long sip, then twisted it in her hands. She still wore her wedding ring.

"It's fine," I said. This wasn't the mom I wanted to talk to. I wanted yelling or jazz hands. But not this.

"Will you tell me what you like about him?" She tucked her feet beneath her and leaned forward, and I was reminded of how she once sat when she used to read to me. Blythe liked to read to herself, but I'd always loved being read to. It was more intimate, like the words would saturate into me and become part of me only if I could hear them. "I don't know," I said, but she kept staring at me, and I couldn't help thinking of Kai singing "Love Song" to me the other day. "He's funny. And he likes poetry. Well, he likes song lyrics . . . which are kind of poetry."

"But you're still not happy here." Her jaw set, and I knew: this had only been the warm-up. "Blythe says you sabotaged our inspections. She said you found out how the inspections could go wrong, then helped them along. Do you hate it here that much?" She stared at me, her eyes darkening, and I knew what that returned rug felt like.

"Mom, I don't hate it." I glanced up at the rehabilitated chandelier shooting diamonds of sunlight around the room. There was something about number six Magnolia I'd always kind of loved. "But I hate that every time I see Charlie, I feel like my life with Dad was fake." She stared, waiting for me to go on. "I hate not having a real home. Even once we're in college, I want a place to come home to. I don't think it's too much to ask. It could be an apartment. Or something small, like the cottage."

"It's not like this is what I wanted," she said. "Do you think I married my college sweetheart hoping in twenty years he would die and leave me this ridiculous house and Charlie?" It was clear she was not looking for an answer. "I'm doing this because your dad and I agreed. We loved each other enough to make a polyamorous relationship work, and to fund this dream slowly. We didn't know your dad would die so soon. It was . . ." I waited for the words that would explain my life. The words that would make everything make sense. The words that would stop me from poeting when I was nervous. "A fluke."

I ground my teeth. "You should have told us everything. And you should have sold this house."

She set the mug down and leaned toward me. "I would have told you everything. And I'd planned to sell the house. But even if Charlie had agreed, what then? I couldn't afford our old house on my own. And we don't have family to help us. Combining our resources seemed like the best idea."

"So now we get to live here with a bunch of strangers." I was so mad at her for keeping Charlie a secret, for keeping this house and everything it meant to Dad a secret. And then I realized, it wasn't her I was mad at. It was my dad. I crossed my arms. "Can't we figure out selling? Don't you want a place of our own?"

She shook her head. "I can only deal with one problem at a time." I couldn't help but notice that she hadn't answered either question.

"So . . . am I grounded?" I shifted on the divan, shoving my hands under my legs to keep myself from poeting at the thought of not attending the dance. When that sewing machine showed up, all my grandmother's long-ago lessons in sewing came tapping back to me, and I came up with an idea for a costume for the dance. Nothing to compete with Emma and Kai, but something I could feel proud of. And if I didn't get some time alone with Kai soon, I was afraid I would implode from the weight of my crush. "See, there's a dance tomorrow night, for Halloween, and Blythe and I and some friends and—"

"You can go," she said. I waited for the *but*. "You'll think of a way to make this up to me and Charlie, I'm sure. If nothing else, there's gravel to spread in the yard." I grimaced and waited for her to list other menial tasks for me to do, but she didn't look up from her papers.

I slipped upstairs and into the empty sewing room. It was

dark, and the only light was from the setting sun. The sun's rays shot through the street trees, turning the bare branches hot pink and canary yellow. I sat down at the sewing table and flipped the machine on, illuminating the room. I pulled out the feathered fabric I'd found in one of my mom's FUTURE DÉCOR boxes; it had been a modern throw blanket, but now I was trimming and stitching it into a short, feathered skirt. On the table were a white tank top and three of Blythe's best Sharpies. And my book of Emily Dickinson poems.

I worked the rest of the evening. When I was done, I held the costume up, proud of the simple creation. When I tried it on, my first thought was that Dad would have loved it. I tried to push the thought away, but it stuck. Even if no one else got me, I knew he would have. I fluffed the feathers of my white skirt, fluttering them, and thinking of my dad's smile.

The thought should have made me happy. But all I felt was empty.

IF I CAN STOP MY
HEART FROM BREAKING

I did not need to worry about accidentally winning the Rolly Halloween dance costume contest—even if I hadn't chosen "weird and obscure" as a themed category. When we arrived at the school, it was to a Marie Antoinette with removable rubber head, a Helen of Troy complete with mobile papier-mâché boat, and a miniskirted Dorothy with a live Toto in her basket. I didn't stand a chance.

We joined the line of Hollywood extras, and I slipped my hand into my feathery skirt pocket to touch my dad's letter. Before I left the house, I'd grabbed it. For luck, I guess. Beside me, Blythe was wearing a skintight black bodysuit, a kitten headband, and eyeliner whiskers, along with an aggressively catlike demeanor. The best thing I could say about my befeathered, drawn-on costume was that no one would mistake me for Blythe tonight.

As we waited our turn in line, I saw a dark-haired guy wearing a tuxedo top and a wet-suit bottom, like his deep-sea dive was about to be followed by a black-tie event. James Bond spoofy. Clever. And the guy could fill it out, too. He turned, and it was Kai. My heart slammed against my chest, and I started to push through the crowd. He looked amazing. But just as I got close enough to call his name, a beehived blonde wearing nothing but gold paint ran out of the gym and into his arms. He caught her and spun her in the air. When he put her down, they high-fived each other and posed for a picture. *Goldfinger.* And they looked perfect.

I slinked back to the line. They hadn't seen me, and I was going to keep it that way until I could breathe again. Blythe hissed and meowed behind me. I thought she might be sympathizing, but then I saw Nate walking up wearing a white curly wig and an old-fashioned burgundy suit. And carrying a grocery bag.

"Meow." Blythe deadpanned and scratched at Nate's Whole Foods bag like a rat might be in there. "Sir Isaac Fig Newton?"

"You amateurs forgot your canned goods." He shook the bag of clanking cans. Of course Rolly couldn't just have a dance. They had to make it a charity event so we could put it on our college applications.

"It was an act of anarchy," I said. Blythe pulled two cans from Nate's bag and handed me one. Nate's eyes roved over Blythe's leave-nothing-to-the-imagination costume. I thought he might say something obscene, with the look he was giving her. But he didn't.

"Where's your tail?" he asked.

She hissed again. "I lost my tail in a catfight." We pushed toward the front of the line. He laughed and they hissed and meowed at each other as we crept slowly toward the entrance. Beside the gym doors, PTA moms were checking student IDs and collecting canned goods. I hefted my can in the air and stepped up, trying not to look around frantically for Kai and Emma. They were dates in costume only, I reminded myself.

Our neighbor, Mrs. Costello of the gingersnaps, was at

registration. "Look at you two! I'm glad you're here. I never called your mom back about the neighborhood association. Tell her to talk to Mr. Cade in person. He knows *all*."

"Address?" Blythe asked. "Hold it out—I'll take a picture." Mrs. Costello looked at Blythe like she was asking her to rewire a computer.

She cleared her throat. "He lives on our street." She leaned in close, as if she had a secret. "He's *Mr. Pumpkinhead.* You should go by on your way home. It's a hoot."

Mr. Pumpkinhead? How was that an address? "This place just gets weirder," I said.

"Actually"—Nate adjusted his wig—"Mr. Pumpkinhead is quite awesome. I'm still not sure how he does it. Maybe he rewired his security system?" I started looking for Kai again as Nate explained the possible logistics, leaving Blythe behind to argue about how it might be done. Whatever *it* was.

Inside, the light was dim, and it smelled of fog machine, dirty socks, and handball. Pop music pumped from crackly speakers, and cardboard headstones and black streamers hung from the ceiling. And everywhere, kids in expensive costumes hopped around, hands in the air. And in the middle of everyone were Kai and Emma, the most creative, the most perfect to their characters. A matched pair. That was their trick, really. There were two of them; they could tell a story. I stared for a full minute before Kai looked up from his Bond girl and saw me. He waved me over, but I just smiled.

When the song ended, he skidded across the floor. "Guess!"

"*Goldfinger?*" I said, smiling at his enthusiasm.

"So, you know James Bond." He crossed his arms over his dress shirt. "If only you'd known the Cure, you'd be practically perfect."

"I know the Cure!" I tried to look mad, but I couldn't help laughing at his feigned dissatisfaction with my level of pop-culture knowledge.

"Well, now that you're with me, you do." He took my hand, and I stepped closer. "And you've accepted that it's pure poetry, of course."

"'Charlotte Sometimes' is poetry . . . maybe." I gave him a little smile, waiting for him to start singing, but just then Emma hopped over to us, and Kai and I dropped hands.

"You two look amazing," I said, because they did. "Tell me about this. Is it a real wet suit?"

Emma nodded. "I sewed his old, worn one to the shirt, and it unzips in one piece." I tried not to think about her zipping or unzipping Kai. And I tried to ignore that she was dressed in what amounted to a gold bodysuit. And that her glasses were gone and her blond beehive wig glittered under the disco lights like a goddess.

"Did you see Helen and the boat?" Kai asked Emma.

"Yeah. The judges love literary." Emma glared in the boat's direction, then looked at me. "What are you supposed to be?" She looked genuinely curious, so I turned so she could see my back, where the rest of the poem was written. Across the chest, I just wrote HOPE . . . , but on the back, I wrote the rest of the poem, then drew a feather. It was obscure and nerdy, but I didn't care. I tapped the letter in my pocket. I knew my dad would have loved it. I tried not to think how badly I wanted Kai to love it, too.

"I don't get it." Emma tilted her head. "You're, like, half bird, half girl?"

I gritted my teeth. Even after the incident of the costume room, I didn't feel angry with Emma. I didn't know why I did now—except that maybe I thought she'd like what I'd made. "I used your sewing machine to make it. But don't worry; I bought new thread. Thanks, retroactively."

The smug look dropped from Emma's face. It was clear she was surprised I'd made it, but she didn't say that. "So, what are you?"

"Isn't it obvious?" Kai laughed, still on a costume high. "She's hope—and hope is a thing with feathers." He pointed to the words written down my back. Then he took my hand. "Come dance with me, Queen of Feathered Things."

Emma crossed her arms over her golden chest. He didn't see how her expression darkened as he tugged my hand. But I did.

Kai spun me in a circle then pulled me close even though the music, in a blatant attempt to keep everyone at arm's length, was insanely upbeat. He dipped his face to my ear. "I feel like we haven't seen each other in weeks." He hummed a few bars of "Charlotte Sometimes," then sang into my ear, his voice gravelly and soft. I melted closer to him.

Kai tapped my nose with his own. "Sing along to the poetry." I sang along, and he grinned, the sparkling lights reflecting in his eyes, making me feel dizzy. How was it he filled up all the empty places inside me? How did he make me love everyone—even myself?

"I missed you, too," I said. We danced together, ignoring the frantic beat of the music and instead spinning together, moving only as fast as we wanted, our hands never moving far from one another. When the song ended, we took a few steps off the dance floor, making way for some wild dancers with no sense of personal space. I leaned against the wall, fluffing the feathers of my skirt.

Kai straightened his bow tie, looking me up and down. For once, I wasn't wearing boots but little white flats that didn't take attention from my feathers. His eyes lingered on my bare calves. "Did you really make this?" he asked, fingering a feather. "It's beautiful." I nodded and shrugged. It wasn't hard to make a skirt or sew a premade tank to one. But it did fit pretty well.

So slowly that my heart rate increased as I watched, he gave me that lopsided smile I loved so much. He pressed his lips together and threw a glance over his shoulder. There wasn't anyone too close to us. He slipped a hand around my waist, and I stepped into him. "I really want to kiss you."

"So kiss me," I said, surprised by my own boldness. I met his eyes, and the past week of awkwardness disintegrated as we kissed. When I pulled away, he dipped his nose into the pile of curls on my head.

"I love the way your hair smells. It reminds me of that purple rose." I knew the one he meant—Barbra Streisand—but my mind was too hazy to get the words out. He kissed me again, slowly, like we had all night. Ignoring the muggy air and the pound of the music, I flattened my stomach to his, feeling the rubbery neoprene of his suit against my knees. He nudged my lips apart, and we sank into each other. That's when the back of my neck prickled, as if we were being watched. I pulled away a breath and glanced around.

Emma stood still in the middle of the dance floor, glowing gold under the disco lights. Just—watching us. She didn't look angry. She looked . . . bereft. I shut my eyes and willed myself to ignore her—to let Kai make me feel dizzy and happy. But I couldn't do it; the guilt was too much. I touched my nose to Kai's once more, breathing in the scent of his skin, then stepped back. Kai's eyes snapped open.

"I have to tell you something I should have told you before," I said.

"Okay." He traced a finger down my cheek and over my bare shoulder. His hand was warm and dry, and I shivered, almost losing my nerve. But unless I told him what I'd done, being with him felt like a lie—a lie that was hurting Emma more than I had already hurt her. I was done with everyone's secrets. Even mine.

"It was me." I swallowed down fear and poetry. "I told Mrs. McMichaels that Emma was staying with you." His face contorted, like he'd finally noticed the gym's handball smell. I was brave for thirty seconds too long. I should never be brave again. Ever.

"Wait, what? Why would you do that?" He stepped back, but his hands lingered on my elbows, giving me a chance to explain.

"I did what I thought was best for Emma. I know you didn't see the harm in her living with you, but she couldn't stay forever, could she?"

He shook his head. "No, of course not." He tugged my elbows, and I stepped closer to him. "But I told you what she was afraid of. I told you what might happen if her grandmother found out at the DUI. I thought you understood it was a secret."

"I did." I shook my head, trying to explain. His eyes looked so dark in the low light—almost black. Unfamiliar. I covered my mouth and tried to focus, to think. I had good reasons. I *did*. "But some things shouldn't be secret. Some things can't stay secrets for everyone's safety."

He bowed his head, dropping his hands from my arms. "I feel like you're talking about your family's secrets. But this is Emma's life." I bit my lip, feeling poetry climbing my throat, trying to rob me of my own words. He was right. I was talking about my own family's secrets . . . but it held for hers. She *should* be protected from a dad who needed help. But I wasn't going to convince him unless I told him the whole truth. And that wasn't nearly as charitable.

"I didn't want her so close to you after . . . what I saw." The air felt sucked from me. "Emma's *into* you, and I didn't want her living with you. Not when something was starting between us, because I might . . ." I gestured between us, unable to use the words that were right there in my mind: *be falling in love with you.* I knew it was true, too. It was him—his quirky sense of humor and the way he smiled at me. But it was also the way I felt about myself when I was with him. With him, I could laugh, be honest about my family, and let him see pieces of me only Blythe had ever known. He had sewn himself into my heart, like a patch over a bleeding wound. It would hurt like hell to tear those stitches out.

"Sabine." He took a deep breath and reached for me again. "Emma told me how she feels that day in the costume room. When you saw . . . what you saw." I sucked in a breath.

"But if you know how she feels, why are you . . ." I wanted to ask him why he would lead her on with this whole costume thing? Why was she still jumping into his arms if he knew how she felt? Did she think there was a chance? *Was* there? The word *polyamorous* floated through my mind, and my stomach twisted.

Kai's hands tightened on my arms. "Sabine. When no one in Thornewood would speak to me because I wore hand-me-downs twice over, Emma did. She made every day of elementary school easier. And every day since. I owe her. But I don't owe her *you*. When I'm with you, it doesn't matter that I have to work two jobs or that I never get enough sleep or that my hamstrings are always killing me. You get me in a way no one else does. I've been thinking of nothing but you and your crazy poetry since the day we met. So I told her I loved her *as a friend*, but that was it. I told her it's you and me."

You and me. I looked up to the ceiling. It twinkled like a night sky. I could feel Kai's grip on my arms, and it felt a little like without him tethering me here, I might float away. "I should've told you," he said. "If I had, maybe you wouldn't have made that call."

I closed my eyes, admitting it to myself. "I was afraid," I whispered. "I feel like you get me, too. In a way no one has. I was afraid to lose that."

He let his hands trail down to my wrists and took my hands. "But you didn't trust me?"

I shook my head and squeezed his hands, hoping he would understand. "I didn't trust the *situation*. So I freaked and called Mrs. McMichaels."

He squeezed my hands back. This was a misunderstanding; we could get past it. I breathed a sigh of relief as he pulled me closer. I tilted my head, about to place it on his chest, when he stiffened.

"Please tell me I misheard you." It was Emma. Kai stared over my shoulder, then quickly let me go as Emma stepped between us in the narrow space.

"*You* called Grandmamma?" Her sparkling face was inches from mine. "Do you know what you've *done*? I may not see my dad for years. He could go to *jail*."

"Emma. I'm sorry." I squeezed my hands together, trapping my thumbs. "I didn't know what would happen. I just wanted you to have a safe place to live."

Emma curled her lip at Kai. "You told her *everything?*"

"Emma." Kai's voice was low. "Sabine is your friend. Friends care about each other, even if they're mis—" Kai grabbed Emma's arm as she tried to round on me, her glittering hands in the air.

"You think she cares about *me?* She only cares about *you.*" Emma yanked away from Kai and stepped so close I could see the droop of her fake eyelashes. "Why do you think my sewing machine is at your house? I can't even *have* it with me at Grandmamma's. Now I'll never finish my collection. I'll never get into fashion school. And I'll never get out of Thornewood. Thanks to *you.*" She was crying, black eyeliner sliding over her golden cheeks. She just let the tears fall, ruining her perfect gold makeup. I lifted a hand to touch her shoulder, to comfort her, but Emma threw herself against Kai, her hands covering her face.

Blythe was suddenly there, her cat-ear headband in her hands. I looked from it to her, then to Nate, who hurried up behind her. "What's going on?" Blythe asked.

I gestured to where Kai was trying to soothe Emma, patting her shoulder and murmuring in her ear. She reared back from whatever he said. "But if I *don't* do what Grandmamma says, she'll press child-endangerment charges." My stomach twisted at Emma's words. *Child endangerment?*

Blythe poked my shoulder, waiting for an answer. "I might have . . ." I wrung my hands, feeling the creep of poetry again. "Emma might not be able to see her dad for a while. And I guess he may have to . . . serve time?"

"In *prison?*" And it was like Blythe turned into her costume: cat who just lost her tail. "What does that have to do with *you?*"

"I told Mrs. McMichaels that Emma's dad was in rehab and that she was living at Kai's?" I hoped it didn't sound as bad as it seemed to.

"Rehab is no joke, but why couldn't she stay with Kai?" Blythe asked, and looked from me to Emma, and back to me. "You just didn't want her living there, did you?" I flicked my eyes to his. Kai met my eyes, listening. There was a look on his face that was both sweet and sad. I didn't like it.

"It wasn't only about Kai," I said, searching for other reasons that would sound less like I was being a jealous jerk.

"You can be so selfish sometimes," Blythe said, shaking her head. "I can't believe you. First you tattle on Emma's dad to the Wicked Crone of Thornewood, then you saddle the house with so many fines we could end up homeless."

Kai's eyes found mine over Emma's blond beehive. "Is this about . . . what we did at the house?" Kai glanced between me and Blythe, frowning. "I thought you both wanted to sell your house."

Blythe gave him a scowl. "*She* does."

Kai's brows drew down in confusion. He shook his head, his eyes clouding with guilt. "You said it would be okay." Kai looked at me like he wasn't sure who I was.

I shrugged. "I thought it would, and it may still."

"It won't be," Blythe said. "We're going to have to move far away."

"Wait," Kai said, pushing Emma from him. "We did all that because you want to move *away* from Thornewood?" I tried to shake my head, but I couldn't deny that I'd wanted to get away not just from the house, but from Thornewood and everything it had been to my dad. Kai looked at me for a long time, his eyes growing hard.

"Yes," I said. "But I didn't want to leave *you*." I thought that sounded okay, but his face fell as if he'd just been handed a costume contest participation prize.

"I can't believe you didn't tell me you wanted to *leave*," Kai said, his voice gravelly. "I wouldn't have helped you if it meant you were just going to leave Thornewood." He turned back to Emma, holding her close as she cried. I thought of the day in the rose garden, when his stare made me feel like I was on fire, when all I wanted was to kiss him. And I almost did, even though I knew Emma cared about him, and that he might care about Emma. It was unfair of me to let the way he made me feel take over. Unfair to Emma. Unfair to Kai. Because I could see now . . . even if Kai had feelings for me, maybe it would always come back to the two of them.

"I'm sorry," I said, but the words were breathy, hollow. I felt my sister's hand on my shoulder, but I shrugged her off. I tried to shove my hands deep in my pockets as Emily's words flitted through my mind, like they had wings. But, like birds, I couldn't keep them caged. I swept my thumb over my lower lip. "If I can stop one heart from breaking." My fingers, as if my hope bird had come alive beneath my skin. "If I can stop one heart—if I can—I will stop my heart from breaking, I will stop your heart from breaking—"

Blythe hissed. "Stop the *poeting*! It's not cute. It's *crazy*." I broke off and shoved my hands back into my skirt pockets, feeling like I might be shrinking. The pounding music waned. The lights bent away. The students swayed more slowly. I could feel Kai's eyes on me, but I couldn't meet them. I couldn't be with him. Wanting him had made me a liar, had made me mean and thoughtless. I should let him go back to Emma. If I wasn't here, maybe he would want to be with her. I took a step back. Then another one. Then I turned, and I rushed toward the door.

Kai's voice sliced through the silence in my head. "Sabine!" I didn't turn around. I hurried outside into the cool air. But I stopped, for the same reason I'd called Mrs. McMichaels. I stopped because I was overwhelmed by how much I wanted to be with Kai. So I gave him one long moment to find me, to keep me from leaving. I already missed the feel of his hand in mine; I already regretted rushing out. But it wasn't Kai who followed me. It was Nate.

"Do you need a ride home?" He held his wig in his hands. His black hair staticked out from his head like Einstein. I felt a pinch of humiliation in my heart. Kai wasn't coming.

I scowled at Nate. "Why do you wear your hair so weird all the time?"

His eyebrows lifted. "I rotate through decades." He didn't look offended that I'd asked. "I include a speculative future."

I barked out a laugh. "You and my sister are perfect for each other."

"I agree. Will you let me take you home? I don't mind." Nate held his wig over his heart, looking more dashing than his costume gave him the right to. I shook my head and stepped into the night.

I passed two chaperone moms, who waved at me. I waved back, but they didn't try to stop me, or ask me where I was going. Then I was in the parking lot, and then I was halfway down the hill toward Magnolia Street.

Suddenly, trick-or-treaters swarmed from a front porch

and surrounded me, pulling me into their revelry. I slowed my pace and stepped aside to let them run ahead as their parents followed, wishing I'd hear feet stomping after me. I wanted so much to hear the sound of my name from Kai's lips. But I kept my eyes straight ahead. He wasn't there. I'd let him go, and he wasn't coming after me.

If I can stop one heart from breaking, I shall not live in vain. It didn't feel like my heart was breaking. It felt like I was keeping it from breaking. My hope bird was very quiet as I walked down the road, weaving in and out of trick-or-treaters, silent and dry-eyed.

ONE SISTER HAVE I
IN THIS CRAZY HOUSE

I walked into the pocket park on the corner of our street to escape the stream of costumed kids. I sat down on a bench and fluffed my feathered skirt, pretending I wasn't about to cry. I totally got why Emily Dickinson never left her house. I checked my phone, but there were no messages. Why did I mess everything up so badly? It was almost as if I wanted things to go wrong—as if I were pushing to see if they would. But I needed to tell the truth, not matter what. Still, I wished I hadn't left the dance.

For the first time in weeks, I wished my dad were there.

I wished so hard that on this night of spirits he would appear, tuck my hair behind my ears, and tell me how I would meet a wonderful guy someday. How, if it wasn't Kai, there would be someone better. I could hear his voice like he was beside me. I could almost see him through the mist. I shivered.

Then I remembered the tiny piece of him I'd hidden in my pocket. His letter. I pulled it out, running my fingers over the crumpled edges, afraid to open it. Then I took a deep breath and lifted the envelope flap. My dad's handwriting scrawled across the page. I lifted the letter close to my nose and breathed in. Old Spice and manila folders. I held his words, looking them over but not reading. Would his letter tell me he'd been the dad I thought I knew? Or if he'd been someone I never knew, and now never could?

Or maybe it was another letter about mediation.

Dear Charlie,

It's a strange thing, parenthood. I wish we could do it together. But the girls need their mother so much. This weekend Blythe got her period. I know, I know. You wouldn't believe the commotion. Not because of girl issues, but because Sabine wants hers, too. She cried and slammed the door over and over. I told Maryann I was going to take their door off its hinges if she slammed it one more time, but Maryann just looked at me. It reminded me of the way you look at me sometimes. Like—Oh, please.

Of course she's right. They need autonomy. They should probably even have their own rooms. But don't you know, it was really me who wanted to cry and slam a door.

My little girls are growing up. I want to believe that I'll be around to tell them everything will be okay. Be there when they get married and have kids of their own. But I worry that I won't. Maybe all parents have that same fear. I can hear you saying, Don't fret—you'll be there. I hope so. And I hope that by then, you'll be there, too.

Maybe all kids need three or four parents. The job is too hard for just two people. And you'd make such a great dad. I know someday they'll love you like I do. And that they'll be better for knowing you and

Maryann both—my two great loves. They'll be better for being part of our dreams and part of our love. Slammed doors and all.

Mick

My face burned. Charlie knew about the time I screamed and kicked because Blythe got her period before me? Why would he write something so embarrassing? I crushed the letter, my cheeks sparking flames. *That* was what he wrote to Charlie? How I'd gotten mad and slammed the door? I covered my mouth, laughing. I had slammed that door so hard the paint chipped off. He was *so mad.*

I pressed my lips together and took a deep breath. Then I reread the letter. And my stomach sank when I got to the ending. He wasn't pretending to be a dad. He *was* our dad. He wasn't some stranger. He was the father I'd loved. He always was. My hope bird burrowed into my heart as tears pierced the corners of my eyes. What would Dad think of what I'd done? Charlie had every right to hate me. Blythe was disgusted with me. Emma was probably planning to poison me. And I'd walked away from the only person who'd let me try to explain. I might not have bought number six Magnolia, but it was my fault we were going to lose it. To lose Dad's dream.

I thought of our pink room, with its view of the willow tree and its wide glass windows. Of the pink chaise that was my favorite place to study. Of how when I looked at the tall redwoods lining our driveway, I thought of the day I met Kai. And I didn't want to go. *I didn't want to go.*

A boom and a cackle came from down the street, and I jumped. The trick-or-treaters screamed, and I craned my neck to look. A burst of strobe light shone through the trees, and a little kid's high-pitched Muppet voice cried out: "Mr. Pumpkinhead!"

Mr. Pumpkinhead. The neighborhood association guy? What had Mrs. Costello said? Just go by? Maybe I could. Maybe . . . he could help. At least I could say I tried.

I stuffed the letter back in my pocket and pushed the tears out of my eyes. Around the corner, a line of kids led to a little in-law cottage beside a much larger house. I almost turned away, because 1) clearly Mr. Pumpkinhead was busy tonight, and 2) what could really be done now? Would he know anything I didn't already know with my city hall snooping? But I still followed the crowd down the well-lit path. I was pretty curious about this famous Mr. Pumpkinhead.

"BWAAAHAHAHAAAA!" I jumped as a giant pumpkin head lit up and flashed, cackling. "I see we have a ninja, and a fairy, and are you a ghost? Boo!" I looked around. Clearly, this guy could see us and was talking into a mic or something. It was pretty cool.

"And Iron Man has come, too. What an honor. And I see a swan princess—a little old to be trick-or-treating, ha ha ha, but Mr. Pumpkinhead welcomes all ages—wait. *Sabine?*" The mic cut off, and the door flew open.

It was Monsieur Cade.

He shoved a basket of candy at the kids, saying, "It's okay, take two," but his eyes stayed on me. When everyone had their treats, Monsieur Cade gestured me to the door.

"You're crying." He motioned to where my mascara had probably smudged beneath my eyes, and I quickly wiped my face. "Why aren't you at the dance?"

"I was. I just left. I—are you Mr. Cade?" I kept tripping

over my words, thinking I should be speaking in French. "I know you *are* Mr. Cade. But are you the head of the neighborhood association?"

"Mais oui." He handed me a mini candy bar. "Sorry. No French. Do you want to come in?" I'd never been inside one of my teacher's houses before. It was surreal. I almost expected there to be chalkboards everywhere. But his walls were white. And bare. He saw me noticing. "I've been living here for three years, but I have no talent for design. Not like you."

I smiled. "My mom's an interior designer."

"Yes. The lovely Maryann. I met her last week at the school board meeting. But you were telling me why you left the dance?"

"That's a long story. I'm actually here because I was wondering about the neighborhood zoning vote on our house? Number six Magnolia? It didn't pass. I just wondered what happened."

"Oh yes. It was housing, right?" He sat on the edge of a stiff-looking couch. "Something in conjunction with a well-regarded charity. The community concerns were noise and parking—of course. But at the meeting, Mr. Parker addressed those issues. Everyone seemed satisfied. I thought it had a good chance of passing. But it's hard to get an eighty-five percent vote. Some people just don't want change."

"Is there a way to get a new vote?" I asked.

Monsieur Cade sighed. "On the same issue? Not for five years. Thornewood has very strict rules."

That was two years from now. Maybe we could hold off Mrs. McMichaels with legislation, until we could have another vote. "Is there a way to find out why people voted no? To address any issues?"

"I didn't collect the vote myself, though it is my job. Mrs. McMichaels was happy to help." He spread his hands on his knees. "Maybe folks let her in on their concerns."

"Mrs. McMichaels?" My knees buckled. "She collected the votes? And tallied them?"

"Oh yes." He stood as the doorbell rang repeatedly. "We're so lucky to have her." So lucky. So, so lucky. I swallowed the candy and unwrapped another. "The votes are kept at city hall with the permit applications," Mr. Cade said. "You won't find names, but if folks made comments, they're public record."

"Okay," I said. But if there'd been a bunch of votes with our file, I would have seen them. Emma and I went through every piece of paper in there. I suddenly wanted to personally check with every neighbor. To ask them how they voted. I knew it was crazy—the Historic District was a square of five blocks. And Mr. Cade was probably right: some people just didn't want change. But . . . even if everything Mrs. McMichaels did was legit, maybe her math was off?

I thanked Mr. Cade, and he gave me another candy bar before I waded through the group of kids looking wistfully at the quiet pumpkin head.

"Sorry!" Mr. Cade's amplified voice boomed over my shoulder. "Mr. Pumpkinhead needs potty breaks, too!" The kids giggled, and I headed toward the street, wondering how long it would take to ask all of our Historic District neighbors how they'd voted. All night, I guessed. I stopped to make way for a cluster of superheroes. I scanned the street—every light was on except for ours. Every neighbor was home, handing out candy. Everyone. There might be no better night to meet our neighbors.

I headed down Magnolia, glad I'd decided to wear flats. Maybe we would still have to move. Maybe it didn't matter what I did tonight. But at least I could tell Blythe that I'd tried—I wasn't just thinking of myself. I was thinking of our family. And of Dad.

I knocked on the first door I came to. I asked a different question from the one they were expecting, but our neighbors were ready with candy, and with answers.

Seven Baby Ruths, three Butterfingers, five Reese's peanut butter cups, and sixteen unacceptable candy options later, I was still knocking on doors and inquiring as to our neighbor's voting records. I was so busy, I didn't check my messages once in three hours.

IT WAS AFTER ELEVEN WHEN I tiptoed into our room, thinking Blythe was already asleep. I tried not to imagine the fun she'd had while I'd canvassed the neighborhood, getting blisters and ruining my secondhand Dior ballet flats. As quietly as I could, I brushed my teeth then began to look over my notes as I slipped on my pajamas and climbed into bed. I'd collected forty-two names and forty-two *yes* votes. Yes, yes, yes. No one I spoke to said they'd voted *no*—not a single person. I closed my Notes application with a smile. There had been three dark houses that clearly didn't want to be bothered, but even counting those as *nos* . . . Mrs. McMichaels's math was suspect. Wasn't it?

I got my phone back out to calculate. And that's when I saw fourteen missed messages from Blythe. I looked over to her bed and realized she wasn't in it. I threw back the covers and got up.

"Blythe?" I swallowed hard. Where was she? She should be home by now.

There was a commotion, and snuffling. I turned on a light as Blythe's armoire door swung open. Blythe sat there, her face illuminated by the yellow harvest moon that shone fat and round through the window. She hiccuped.

"Why are you in your closet?" She was still in her cat costume. Her whiskers were smudged across her cheeks. I knelt down, but she just kept crying quietly. When she didn't move, I sat down on the floor beside her. "Are you okay?" I looked for blood or bruises, but she wasn't hurt. Not that I could see. "Did something happen?" She tried to speak through hiccupy sobs as I rubbed her back, but she couldn't get a word out. If Nate had upset her, I was going to tie him down and pluck every hair from his head. "Hey. Take a breath, okay? You're freaking me out." When she still couldn't speak, I felt panic rise. I'd left her behind at that dance—something Mom was always saying not to do. *Stay together* was her one big rule. If something had happened—

"I didn't—I didn't . . ." She took a haggard breath and swallowed, wiping her nose. "I didn't know where you *were.*" She gestured to her dripping nose, and I got her a tissue. "I looked *everywhere* for you. I tried your phone. I sent so many messages."

I dug my thumbs into my palms. "Does Mom know I missed curfew?" I was in enough trouble already.

She shook her head. "When we got home, you weren't here. And you didn't answer your phone." Her eyes were wide and shining. "And Emma and Kai didn't win the contest, that boat did, and everyone was mad and crying. And where *were* you?"

"I was . . . talking to the neighbors." I bit my lip, thinking about how upset Emma would be. I didn't think Kai would care much, but I knew it would wreck Emma. Blythe stopped hiccuping and drew her leotard sleeve across her nose.

"What? Why?" Her cat ears were lopsided.

"I was asking about the neighborhood vote." I took her headband off and pushed her hair back behind her ears. "I thought you'd be happy."

She slumped against the side of the armoire, her hanging clothes falling over her face. She pushed them off and wiped at a fresh set of tears. "The vote? *Sabine*. I thought you'd finally listened to something I said and *left*."

"I didn't leave." I would never leave my sister.

"I didn't back you up tonight." She bit her lip, hard. It looked like it hurt. "And I called you crazy."

"Yeah." I dug my thumbs into my hips, trying not to be crazy right this second. "That was uncool."

"I shouldn't have said that. I know you're not crazy." She sniffed. "But the poems . . . They remind me of him." When I just looked at her, she shook her head. "Of *Dad*. They remind me of Dad." I didn't know what to say. I couldn't believe she remembered the poems, too. Had she found the words inside her, too, like flowers growing in a garden? She wiped her nose again. "Did you really talk to the neighbors?"

I nodded. "Forty-two houses—"

"—they all voted yes."

I tilted my head. "How did you know?"

"Emma said you didn't see any votes at city hall." She held up her hands. "If there weren't something to hide, why would they be hidden?"

I shook my head. Hidden? Where could they be? "Let's think about it in the morning." I yawned, and she did, too.

"Sabine?" Blythe tilted her head to my shoulder. "I think I want a home, too."

"Yeah. We'll figure it out." We could think about *that* in the morning, too. I offered my hand, and she clambered out of the armoire. I helped Blythe out of her cat costume and into her pajamas, then I tucked her into bed.

I was in bed with my eyes closed, drifting off to sleep, when she spoke again.

"When you disappeared, it felt like Dad. Like after he died." Her eyes were gleaming again in the moonlight. "You're not going to leave again, are you?"

"No." Emily's words floated in. I rubbed my thumb over my lower lip. "One sister have I in this house. And you're it. Forever."

26 THIS IS MY LETTER TO FORGIVE

Sun pushed beneath my eyelids, bringing back the night before. My heart seized up as I remembered how Kai had looked at me like I was a stranger, how he'd held Emma, and how he'd let me go. On my phone was a message from him, asking me if I was okay. I wasn't. So I put the phone away without answering.

Blythe was already up, muttering to herself as she organized the mess that was her desk. When she saw that I was awake, she paced, pressing her hands together. This was Blythe in planning mode. "If you're right about the neighborhood vote, then we just need to prove it." She spoke as if we'd been in the middle of a conversation. We probably had been—in her mind. "That alone would cancel the majority of the fines."

"What? How?" I rubbed sleep from my eyes.

"Two reasons: Our fines are linked to the original permit denial. And if number six was zoned business, there would be no fines for the apartment, either."

"But what about the historic violations?"

"I'm not sure, but I did look at the city's handbook." She rolled her eyes, and I remembered the hundreds of pages that Mrs. McMichaels had dropped off our first week in Thornewood. "The requirements are different and less strict. I think Charlie's been counting on the *next* neighborhood vote going

229

his way. But if we're right, we won't need another vote. We just need to find the original votes." I blinked. She was way ahead of me, thinking-wise. Blythe paced the ten-step width of the room. "If we work under the premise that you didn't miss anything at city hall, it stands to reason the evidence is elsewhere."

"The recycle bin?" I asked.

"Emma said Mrs. McMichaels's house is like *Hoarders: Antiques Edition*," Blythe said. "I doubt she throws things away. And if we accept that as fact, then the documents must be somewhere in her house."

I gave her the side-eye. "It's not like she'll let us look through her underwear drawers."

"No." She sighed and sat down on the bed beside me. "But there may be another way. We need to tell Charlie."

"Okay," I said. But something tugged at me. *Charlie.* I pulled the letter out from under my pillow. "Before you talk to him, I think you should read this."

"Sabine." She gave the letter the kind of look Mom gave seasonal plaid throws. "You have to give that back."

"I know." I pushed it into her hand. "But please read it first." She blinked, turning the letter back and forth. I was afraid that she would refuse and say it wasn't our business. But she opened it. I watched her read, wondering if she would feel the way I had: that it was like being with him again. She covered her mouth, murmuring, "door slammer," then her eyes turned down at the edges. She folded it, then handed the letter back. I placed it carefully into its envelope.

I let her sit with it as she looked out the window, her eyes unfocused, filling with tears. I waited. Finally, she picked up my pillow and looked at me. "When Mom and Charlie told us," she said, "it felt like one theory of our life. But now there's *proof.*" I followed her eyes to the weeping willow outside and thought of the photograph of Dad. I'd seen the proof before she had, and it had wrecked me.

"He's still the dad we knew," I said, but I wasn't sure she was ready to hear it.

"You talk to Charlie," she said, and curled up in my bed. "You owe him an apology anyhow. I can't look at him for a little while."

I knew the feeling. I patted her shoulder and slipped out of bed, leaving it to her. "Try not to break a window, okay?" I left her there, burrowing, and got dressed.

I swung through the kitchen and grabbed a Pop-Tart before heading up to the garage apartment, the letter heavy in my pocket. When I got there, wiping crumbs from my face, I knocked, but no one answered.

I glanced in the big windows of the former four-car garage, wondering what was in there. Storage? It could practically be a second apartment. But no Charlie.

I turned to the garden and saw that the old, dead ivy and blackberry brambles had been cleared from the brick retaining walls. Now, the three wide, flat terraces of the yard were visible: the willow tree and its surrounding field, the would-be rose garden, and the crumbling pond. So much potential. I heard the skitter of gravel and called out for Charlie.

"Sabine?" Charlie came from the upper garden wearing one of my dad's old MIT T-shirts and a pair of ripped shorts. I'd always seen him perfectly put together. Like this, he looked a little bit more human.

"Bet you thought I'd be packing," he said, his mouth set

in a thin line. "But I'm not giving up. I'm gardening. Helps me relax."

I touched the letter in my pocket. "Gardening?" He gestured for me to follow. Around the corner, he was working on three newly constructed raised beds, half-planted with sage and thyme and marjoram and basil.

"I know Maryann didn't want anything done with the garden, but I decided to let out some aggression on a few two-by-fours." He glanced at the window I'd broken, whole again now. "Safer than using glass."

"Oh," I said, guilt nibbling at my stomach. "Sorry about the window. I can pay for it. Eventually." Charlie picked up a trowel and a small plastic bin of lemon thyme.

"It's okay, Sabine." He stopped what he was doing and looked at me for a long moment. "Believe me, I know it's a lot to handle." He went back to digging. "How can I help you today?"

"Well . . ." I wondered how much to tell him. "I talked to Mr. Cade last night. He's my French teacher. And what he said made me think we should double-check the neighborhood votes. So, during trick-or-treating time, I talked to forty-two of forty-five houses."

He patted the thyme down. "And?"

"They all voted *yes.*"

"Interesting. I hadn't considered a miscount." He picked up his spade and scooped another hole then squeezed a basil plant into the fresh soil. The smell of it was soothingly familiar.

"I don't know that it was a miscount," I said. "Mr. Cade was supposed to collect the votes, but Mrs. McMichaels did instead. And he said they should be at city hall. But they're not."

He paused and eyed me for a moment, like he was wondering how I'd been snooping around city hall. But he didn't ask about it. Instead, he pressed his lips together and sprinkled soil around the bases of his newly planted herbs. He took up the next bin before he met my eyes. "So, no votes. Are you saying what I think you're saying?"

I lifted my eyebrows. "If you mean that Mrs. McMichaels lied about the vote, yeah," I said. "That's what I'm saying."

"That woman and her DENIED stamp." Charlie shook his head. "Probably sleeps with it."

I laughed. "And in her hat."

"Stranger things, Sabine," he said with a little smile. "I'm trained to believe people are innocent until proven guilty. But . . ." He set his jaw. "Tomorrow I'll go to city hall. I'll talk to the mayor. Let me handle this from here. All right?"

I didn't trust him or my mom to fix anything. How could the mayor help? Did he know where Mrs. McMichaels kept her secret vote stash? Not likely. But I nodded, my mind turning to the real reason I was here. "There's something else." I fished the rumpled, tearstained letter out of my dress pocket. "This is yours." He brushed his hands free of dirt and reached for the letter. I held on a second too long.

"I'd lecture you about property rights, but it's a little early in the morning," he said.

"Possession is nine-tenths of the law." I smiled.

"Your father's daughter." He squinted as the morning sun leveled with his eyes. I couldn't tell if I was imagining it, or if he looked nervous. "How many have you read?"

I kept my eyes on the herbs. "How did you know I took them?"

"I saw you." He fingered the letter before putting it in a pocket. "How much did you read, Sabine?"

I forced my eyes to his. "Just a few. It seemed like work stuff. I guess I was dumb to think that."

"You understand why I had to take the letters back." He wiped his fingers on a tea towel he had over one shoulder, like he was cooking, not gardening. "But I know we should have told you. You all have been more understanding of this . . . situation . . . than Mick thought you'd be."

I swallowed hearing my dad's name. "Really?"

"Yes." Charlie nodded. "He was very worried. In the South, there's no name for a man with a fluid sexual identity, let alone polyamory. Gay marriage wasn't legal back then, and where we were from, it was dangerous to even talk about enjoying the company of *both* men and women. I'm not sure he knew how to explain his choices. Maybe because some of those *choices* led to him contracting HIV."

"So, you didn't give him . . . I mean . . ." I was really regretting coming up here.

"I'm negative, Sabine. If that's what you're asking. He made some regrettable choices before we met, which led to contraction of the disease. It was when he was discovering who he wanted and needed to be for a fulfilling—"

"Maybe I don't need to know *everything*," I said, pushing away the thought of my dad as a lothario.

"All right." For a moment, Charlie looked very dad-aged. He picked up another plastic bin. French lavender. "I'm not sure I'll ever forgive him for not telling you his story himself." He brushed off his hands and took a step toward me. "It would be better in his voice. Would you like to read more of your dad's letters? He mentioned you a great deal, Sabine.

The poetry you read together, how you used to quiz him on botanical plant names, even your fashion commentary. A Vivienne Westwood fan, am I right?"

Memories zinged to the surface of my mind. "Sure. But McQueen could do no wrong." I could hear my dad asking me to give him "the fashion faux pas and yes pas" of Milan or Paris. And, even though my heart hurt, I smiled.

"Maybe we can talk fashion sometime," he said. I looked away, out across the yard. Charlie took a step closer to me. "You know what Mick liked best about this house?"

"The garden," I said. Charlie nodded. I knew my dad. Not everything, but the important things. My hope bird dug into my chest with sharp, pointed claws.

"He had dreams of maple trees and wide patios and raised vegetable beds." Charlie set his gardening gloves aside. "And I wanted that for him. I wanted it for all of us. I know I may not get it now, but I still want it. Your dad's not here to want things for you, Sabine, but I am."

He'd made these raised beds for my dad. He'd made them so we could remember who my dad had been—not just to him, but to all of us. And even though he could have left and started a life of his own, he'd stayed here, to help realize the dreams my dad had and could never fulfill. "Call me Bean," I said.

Then I couldn't stop myself. I launched into his arms.

He caught me, wrapping one arm around my shoulders and patting my head with the other. "There, now. Don't I know it." His voice cracked. "It's going to be all right."

I was crying, really crying. But I didn't care. I might not have my dad anymore, but I had Charlie. And having him was like having a piece of my dad—only a piece of my dad I never knew.

When I stepped back, wiping my eyes, he smiled, his blue eyes shining. I could see what my dad saw in him—when he smiled, he sparkled. Maybe I had to accept that people were infinitely imperfect. I sure was.

I needed a chance to get to know Charlie, and the dad I wished I'd truly known. Just a *chance*.

But the only way I could have that chance was if we kept the house. And to do that . . . I needed to find the votes. And the only person who might be able to help me do that was Emma. Emma, who had let me wear her handmade designs on my soda-sticky self. Emma, who loved fashion as much as I did. Emma, whose would-be boyfriend I had tried to steal, and who now hated me. I didn't know how I was going to get her help.

But I knew I had to try.

A FACE DEVOID OF LIFE

Just after five, Blythe and I walked up to the McMichaels mansion. It was a tall yellow Victorian with white trim surrounded by neatly clipped boxwood hedges. An old-fashioned streetlamp cast a yellow glow on a plaque proclaiming it THE SECOND-OLDEST HOUSE IN THE FINE CITY OF THORNEWOOD. Another sign said: NO SOLICITORS.

Add to the list of Thornewood favorites: signage.

We stepped into the courtyard. It was thick with the smell of last season's roses and perfectly kept. But as we approached the front door, the rose smell was replaced by a dank basement smell, like overcooked beets. Blythe hesitated before knocking. Emma answered the door wearing Kai's soccer sweatshirt and a bored expression. The sight of the sweatshirt pushed a knife in my stomach. It had taken less than forty-eight hours for Emma to go further with his sweatshirt than I ever had. That sweatshirt had only touched my knees. Then I internally bled out as Kai himself emerged.

"I was just leaving." He slid into his Nikes in the shadows behind Emma. He glanced at me, then at Blythe. Blythe blinked, looking from Kai to me, then Kai to Emma, then Emma to me. She sighed audibly and pushed past us into the dark foyer. She peered around, already searching for evidence.

"Do you want me to stay?" Kai glanced at Emma, and I wished I'd answered his message—at least I could have told him that I was sorry I'd left, even if now it seemed like I'd been right to leave them alone together.

"No, go." She squeezed his bicep. "You've been playing like crap. Get some rest." It wasn't until Kai slipped past me that I realized he must not be planning to quit soccer after all. I was watching him ignore me when Emma spoke. "Kai! Your sweatshirt!" He stopped and turned around. She took it off, revealing a very ladylike blouse. She was about to run to him when she saw Blythe making a nuisance of herself with the entryway mail. She handed me the sweatshirt. "Give this to him." His sweatshirt was still warm. It didn't smell like him anymore, but like Emma: gardenia perfume. Still, I held it close as I walked out to the sidewalk, where he was waiting, flipping a skateboard back and forth between his feet.

I'd never seen him with a skateboard, not that it was surprising. It just made him seem like more of a stranger, with his gardenia-scented sweatshirt and his Element board.

"Probably can't live without it." I said, and handed it to him. He took it from me and swept it over his head. Then he made a face, as if he thought the perfume was a bit much, too. I was fully expecting him to kick off and take to the street, weaving his way back home, but he didn't. He kept flipping his board. The noise was incredibly loud. Flip. Clunk. Flip, flip. Clunk.

"I'm not a bird, you know," he said. I stared at him for a long time before realizing what he meant. The poem: *if I can stop one heart from breaking*. It was about saving a robin by putting it back in its nest. It didn't mean a literal robin, and I didn't think he thought it did. But the fact that he'd gone home, looked up the poem, and thought about how it *wasn't* about a robin made me feel impaled. At the dance, he'd been holding Emma. It felt like he'd chosen her, like he would always choose her, like she'd always be there, between us. But he'd gone home and looked up the poem.

I didn't know how to say the things I was thinking. "It's not about a bird." Flip. Clunk. Flip, clunk.

"I thought it was deep. The poetry?" He looked up from his skateboard, eyebrows knitted. "I thought it was awesome. But maybe it *is* crazy. I mean, do you want to be like her and hide in your house? And just write poetry? And never love anyone?"

"What?" I tried to ignore the *crazy* part. "Dickinson did more than just write poetry."

"She was a shut-in." He put his foot on the board to stop it.

"She had her reasons," I said, thinking of her loving someone who couldn't love her back. The crushing pain of *wanting*, of *loving*, gripped my heart. He crossed his arms over his chest, and my traitorous mind thought about what it was like to place my head there. For one second. One and a half.

"Why did you leave, Sabine?" He tipped his board again, and I found myself missing the Hacky. Flip. Clunk. "Why didn't you answer my message? You owe me an explanation."

I swallowed over the tightness in my throat. I wanted so badly to go to him as if nothing had happened with Emma. As if he hadn't kept her secret, even as I stood by wondering what was going on, as if he hadn't comforted her at the dance instead of following me. But if I went to him and apologized, and told him how much I regretted leaving the dance, he might choose her again. "Would it have mattered?"

His feet stopped, and he looked at his board. He licked his lips. Then he shook his head. "What do you mean? Of course it matters."

"But you're here, aren't you?" I said. "We don't talk for a day, and she's wearing your favorite sweatshirt? You'll choose Emma over me, and maybe Emma over everyone. And maybe that's how it should be."

"My life will be what *I* want it to be, not what Emma or anyone else wants it to be." He kicked his board, and it flipped in a perfect circle. "I'm sick of everyone thinking they know best—I should work for my dad, I should get a soccer scholarship, I should take Emma to the dance. *I* get to decide, Sabine. No one else."

"Oh yeah? Then how come you chickened out on quitting soccer?" I don't know why I said it, except that my internal bleed was getting worse by the second, and I wanted him to fix it or to go.

"That's not even . . ." He shook his head. The he pushed his shoulders back. "Go ahead, Sabine. Tell me I can't choose you. Tell me I don't have choices. Be just like everybody else. It will make this a whole lot easier." Then he stepped onto his board, pulled his hood up, and took off, dragging my heart behind him. I felt for my hope bird. But there was nothing. No sound, no flap.

It wasn't until I was walking back to the house that I remembered what he'd said about Emily and me. *And never love anyone.*

Love. Never *love* anyone.

He'd said *love.*

SWAMPY SWEET SECRETS

The door to the big yellow Victorian was closed. I stood there looking at it, shifting on my feet. What I wanted to do was: a) run back home and get into bed for the next three years or b) run after Kai and throw myself on the mercy of his skateboard. But instead I had to stand there looking awkward and wonder if someone would open the door or if I had to ring the bell. And if I did, whether I could apologize to Emma. She must hate me for kissing Kai and tattling on her to her grandmother. And I still kind of hated her for deleting the only evidence that Kai and I were ever together.

Just thinking about that day in the city and that selfie made me want to sink to the aged brick steps and cry, so when Emma pulled the door open and stared at me as if she was telepathically thinking: *You brought this on yourself, dummy*, I didn't say a word. I just stared back. "Why should I let you in?"

I could hear Blythe somewhere inside, chanting poetry I'd forced her to memorize. I didn't know what to say to Emma, but I made myself meet her eyes. Kai's sweatshirt had been hiding a blouse—nothing I'd seen her wear before. It was pale pink, like she might have borrowed it from someone at school. She was wearing plain dark jeans. And her feet were bare.

"Where are your boots?" I asked.

"No shoes in the sanctuary," she said, and I looked down at my own boots—the tall black ones, for extra power.

"She really is evil."

"At least we agree on that." She smiled, but it was forced. Emma's hair was different—tied back instead of swishing into her eyes like it usually did. I wondered what was with the make-under. "It's cold. Just come in." She threw the door open and gestured to a shoe rack. When you plan to run out of a place, you want your shoes on your feet, not on a brass-knobbed shoe rack. But in the interest of peace, I pulled off my boots and padded behind her into the dark, overfurnitured living room.

I could see why Mrs. McMichaels had our house in mind for a museum; the museum she owned was full. It was a hodgepodge of different styles and eras, and every inch of space was covered with something—even the furniture had furniture on it. Deep red velvet pincushion-button chairs supported carved black plant stands and tufted ottomans. The dark wallpaper had gold painted through it, but you could barely tell for the landscapes and portraits covering the walls. And everywhere: tchotchkes. Little wooden carvings and porcelain figurines and jade elephants. Even the old guy in the wheelchair in front of the unlit fireplace looked like he belonged in a museum.

"This is my great-grandfather. Noni." He made a noise that might have been *hello*, and I lifted a hand. Emma adjusted the blanket that covered his knees, and he opened his eyes for a moment. He had those same light blue Emma eyes—his milky with age. She stood, and he closed his eyes once more. All I could think was we would never, not ever, find anything in this hellhole of stuff.

But Blythe was already somewhere inside, snooping per our plan. My job: apologize. Her job: explore.

"Emma? Can we talk?" I asked, trying to look as contrite as I felt.

She nodded slowly. "Blythe is in my room, and Grandmamma's at a constituent thing. Let's go to the kitchen." I followed her through a narrow, book-cluttered hallway.

"So, you really have a great-grandfather?" My grandparents were all gone. I'd never known most of them—only my mom's mother, who'd taught me to sew, was someone I'd had a chance to know and love.

"Grandmamma's dad. My mom grew up with him after her dad left. Noni's ancient. But Grandmamma still drags him to church on Sundays. Her freakish strength comes in handy." I wanted to ask about that lightly mentioned tragedy of another lost dad. But I was afraid if I started talking dads, I would never say what I'd come to say. Then we could never do what we'd come to do. So I kept quiet.

Emma led me to a kitchen that was also full of stuff. But it was light and bright yellow, and there were about a hundred shiny copper pans hanging from different racks around the room—not cramped but cozy. Emma gestured to two ornate, metal-backed stools beside the cookbook-covered kitchen island. Then she opened a cabinet, yanked down a big plastic tub of Red Vines, and dropped it in front of me. "The favorite," she said.

I took four. It was only after I was done with the first twist that I could look her in the eyes under that bright kitchen light. "Could you please take that stupid clip out of your hair?" I said. "It's freaking me out."

Emma's hand shot to the pink-and-white polka-dot bow

decorating the back of her head. She snapped it out, her cheeks coloring. "I forgot I had that in," she said. "Grandmamma bought some things for me."

"I figured." I stared at her silky blouse. "Are you okay?" Her cheeks darkened. I'd never seen her look so self-conscious and so little like the Emma who I knew.

"You were right." She shrugged. "In a way. I mean, I have my own room. I have clothes. I have Red Vines." She tapped the top of the plastic tub.

"But?" I pressed my lips together not to chew them. She took a deep breath, and the air caught in her throat. I was afraid she'd cry, but she just shrugged again, her bright eyes flashing.

"It sucks—of course it sucks." She sighed. "My only sewing machine is at your house, and Grandmamma wants me home right after school every day. So I can't work on my designs. And my dad gets out tomorrow, but I can't even be there to meet him because the courts say I need to wait until his mental stability is assessed before I can have a supervised visit. That's *if* the restraining order is lifted, which it may not be. And *if* she doesn't press the child-endangerment charges, which she might. All because Grandmamma blames him for my mom's death."

"Wait. What?" I'd been waiting for her to place all this blame on me, where she had before.

Emma shook her head, and her hair took its usual place across her forehead. "My mom was driving to pick my dad up from a bar. It was raining, and the truck just didn't see and . . ." Emma's shoulders slumped. "He's always had a bit of a drinking problem. Before she died, he didn't have a *problem* problem. He just liked to have a drink with coworkers on Fridays. And he never drove drunk—they had a deal. He would always call a car or my mom to pick him up. More than once, she shoved me in the Toyota in my pajamas so we could go get him. I used to cry because it was cold, and I didn't want to get out of my warm bed. But she always said that it was safety first."

A terrible thought occurred to me. I tried, but I couldn't keep it inside. "Were you there? That night? When it was raining?"

Emma looked up from beneath her bangs. "Yeah." I imagined a young Emma, sleepy in pajamas in her padded car seat. I started to lift my thumb to my mouth, but stopped, thinking of Charlie's memories of my dad. I wasn't the only one holding his memories, holding the things my dad loved inside me. I could share that burden. Then I thought, but didn't say: *Sweet is the swamp with its secrets.* Swampy, swampy secrets. I pushed my hand down again, letting the poem go. I swallowed, knowing the poetry would stay inside me until I wanted to let it out.

Emma stood abruptly and opened an overstuffed cabinet for two water glasses. She set my drink down. Then she pulled up the sleeve of her silk shirt to the shoulder. A thick, ropy scar speckled with red bumps disfigured her bicep and elbow. It looked like hamburger meat someone had been taking bites of. I reached out, then pulled back. It looked like it hurt.

"Emma," I said, and my voice sounded faraway. "Oh, Emma." Her one-armed creations were all to cover this—to cover her injury. She and my mom had the same style: only show the perfect parts.

Emma's voice was soft. "When the truck hit us, it hit my

mom mostly. But the window and part of the door sliced into my arm. There are still tiny pieces of safety glass stuck in my arm. They were trying to save it, you know. But some of it is obviously missing. I'm supposed to be *grateful*." She barked a short laugh.

I winced at the sound. "You don't have to be happy about losing something," I said and reached out and squeezed her hand. "Or losing someone." It was hard to feel grateful for the remnants of a shattered life. I knew that. I released her hand, and she took a deep gulp of her water then sat down across from me. She slid the silk back down over her left arm.

We looked at each other in silence then both dipped into the Red Vines bin.

I tried to think brave. "Emma, I want you to know why I called your grandmother. I know I was wrong. But I had no idea how bad—"

"I know what you're going to say. You don't have to," she said. "Kai. It was because of Kai. What else is there to say?" I sank into the cowl neck of my sweater. She'd stolen my sorry steam. But she deserved a real apology. And maybe I had to give her one.

"I still want to get this out." I took a deep breath. She looked like she was about to roll her eyes, but I told myself to *keep going*. "When you told me you had feelings for him, I told myself to forget about him. I really did. I've only ever had crushes, so it wasn't like I wasn't used to my heart being trash-compacted. But then he asked me to the rose garden, and even though it didn't end up a real date, it was the first time I'd ever seen what it could be to care about someone in this . . . *romantic* way. He loves words and really *listening* to music. And he loves my poeting. And I forgot about your feelings." Emma looked up, her eyes hard, chewing two Red Vines at once.

"And . . ." I said quickly. "That was wrong, and I'm so incredibly sorry." I could feel my cheeks heating, but I forced myself to go on. "I called your grandmother because I was jealous. I could tell there was something between you that was serious, and I was afraid he'd turn around and see how awesome you are and realize he wanted *you*. And I shouldn't have tried to stop it. And I'm going to try to be happy for you both." Maybe in my next life, I thought. In this one, I was going to back off but be miserable. When I looked up, she was staring at the Red Vine in her hand. I wanted her to deny it, to tell me that she and Kai hadn't ended Halloween night together.

She ripped a Red Vine in half and pushed the plastic tub toward me, but I shook my head. I was feeling pretty sick from all that apologizing. "Thanks," she said. "I owe you an apology, too. For the photo of you and Kai. And that day in the costume room. I knew you'd come back for your phone. I knew it, and I still . . ." She took a bite and chewed for a moment. "I felt like he'd stopped seeing me. So I made myself hard to ignore. But it's not that he doesn't see me. He just doesn't see me *that way*." She pulled into herself and her hair drew a curtain across her face, and I had to stop myself from asking if that was really true. "Without him, I'll probably never leave Thornewood."

I wrapped my fingers around the edge of the kitchen island, pinching hard. I told myself to focus on Emma, not on Kai—not on what she'd said and how it made my heart thunder in my chest. "You don't need a *guy* to get you out of Thornewood. You can do that yourself."

"I'll never get away from Grandmamma," she said. I didn't know how true that might be, but I knew in that moment, we had a common enemy.

"Emma? What if we could help you? Me and Blythe?" She lifted her head, eyeing me warily. "Okay, so Blythe and I are looking for something—here, in this house. And if we find it, it might give you . . . leverage. Over your grandmother."

Her light blue eyes were locked on me. "What *kind* of something?"

I told her everything. About talking to Mr. Cade about the neighborhood vote. About how much we owed on the house—and how it wasn't really ours anymore. She listened to everything without comment, even my suspicions about her grandmother, and didn't call me crazy. Blythe walked in as I was talking, took three Red Vines, and twisted them into a jumbo-Vine.

"We only have forty-eight hours," I said. "We have to find evidence soon, if it even exists." Blythe swallowed with difficulty and lifted her hand, as if she was asking for permission to speak.

"Does your grandmother keep filing cabinets?" Blythe asked.

The confident Emma-ness came back into her eyes. "I know where to look."

SAFE IN THEIR
ALABASTER CABINETS

We were heading out of the kitchen when the front door opened and Emma's Noni croaked his hello. "Grandmamma's back," Emma whispered. She shoved me and Blythe down the narrow hallway. "First door on the left."

"Emma?" Mrs. McMichaels called from the front of the house. "A little help, please. Emma? I have bags." We didn't wait to hear Emma's reply. We hurried down the hall and closed the door behind us.

Blythe clicked on a lamp, and a cavernous room stacked with books and literary oddities rose around us. As much as I wanted to pause on the books—they were fancy ones, like first editions and whole collections—I forced my eyes to a low row of stark cabinets glowing like white tombstones beneath the far windows. They had to be her files.

Blythe's hands were on the first drawer in a flash. She tugged and twisted the handle, but it didn't budge. I tried the one beside it, but it was also locked. I felt the poetry burble in my mind. "Look at them. It's like Emily said. 'Safe in their alabaster chambers. Untouched by morning. Untouched by noon.'"

Blythe gave me a sidelong look and glanced at my hands. I wasn't poeting. I was just . . . poeming. "Unfortunately," she said, "they're also untouched by us."

"Because they're like graves, see?" I gestured to the cabinet, but Blythe wasn't paying attention. She pulled out the little Swiss Army knife that decorated her key chain and began picking at the center lock. I looked over the stark white cabinet, thinking it looked like something our mom would buy. It didn't match the antiquated décor at all.

Blythe's hand slipped, and her knife nicked her knuckle, taking out a chunk of skin. She hissed an expletive and grabbed her hand as blood welled up. Blythe was not good with pain. Or with the sight of blood. I grabbed a tissue from a side table and wrapped it around her finger. She hissed again, and I held up a finger to my lips. In the hallway, footsteps passed. We stood behind the door, me holding Blythe and both of us holding our breath. But whoever it was went by without stopping.

When I let go of her hand, Blythe bit down on her lip, her eyes tearing up. I steered her to a chair and forced her to sit. I took the pocketknife from her, but I had no idea how to pick a lock, so I put it in my pocket. Then I stood back and stared at the cabinet. Something was really off about it. Why didn't she have big oak filing cabinets that had been in her family for generations? This looked like a recent purchase from Design Within Reach.

I walked around the side and moved a stack of books out of the way. The side was split from the front in a line. The files weren't drawers at all—it was a false front. I was reminded of our mom's cloth-covered bedside tables. When you pulled a hidden rope, the cloth revealed a bookshelf. That way you could store all your bedside items without the room looking cluttered.

So where was the rope? I skimmed my fingers along the

top of the cabinet, then along the sides. Nothing. I got down on the floor and ran my hand along the base of the cabinet, finding nothing but dust bunnies. But when I came to the center, my finger caught on a slim piece of metal. I got down on my hands and knees and shoved my face practically to the floor to see the lock. But it wasn't a lock. It was a letter R, like from a sign, welded to the base of the filing cabinet.

I flashed on the signage in city hall: RECO DS. Mrs. McMichaels hijacked the R. This was it—her private city hall. I moved my fingers slowly over the R again, and it shifted but didn't move. Maybe it had to be pushed or twisted or turned or something. I tried all those things, but none of them worked.

I walked over to Blythe. Her breathing was taking up a lot of the air in the room. "Hey. Can you look at me?" She was holding her hand where a not-insignificant amount of blood was saturating the tissue.

"It hurts," she said.

"I know." I squeezed her other hand. "You can have a cupcake bandage when we get home. But right now, I need you to think. There's a latch thing under the cabinet. But it won't twist or turn or pull."

"Mrs. McMichaels is too old to crouch down. It's a bottom latch, it would go up. Maybe she kicks it up, or uses something to lift it?"

I walked back to the cabinet and paused, listening for footsteps. When I heard nothing, I crouched down and placed both thumbs under the feet of the bronze R and pushed up. It clicked, and the front of the cabinet door popped open, almost knocking me over. Then it slid up like an old-fashioned roll-top desk. And I was faced with three dozen narrow slots, like a mailroom wall. Each slot was numbered.

Blythe came to sit beside me, cradling her thumb. We scanned the numbers, but there was no discernible pattern. "What kind of system is this?" Blythe looked personally offended. There was 133 next to 17 next to 209. I shook my head, but then I saw a six. Number six.

"Addresses. They're *addresses.*" I yanked the number-six box into my lap, and there they were. A pile of quarter-sheet ballots with a single typed question: *Shall the illustrious city of Thornewood allow the residential home at number six Magnolia to be rezoned for commercial use by the Mission Project–funded charitable subsidiary named "The Sisters"?* I could hear my dad's voice. He used to make fun of us that way. "Hey, the sisters, come in to dinner." Like we were a garage band. I held the card out to Blythe.

"The sisters," I said. "You and me." Blythe looked at me, her eyes glassy. Her mouth was open, but she didn't say anything. She just looked back down at the papers in the box.

She let out a long breath and pulled the ballots out. "Start counting." But instead, I sat back on my socked heels, numb. If this one box was our house, what were the rest of these dozens of boxes? I pulled another out at random. More ballots. This voting sheet said, *Shall the illustrious city of Thornewood allow Elm Park to be redesigned to include a skateboarding area for youth?* A quick skim of the votes showed that they were mostly yes votes, but I think I would know if there was a cool skate park in Thornewood. All the parks were those corner pocket parks, without even a jungle gym. For sure no half-pipes.

I could guess what the rest were. People asking for changes

in Thornewood. And Mrs. McMichaels was making sure they never happened, no matter what the neighbors or the city wanted. Just like our project, a skate park or a new apartment building would change Thornewood. And it was clear she thought it was better the way it was.

Beside me, Blythe was making two piles of the votes on our house. So far, the *no*s were three, the *yes*es not countable at a glance.

I started taking photographs with my phone. I got the inside of the cabinet and the votes and the files. I took a photo of the whole room so someone could see that the cabinet was really there and not fabricated by a computer program.

Blythe put the last vote down, looked up at me, and smiled, just as the doorknob turned with a sudden creak.

Mrs. McMichaels stood in the doorway, looming over us. "What, may I ask, are you doing rummaging through my personal effects?" Blythe's mouth was hanging open, but for once nothing smart came out of it. A drop of her blood splattered onto the top vote on her pile. Mrs. McMichaels sucked in a horrified breath. "Put down those papers, get up, and leave this house if you want to avoid an altercation with the Thornewood Police." When we hesitated, she crossed her arms. "I hear colleges frown on applicants with criminal records." Blythe paled.

I stood up. Without my boots, I reached approximately to Mrs. McMichaels's collarbone. "No problem. I already photographed everything here and sent copies to the cloud. So go ahead and call the police. They might be interested to see your personal city hall."

Mrs. McMichaels smiled, crossing her arms. "You can't think that the illustrious members of our town would believe

253

that I, council member-at-large, would ever do anything untoward in Thornewood. This is my town more than it is anyone else's."

"More like no one else's," Blythe said.

"I have served nine concurrent terms," she said. "And I have kept Thornewood the pure, separate community it was meant to be, as intended by my father and the other founding members of the Thornewood Beautification and Historic District Society."

"By killing valid votes," I said.

"By helping people understand what they really want. No one moved here to have a discotheque in the middle of town or a fast-food restaurant drawing all the little peons from neighboring cities to the nice, clean burger house in Thornewood. People come to Thornewood and stay for generations because we are a special city. Thornewood was meant to be beautiful, to honor our history, and to celebrate the vision of our forefathers. Not to become Little San Francisco. People want picnics and parades and pancake breakfasts. They don't want the great unwashed next door."

"Unwashed?" Blythe raised an eyebrow, perhaps thinking of Charlie's fastidious hair. "Hardly."

"The housing was meant for people like *us*," I said. "People who need help because their families are complicated." Even after seeing the pictures at the Mission Project, I'd never really thought about why someone would need temporary housing in a safe LGBTQIA+ space . . . but now I did. Maybe because they had unaccepting, slightly insane grandmothers, like Mrs. McMichaels, who didn't like who they were.

"People like you?" Mrs. McMichaels sneered. "People like *you* are exactly who we don't need here."

Blythe stood slowly, wrinkling her nose. "You're a twin-ist?"

"I'm a conservationist." Then Mrs. McMichaels stepped into the hallway, her hands on either side of the door, and began yelling for Emma in a steady stream of "Emma! Emma! Emma!" until Emma sauntered in.

"Oh, there you two are," she said, glancing at the cabinet in surprise. "Got that thing open, huh? Good work."

Mrs. McMichaels whirled on Emma. "Your friends were just leaving." I met Emma's eyes, and she winked. She stepped across the mess Blythe and I had made on the floor and stood between us and Mrs. McMichaels, whose hand-drawn eyebrows spiked.

"We'll leave," I said, "when you agree to drop all the fines against our house. And rezone it commercially."

Mrs. McMichaels snorted. "That will never happen."

Blythe picked up one of the boxes. "Then I guess we take all these fancy files of yours to the *Thornewood Post*."

Mrs. McMichaels hissed, her hands on her narrow hips. "Do you think there's a single corner of this town where I don't have friends who *owe* me?"

"*Fear you* is more like it." Emma met her grandmother's eyes. They stared at each other for a long moment before Mrs. McMichaels wet her thin lips and turned her gaze on Blythe.

"No one will believe you over me," Mrs. McMichaels said.

"They don't have to believe," I said. "We have photographs."

"By the time you leave this house, I'll have everything gone. Burned. And you'll just be two teenagers who tried to play a joke on an esteemed Thornewoodian." I narrowed

255

my eyes. She *could* probably do that. But I didn't think she would. These papers were like trophies, the way serial killers kept people's jewelry or ears or whatever. She kept their useless little ballots. And I wondered for a minute how crazy she really was.

"No," I said.

She turned her pale eyes on me. "Excuse me?"

"No way. You won't take the chance. Just a whiff of scandal could be too much for you. You need everything perfect in Thornewood. And everyone has to see you as perfect, too. But they won't if there's a scandal. They'll look at you with doubt. They may even—"

"Unelect you," Blythe said. Mrs. McMichaels paled.

"So here's the deal. You'll give us our house back, drop the fines, and rezone it. Because otherwise, we'll spread these photos all over the *Thornewood Post*, all over the Berry Market, all over Rolly. And even if we *can't* prove that you 'miscounted' all these ballot measures, people will start talking. And maybe there'll be enough talk that they'll vote someone else in to avoid a scandal. But all it will cost to keep your secrets is a house. Just one house."

Emma raised her hand, like we were in class. "And tuition to FIDM." But Mrs. McMichaels didn't even look at Emma. She was still staring at me. And I have to say I was barely standing under the pressure of that gaze. I didn't know how I'd gotten all those words out; it was like my dad had been feeding them to me. Then I heard him, like a whisper in my ear. *In arbitration, everyone needs to feel like they've won something.*

"We'll keep the historic details," I said, thinking of what I loved about number six. "The butler's pantry signs, the telephone booth. And we'll follow historic code for the exterior."

She dropped her arms from her hips. "No Silver Cloud?"

I shook my head. "No Silver Cloud." The silence in the room thickened until I was sure I couldn't take another breath. Then she walked over to a bookshelf and pulled out a file. It was the file for number six we'd seen at city hall. I reached for it, and we each held one side of the manila folder. Then she let go. I crushed the file to my chest, sagging under its heft. Blythe snatched the number-six box from the floor. She cradled it and her bleeding thumb as she sidestepped to the door. Mrs. McMichaels watched the box leave as though Blythe held a baby in her arms. Then she slammed down the false front of her filing cabinet. She didn't say anything as we hurried into the narrow hallway. I stopped, feeling like I should say thank you. But when you've just blackmailed someone, *thank you* doesn't seem appropriate. So I said something else.

"We're taking her, too." Emma grinned at me and reached down for an overstuffed duffel bag just behind her. Mrs. McMichaels's mouth fell open. Even after Emma's little stab about people being afraid of her, she hadn't realized that Emma had only ever been playing at good granddaughter. In fact, she was the worst kind of granddaughter and the best kind of friend—the kind with her own ideas. Mrs. McMichaels sputtered for a minute before she came after us.

"But they're not even from Thornewood!" she shouted after us, hands in the air.

Blythe had her feet half stuffed in her Converse and the door half-open. But I had to sit to pull my boots on, and that's when Mrs. McMichaels caught up to us.

"Emma. Think about this," she said. "There are consequences. If you leave this house, I will call the police to bring you back. And then I will make absolutely sure that you never see your father again, that he will never get his driver's li—"

I clomped into my boots. Then, using every centimeter of the three inches of height they gave me, I held the file up in front of Mrs. McMichaels's face. "While you're making fines disappear, how about you disappear that restraining order, too?"

"How dare you step into my family business?" She held her hands in front of her, like she was thinking of wringing my neck. "Emma's father is a danger to himself and to her, and he should not be allowed to parent, let alone operate a motor vehicle—"

Emma put her hand on her grandmother's arm. "He needs help, Grandmamma. Not punishment."

"No. Absolutely *not*." She was shouting now. "I concede the permit. But your father is dangerous! He was driving drunk! What if you had been in the van? What then?"

I looked from Mrs. McMichaels to Emma. They both had their arms crossed and their mouths set in similar lines. For the first time, I could see a family resemblance.

"I won't drive with him," Emma said. "I promise. Not ever. But you have to pull the restraining order. You have to let me see him. You have to let us be in each other's lives. He's my *only* parent."

Mrs. McMichaels opened her mouth to speak, but it was Emma's Noni we heard.

"Family first, Bernadette." His voice was deep and strong. "You'll give him a second chance." Mrs. McMichaels's mouth clamped shut. She glanced over her shoulder as if to argue, but Emma's Noni had closed his eyes again, his hands clamped tightly in his lap. She seemed about to say something, but she closed her mouth and turned away.

"I'm sorry," Emma said, her voice just above a whisper. And then we were out the door.

We rushed into the night, Blythe and Emma taking the stairs two at a time.

Outside, Nate's clanking, shaking Volvo idled in the silent Thornewood night. We clamored in, all three of us sitting in the back together—boots and bags and files.

In the car, Emma leaned against my shoulder. "Thanks for rescuing me, handsome prince." I smiled. But I was still thinking about the confrontation we'd had with Mrs. McMichaels, and her weird document-kill room.

"Emma?" I said. "Why would your grandmother have an *R* on her file cabinet?"

She looked up, then lowered her head back to my shoulder. "Maybe for my mom. Her name was Rebecca."

I thought about that as we drove through the silent, perfectly ordered, never-changing streets of Thornewood. Here, everything looked the same, stayed the same. It was how Mrs. McMichaels coped with loss, wasn't it? She controlled what she could in order to keep her long-gone daughter safe. And when her rules weren't followed, she cut off ties—maybe hoping to keep her heart from breaking again?

I wondered whether I'd been doing something similar, trying to keep our family from change. I wanted my dad's memory to be safe. But there was no safety in loving anyone. There was always risk, always the chance of loss—sooner or later. How had my mom kept her love for my dad, and made room for Charlie, too?

My heart squeezed as I thought of Kai, riding off down the street, leaving me behind, protecting my heart. But maybe love wasn't keeping everything neat and tidy and perfect. Maybe it was leaving room for mess. Maybe it was leaving room for people who needed a place to fit in. I tilted my head against Emma. I could think about Kai later. Tonight, I was making room in my heart for another sister.

BECAUSE I COULD
NOT GO TO BED

On the day of the Mash-Up, I was backstage in the dressing room tying Blythe into the costume Emma and I had designed. The night we'd found the ballots, Emma came home with us and fell asleep on an inflatable mattress as we waited for sirens and police boots. But none came. On the third night, as we waited for an eviction that didn't come, Emma called her grandmother, and they decided she could stay—just until her dad got a place. So we converted the sewing room into her room, and spent hours there on the dress that was now before us: a burgundy gown with a tight ruffled V-shaped bodice and a big satin bow. We'd designed it together, me and Emma, and now, as Emma saved us seats, I was backstage trimming the last little threads from the hem and sleeves and wrangling the massive ribbon into a perfect bow.

Blythe lifted the thick fabric of the gown, plucking at nonexistent lint and flattening already-flat seams. "Tell me again why I agreed to do this."

I tied the bow at her back and put my hands on her shoulders. "Because you want an A in your English class?" She was just nervous. I'd drilled her lines so many times she could recite them while mixing chemical solutions. With Kai ignoring me this past week as if he were Giorgio Armani and I were Donatella Versace, I'd had time for school, sewing, *and* rehearsals with Blythe and Nate. I'd distracted myself from the fact that when I tried to meet Kai's eyes in French, he looked right through me, by becoming so busy I didn't have time to hear the faint clunk and thud of my broken heart. "Remember," I told Blythe. "This is school. You're good at school."

"But what if—"

"Nope. Nothing will go wrong." I patted her upswept hair. "Let's go. You're on next." With one last wave, I hurried through the now-familiar backstage props and into a downstage wing. When the second-to-last act finished to warm applause (Shel Silverstein mashed with William Carlos Williams), I ran to set the stage. I placed each cardboard gravestone then dragged the smoke machine out. I hit the on button, but just a trickle of fog came out. I tinkered with the knobs, but the stage manager whispered, "Places!" so I hustled back into the wings and out through the audience door. In the auditorium, Emma patted the aisle seat she'd saved, and I slipped in beside her.

"How's the dress?" Emma asked. I gave her a thumbs-up as the MC tapped the mic and the audience quieted.

"Our last contestants are Nate Fong and Blythe Braxton with 'Because I could not—go to bed.'" The lights flickered and went to a spotlight, and Nate walked onstage, raising hollers with his kohled eyes and bright gash of red lipstick. He winked and flapped his black jacket over his black pants and combat boots. Then he shook out his wild, stringy, Robert Smith–esque hair. It looked like the worst bedhead ever. Then he tented his hands and everyone quieted.

"Virtual writing collaboration. I'm giving it a go. Her name is Emily." His British accent could have used a few more days of practice, but it wasn't awful. "Emily Elizabeth Dickinson. An American poet born in Amherst, Massachusetts, on December 10, 1830 . . . influenced by Ralph Waldo Emerson, Elizabeth Barrett Browning, and William Blake. But I just don't know if we'll be compatible. I mean, she's only published ten poems and one letter."

Blythe walked onstage. I could see her hands shaking. I hoped no one else could.

But her voice rang out strong and loud. "You must be the . . . *person* I'm looking for? Robert Smith. Born April 21, 1959. An *English* musician. You influenced the bands Ivy and The Smashing Pumpkins. I don't know about this. You're not even a writer, are you? I should never have trusted WordLovers. com to find a writing partner. I can't believe I left the house for this." I was pleased when that got a chuckle.

"I am *indeed* a writer. With many successful recordings. But you? Ten poems? And your profile boasted knowledge of *death*. Just look at what you're wearing."

Blythe lifted her burgundy skirt. "Black is not the only color of death, sir. Have you read none of my profound poetry? I speak of nothing but death. That and birds. But how could you understand? You only write *lyrics*, not real poetry—"

"Don't you listen to the radio? NY Rock describes me as 'pop culture's unkempt poster child of doom and gloom,' and my songs a 'somber introspection over lush, brooding guitars.' Let's see your somber introspection."

"Oh, I have that in droves." She swept around him, gracefully avoiding the wobbly tombstones I'd set.

"Recite something for me," Nate said, losing his accent a little.

"*You* recite something for *me*."

"Oh, ladies first."

"*Fine.*" She sniffed. "You're interested in death? I have something for you." Blythe crossed her arms and swept across the stage, her gown flowing out behind her. "Because I could not stop for Death / He kindly stopped for me – / The Carriage held but just Ourselves – / And Immortality."

Nate followed Blythe across the stage. As he began to recite the lyrics from the Cure's "Let's Go to Bed," I couldn't help but look around for Kai. I didn't have to look long—he was four seats over from us, toward the middle of the row.

Kai watched, rapt, as they bantered. Blythe recited Emily, and Nate cut in with Robert Smith, and each time they tried to outperform each other. "The Carriage held but just Ourselves – / And Immortality."

"Just ourselves . . ." Nate gestured between them.

"We *slowly* drove – He knew *no haste* / And I had put away / My labor and my leisure too, / For His Civility –." She turned her back to him, but he spoke softly over her shoulder, his voice amplified and breathy over the speaker system.

I looked back to Kai, who was watching, a strange look on his face. He looked a little like he did when we were reading a tough passage in French class. I stared long enough for him to notice, but his eyes were on the stage. I looked back to Nate and Blythe.

Onstage, they both froze, and the audience hushed. Someone gave a single clap. Then Blythe turned and pushed Nate away from her with one strong shove. "We passed the School, where Children strove / At Recess – in the Ring – / We passed the Fields of Gazing Grain – / We passed the Setting Sun –" Nate took her hands in his and stopped her. Then he stole her line.

"Or rather—He passed us –?"

Blythe set her mouth and lifted the length of her dress, and the sheen of the fabric caught the stage lights and shimmered. Then she reached up and tore out the hairband holding back her wild curls. As her hair framed her face, Nate stumbled back, a hand against his chest. I'd envisioned this as a battle, but now it seemed like something else—like a story that begins with hate and ends with love. I had spent the past week writing what amounted to a love letter to Kai—a letter that acknowledged my part in us being a big mess . . . and asked him to forgive me, to keep me and the mess. But here, I was Robert Smith, and he was Emily Dickinson. Onstage, Nate cupped Blythe's face. They turned to the audience, barely a whisper between them.

Blythe tilted her cheek into Nate's hand. "The Horses' Heads were toward Eternity – toward Eternity—Eternity –" Nate moved imperceptibly closer to Blythe. A pause filled the space around them, and Nate turned Blythe's face to his. I looked over at Kai and found him looking back. He opened his mouth to say something, and as Nate spoke, Kai smiled at me and said the last line with Nate:

"Let's go to bed."

Then Nate dipped Blythe and went to kiss her, but she squirmed away. "Sorry, Mr. Smith," she said. "I like girls." Nate held up his hands in surrender, and then they turned to the audience. Together they dropped into low bows.

I was still watching Kai as howls and cheers erupted from the audience and the curtains were yanked closed. Kai was grinning. I placed a hand over my heart, and I felt my hope bird in there, still alive. Just barely breathing. I hadn't heard the mash-ups that came before Blythe and Nate, but Rolly was filled with overachievers, so they were probably amazing. Still, the clapping for Blythe and Nate seemed very loud. The curtains opened, and all the contestants walked forward, but I kept glancing at Kai's broad smile. He looked the way he did right before he laughed.

Now the audience was clapping for all the contestants, and I turned my attention to the stage. I put two fingers between my front teeth and whistled. When Blythe heard, she grinned. I waved and lifted my hands, clapping as loudly as I could. I glanced again at Kai, but he was looking at his phone. My heart sank. Maybe him looking at me as he recited the last line hadn't meant he'd liked it, or even understood what I was trying to do. I mean, I hadn't really understood until I saw it onstage. Maybe him reciting the line just meant he really liked the Cure. I tried to push away disappointment and focus on Blythe, who was smiling widely with relief and pride.

"Thank you to all our contestants today!" A teacher was onstage, holding a plaque. "We had so many strong contestants. But one pair stood out. Two students brought strange bedfellows together to show how violence, depression, and unexpressed desire are depicted in poetry and in musical lyrics. And they took a chance—breaking one of the time-honored rules to keep meter. But it was in such excellent service to the story that the judges had to credit the ingenuity. Blythe and Nate? Well done!"

Even after her great performance, Blythe's eyes bugged out in surprise. Nate took it in stride and strummed an air guitar. Blythe found my eyes and mouthed, *Thank you!* And suddenly it didn't matter that I was so heart-twisted I couldn't handle sharing Kai with Emma. I had Blythe. I had my sister and best friend. Beside me, Emma grabbed my hand and squeezed. And I had Emma, too. I waved at Blythe, grinning so hard my cheeks began to sting.

Then my phone buzzed. It was a picture. Me and Kai in the Shakespeare garden. When I looked up, Kai was looking back. His eyes were somber, steady on mine. I swallowed, suddenly needing to get to him. I had to tell him that I still had feelings for him. Or, really, that I had bangings and crashings for him. I had to tell him—even if the photo was just a peace offering. I had to tell him that I forgave him for not being honest with me, for protecting Emma the way I wished he'd protected me. And that I was sorry I'd walked away, sorry for protecting my heart instead of giving it to him.

Kai was pushing his way toward me. My heart pounded in my ears. This was my chance. I would say: *Please.* I would say: *Give me a chance to make space in my heart.* I stood to meet him. But everyone else stood, too. Emma took my hand and pulled me out of the row to make way for the other people, and as we stepped aside, I lost sight of Kai.

Beside me, Emma was practically leaping in the air. "Didn't the dress look great? I can't wait to get some pictures. And they were *so* good. I can't believe they won!" She dove at me, and we hugged, tight. She *did* deserve to celebrate—we both did. After she lost the costume contest for the first time ever, she deserved this win. When she pulled away, I looked for Kai in the crowd, but I didn't see him.

As I was about to go searching, Emma took my hand and led me to the man who had been sitting on her other side and introduced me. Her *dad*. He didn't look like a drunk. He was wearing a suit and his face was clean-shaven. He had a sweet smile that looked a lot like hers.

"Thank you for helping me and Emma," he said, squeezing my hand. "We're both very grateful."

I smiled. "We're the lucky ones to have her with us. She's like an in-house fashion designer." Emma was saying something about how I was not a bad designer, either, but I was looking for Kai, and didn't quite hear her. But he'd disappeared.

Emma's dad smiled down at her and touched her scarred arm. "Your work is amazing. Your mom would be so proud." Her dad was talking about going to lunch together, since we had a half day in honor of the Poetic Mash-Up, but I shook my head when they asked me to join them. I almost gave Emma the excuse that I needed to find Blythe, but that wasn't true. We had plans to meet after her class celebration in the quad and walk to the Berry Market for fancy apricot sodas this afternoon.

Instead, I told myself to be brave and tell her the truth. I could no longer ignore the knocking of my heart. "I need to find Kai." I started to explain why, but she knew.

Emma's cat-eye glasses winked under the bright house lights. She sighed. "That mash-up, you wrote it for him, didn't you? All that Cure stuff?"

When I nodded, she sighed again, fidgeting with the vertical ruffles of her skirt. "Try the library." I released every pinch of the breath I'd been holding. I started to leave, then turned back to Emma.

"There's room for all of us, okay?" I wasn't sure I knew what I meant, exactly, just that there was.

"I know," she said. "He'll always be my best friend. But now I have you, too." She gave me a little smile, and I leaned in to kiss her cheek. Then I said goodbye to her dad, turned, and pushed my way out of there.

THE HEART IS
WIDER THAN THE SKY

When I walked into the library, I looked to the couches where Kai had suggested that houndstooth was pictures of dogs, but they were empty. There was no one there except the librarian behind the reference desk. I was about to leave when she looked up and caught my eye. She jerked her head toward the stacks and lifted her eyebrows. *Kai?*

My heart rate doubled and I hurried down the stairs but slowed at the book-theft detector, telling myself to *calm down.* He'd sent a photo, not a proposal. And I still had to somehow tell him in nonpoetry how I felt. Breathe.

I found Kai in the last row of the stacks, writing in the flap of a book. I smiled. "Defacing school property?"

His head snapped up, and he closed the book. "Just some light doodling."

I searched for something funny to say, but my heart was cracking at the edges. "How did you find it?" I asked. "The picture of us?"

He lowered his eyes. "Emma sent it to me before she deleted it. I thought it was from you. Then last night, after I told her I quit the team, she told me about deleting the picture." I sucked in a sharp breath. So they'd really talked. And she knew he probably wasn't headed to Los Angeles with her.

"You really quit?" I held on to the side of the tall mahogany stack, feeling light-headed.

He nodded. "I thought my coach might cry. I almost did." He bounced the book he was holding in his hands, probably wishing for something to throw. He looked both forlorn and a little proud, and I wanted so much to hug him.

I took a step closer to him. "Would you rather hear *I'm sorry*, or *Good for you*?"

"I think the latter."

"Good for you," I said.

"Thanks." We stood there, too far apart, looking at each other. I pulled at my hem. He bounced the book.

"I saw you in the theater." I waited a beat, but he didn't fill in the blank. "Did you like it? Is that why you sent the picture?" I was watching him so hard I saw his Adam's apple bob. Then he gave me a half smile that made me miss his real smile.

"It was awesome," he said. "You wrote it?"

"It was sort of . . ." I swallowed the words *love letter*. "An apology."

"To me?" He hugged the book to his chest, stopping his nervous, bouncing hands.

"Well," I said. "You were right about Robert Smith. He is a poet."

He grinned. "She finally caves."

I crossed my arms. "This by no means is a free pass for all lyrics," I said. "Just his." He saluted me with the book and laughed, shaking his head. He looked so good, I could barely concentrate, but I had to focus. No matter what he said back, I had to tell him how sorry I was. "I couldn't fit it into the sketch, but I'm sorry for running out on you on Halloween.

And for not trusting you with Emma. I thought I was protecting myself, but really I was hurting you."

Kai shook his head and folded his arms over his chest. I had the sinking feeling that this was the real breakup. Right here. "I'm sorry I didn't tell you that I knew how Emma felt. I said we'd tell each other the truth, and I didn't." He blinked hard and met my eyes. "When Emma told me about deleting our photo, I realized I'd been messing with your head by pretending it was all cool."

"And my head's already a pretty messy place," I said, leaning my head against the cool stacks.

"No." He took a step toward me. "It's a beautiful place. I love your poeting because it lets me look right inside your mind." He closed the space between us and handed me the book. "I've been keeping this in here. I got it for you before the Halloween dance. Better than a corsage, right?"

I curled my hand around the book, feeling an expanse within my heart growing wider and wider. "Better than heritage roses," I said. I pressed my lips together, thinking of what Emily said about the sky being wide . . . *the brain is wider than the sky*. I turned the book over. It was a slim volume of poetry called *The Father* by Sharon Olds.

"Nothing against Dickinson," he said. "I just thought you could mix it up." I held it in my hands for a long time, thinking of the day I pulled Emily's book off my dad's bookshelf. This had that same feeling—of holding someone's soul in your hand. "I really like this one poem." He reached to open the book. "It's called 'I Go Back to May 1937.' It's about when her parents met. And she thinks she wants to stop them from meeting, because they hurt each other and they're wrong for each other." He flipped the page and pointed. "But then she says she wants to live. She says that she'll tell their story. I liked that."

My cheeks warmed, and I looked up at him, standing very close to me. "I love it. Thank you." I opened my mouth and closed it, wondering how to tell him that my heart was painfully full. "Emily was wrong," I said. "It's not the brain."

He lifted one eyebrow, hesitation in the set of his mouth. "What's not?"

"She said 'the brain is wider than the sky.' But it's not." I closed the space between us and tapped his chest. "It's the heart. The heart is wider than the sky. It's wide enough to hold the whole world. Wide enough to hold fear and love, to break and to mend again."

He exhaled and lowered his head until our foreheads touched. I felt the steady rhythm of his heartbeat and breathed in cinnamon. I could do this. I could hold all the fear and all the love at the same time. "Tell me you came here to give me a choice." His words fell against my cheek.

I sucked in a breath, feeling the sting of tears. "You always have a choice."

"Tell me I can choose *you*, Sabine." His lips grazed my cheek. I trailed my fingers down his arm and swept the inside of his wrist. I felt the same rush I did when plummeting down the park's cement slide, the same breeze in my hair, and the same openness in my heart—wider than the sky.

"Not if I choose you first," I said.

He smiled. And I smiled. And our smiles met. And as we kissed, I didn't hold back. I didn't stop myself from falling into him, from feeling his heart beat against mine. I leaned in and pressed against him and held on as my heart grew and grew.

32   FORGIVENESS IS LIKE FLYING

Saturday morning, after days of silence from city hall, we found a single piece of Thornewood letterhead taped to our front door. Beneath the fancy insignia was one sentence.

All fines, fees, and expenses incurred on number six Magnolia have been dropped subsequent to the acceptance of all permit applications filed in the past seven calendar years. Permit fee due upon receipt: $982.

Charlie read it aloud three times. "Does this mean what I think it means?"

My mom threw her arms around Charlie. "Whoever you spoke to really came through." Mom said. "Well done!"

Blythe sauntered over and snapped the piece of paper out of Charlie's hands. "Bean has something to say." I lifted my eyebrows. We hadn't prepared for this, but . . . Blythe gestured for me to go ahead.

I looked between Mom and Charlie. "It was me and Blythe. We got Mrs. McMichaels to rezone the house," I said. "And as payment for our services, we want to change the plan."

Charlie sighed, crossing his arms. "I admit it must have been you two," he said. "I couldn't even get in to see the mayor, but if you think that—"

"Wait." Mom held up a hand. "You two did this? You convinced Bernie McMichaels to drop the fines?" Mom looked between us like we'd both been accepted to MIT.

"And we demand payment," I said. Blythe jumped in: "In the form of a new plan."

Charlie shook his head. "No. That's out of the question. We already—"

Maryann Interiors put a steady hand on Charlie's shoulder. "You need to listen to them."

"For real," Blythe said, looking as haughty and annoyed as I'd wanted her to all those weeks ago, when we found out that there was no easy way out of this number-six-Magnolia situation.

I took a deep breath. "We aren't arguing with you, Charlie, about turning number six, which is way too big for a single family, into transitional housing. But we want a home. Something just for us, and for Mom."

"It would help our mental health to have a stable home," Blythe said. I met her eyes and smiled. Then we turned to them.

"We want the garage apartment," we said. We glanced at each other, and I went on. "Turn the bottom floor into two more bedrooms and a bathroom, and let us move in there."

Charlie held up his hands, trying to interrupt, but Maryann Interiors slapped his hands down. I almost laughed out loud at the affronted look on his face.

"And," Blythe said, "Bean promised we'd keep the telephone booth and the period-specific signage. So we might need to keep some of the first floor as it is. And, you know, we have to paint the place white."

"And we want the garden redone as a memorial," I said.

"The Mission Project can have the house and the main garden. But we get the apartment and the garden outside of it." Charlie's mouth hung open. He groped for words, but nothing came out.

I seized the opportunity. "We could use the upper terrace to make a circle of friends around the willow tree. Just like the National AIDS Memorial Grove." I looked at Blythe, and she continued. "That way, we'll have a house with a piece of our dad in it, a place for all of us to remember him, and Charlie—you'll still get his dream."

My mom took the sketch I'd gotten out of my backpack. "Charlie. Look at this." She handed him the drawing. "They spent a lot of time on this."

"I like this. A lot . . . but . . ." Charlie scratched his neck. "Where would I live?"

"What about renovating the attic?" I asked, thinking of a *Swiss Family Robinson*–type apartment. "It has great views, just like the apartment. And there's a bathroom."

Charlie gave a frustrated sigh. "I could never leave the apartment that Mick and I built together; you know how special that place was to us—"

"We gave up a lot to be here," Mom said. "And so far, we're the ones who have made the most sacrifices. The girls left the only home they've known." She turned and gave me and Blythe proud smiles. "I need you to think about Mick. He never imagined we would live here. Or that his children would need something to remember him by."

I wanted to say, *Yeah, Charlie*, but I remembered my dad's arbitration rules. "And if you're in the main house, you'll literally be living inside of Dad's dream. You'll be part of it." I bit my lip.

Charlie gave me an appraising look. "But the plans will have to be redrawn, and the architect was expensive—"

"I just got a new client. Mr. Cade," Mom said, then Maryann Interiors took over talking. "He knows everyone in Thornewood, and he's willing to recommend my services to some wealthy Historic District families so I don't need to keep flying back to Orange County to make money. I'll be here more to help, and I'll have more money to put toward new plans."

Charlie lifted his hands in surrender. "Well . . ." He looked from me to Blythe and back to me. Then he smiled a rueful little Southern smile. "I do love the idea of a garden memorial."

THAT'S HOW, THE SATURDAY AFTER Thanksgiving, Kai, Nate, Blythe, Emma, Kai's brother Keanu, Mom, Charlie, and I watched as the Mission Project volunteers came in like a swarm, dropping off slabs of stone, bags of dirt, and dozens of plants in little black buckets. They unloaded all the one-gallon plants into a staging area, tilted out burlap-wrapped maples, and hauled the bluestone and gravel to the circle. Then they left us with instructions and a dozen pairs of gardening gloves, and were gone.

"We have our work cut out for us!" Charlie pulled on his gloves, and he and Keanu got to work moving the stone. Kai and I looked over my plan, deciding what should happen next. When we'd given everyone else jobs, we got shovels and began digging holes for the trees.

Kai looked at my drawing again. "You know, there's a landscape architecture major at UC Davis." He grinned at me. "I'll go for premed. You go for architecture."

I felt my cheeks warm. "Design sounds good." I tapped a splatter of mud off my boots and gave him a significant look. "But I'm not sure outdoor work is for me." I loved a garden, but what I really wanted, I'd realized as Emma and I worked on Blythe's Emily dress, was to design, like Emma. Or, maybe, like *me*. He laughed, looking at my attempt to wear gardening-ish clothes (knee-high boots, matching tights, and a short minidress with long sleeves under a short red jacket.) The gardening gloves ruined the look, but every time I took them off, Kai handed them back to me. I stepped in close to him now. "I do like the idea of being with you, though."

He smiled, his eyes lighting over my face. "Good," he said, and pressed a kiss to my temple before stepping on his shovel to push it into the damp ground.

I walked around to check everyone's progress. As I did, I could hear my dad's voice reminding me of plant names and of which plants did well in what types of light. His gardening gloves might not be on the kitchen counter, but he was here.

My mom patted down lavender plants, and Blythe pushed mulch over all the uncovered surfaces. Nate mostly whistled. Then, underneath the willow, Charlie and Keanu set the last bluestone. Charlie called me and Blythe over.

"Let's chalk out his name," he said. I waited for Blythe to join me, and we chose where his name would go. I chalked it out, and Blythe added fancy lettering. Everyone was quiet. Even the birdcall faded.

"I'll have the engraver come in the morning. He'll mark Mick's name here," Charlie said. "For us to remember."

Kai came to my side and took my hand. I stepped back and looked up at the willow tree. The branches swayed, dizzying me. I closed my eyes, imagining my dad standing in this exact spot. I'd never know what he was thinking then, in that moment, on that day, but I knew him. I'd always known him, and I always would. My heart felt like it was opening, breathing. My heart felt wider than anything I could imagine.

So this was what forgiveness felt like. It was a little like flying. I felt a pull in my chest, and when I opened my eyes, there went my hope bird flying up and up, until it was just a happy yellow speck against the clearing sky.

ACKNOWLEDGMENTS

It has taken a medium-size village to bring this book into the world. Everyone I thank here played a role in giving me the confidence to share my story. I'll begin at the beginning—with gratitude for women writers who were strong and brave enough to share their words with the world before I could. It was love of books that led me to love writing, and to apply to the undergraduate creative writing program at University of California at Irvine. UCI is where I began to gather the confidence I would need as a writer.

My first thank you is to my writing teachers. From Mr. Rasmussen in high school to my instructors at UC Irvine, you have all given me confidence in my words. A big thank you to Geoff Wolff, my creative writing teacher at UCI, who told me to go to graduate school for writing. Without your support I would not have had the confidence to go, and meet the amazing Brenda Hillman, Carol Beran, John Fleming, Lou Berney, and Lynn Freed, who all took turns helping my confidence grow. In graduate school, I grew close to the woman who would become my writing buddy, my champion, and a friend through all things, Jennifer Chambliss Bertman. When it seemed like I would never figure out the book I was working on, she sent me Sarah Dessen's *The Truth About Forever*, and I realized I wanted to write young adult. I thank her still for the subtle hint. Jenn, thank you for all your support, but mostly for your belief in my writing. Each time you encouraged me, my confidence grew.

I wrote over many years, but it wasn't until I joined a critique group that I truly gained the confidence I needed to share my work with a wider audience. Thank you to the original members of that group and particularly Corina Vacco and Sally Engelfried. You two have been the core of my writing community for so many years. Corina, I have you to thank for a place at your dining room table and a place in your heart. And Sally, there are no words for our journey. I knew we'd be in this together from the first time we met. And thank you to my current critique group, the Panama Math & Science Club: Stacy Stokes, Lisa Ramee, Lydia Steinauer, Sally Engelfried, and Rose Haynes. Thank you for your wise insight, your editorial eyes, your snarky comments, your predilection for wine, and for giving me the confidence to send my first book into the world. And when I faltered in my confidence, a wider community of writers supported me, including my teen reader, Ellie Ryan. Thank you to the Society for Children's Book Authors and Illustrators (SCBWI), Better Books, and the Vermont Studio Center for all supporting my writing financially. And thank you to Darcey Rosenblatt and Lisa Schulman—if you two hadn't staged an intervention, I might never have sent another query.

When I did find an agent, I could not possibly have chosen a better one. My agent never gave up on me, never doubted me, and never allowed me to doubt myself. Rena Rossner, you are truly a gift in my life, and I thank you: sun, moon, and stars. Thank you, too, to Kathleen Caldwell of A Great Good Place for Books in Oakland, California, for supporting

ACKNOWLEDGMENTS

this little book and keeping the faith always, and to Misa Siguro, Jandy Nelson, and Nina LaCour for supporting my work with your wisdom and kind words.

Many editors encourage their writers to think about their manuscripts in new ways, but my editor allowed me to try on his eyes and look at my manuscript in a way I never could have alone. Dan Ehrenhaft, thank you for lending me your gaze; it has made this book everything I hoped it might be. Your patience, kindness, and shrewd vision will be with me always. Thank you also to the entire amazing and endearing Soho Teen team, and in particular Rachel Kowal, Paul Oliver, Alexa Wejko, Monica White, copyeditor Janet Rosenberg, and Bronwen Hruska. And thank you to my cover designer, the incredible Helen Crawford-White, for a stunning vision of the fictional Magnolia Street.

First and last, then, now, and always: thank you to my family for their support. Thank you to my mom for modeling dedication to words and writing, thank you to Rebecca for reading all my drafts and catching all my typos and texting late at night to remind me that everything will be okay, thank you to my young daughters for understanding when mommy has to go away to write, and thank you to my husband. Blake, thank you for listening to me read my work, and with every listening showing me how important my voice is. Thank you for always lending me your confidence when mine goes missing. I love you always.

And finally, the journey ends with a book in someone's hands.

So, my last thank you is to you—thank you, my readers!